From the Author:

I wrote this book after [illegible] the bathroom floor and called an ambulance to take him away from his home on Earth forever. His transitioning in form paved the way for me to continue my relationship with him. He continues to exist. We all continue to exist when we transition into another dimension.

I have seen them and so have you. We have all experienced assaults on our senses that come from dark places. Things we can't explain. Sure, we are surrounded by experts who have logical explanations for those intrusions into our dimension. These unexplainable experiences are found more readily in altered states of being and in places that seem to harness mysteries more aggressively. I have yet to know of a scientific formula to explain the love between all creatures who have, at some point in time, walked on this large rock spinning and flying through space. Some things can't be explained so easily.

The Bermuda Triangle is such place that welcomes that without explanation. I have witnessed these with my own eyes and know, that what I experienced, can't be explained away as normal. I'm certain the laws of physics can explain them, but the "why" question will always remain beyond the horizon of explanation.

I believe firmly that life does not end with our return to beings of light. No one can convince me that the human spirit is extinguished when we take our final physical breaths. The human spirit goes somewhere else, along with those of scientists and even the animals we love. That's good news for them too. My pets are just too damn awesome to simply vanish forever; not mine and not yours.

This book was written with love and ties together experiences I have had into a chain of continuous existence. Our likeness is scattered throughout the known Universe. You didn't recognize them when you saw them...They look just like you and me.

Enjoy this book as it takes you out of this world. I'll see you in any Dimension and anytime you wish to connect.

Misael Guerra

Irvine, California

eleventhdimensionbook@gmail.com

# CONTENTS

# CHAPTER 1: THE BOOM AND FLASH

"What are you doing?"

"I'm sitting on a rock, speaking to you."

"Did you ask that rock for permission to sit on it?"

The old Shaman's question haunted me for the rest of my life. It often entered my thoughts when I found myself in a quiet place, contemplating how interconnected we were with all matter in the universe. The stars above extended my thoughts to distant lands across space. I felt connected to the cosmos. I'd always known my place of origin was among the stars, and to the stars, I would eventually return. I wondered what aliens from distant worlds looked like. I'd never thought aliens looked like me or that I looked like them. Did they ask their rocks for permission to sit on them? I would soon have my answer. There was a certain quiet before the shit hit the fan.

The surrounding hills of the Texas Hill Country sat above the family homes like vigilant sentinels. In the low ambient light, one could see the brilliant stars of the Milky Way piercing through the dark blanket of space. The cool summer night breeze that came with the setting sun and the rising moon had arrived unannounced and brought with it the swirling smells of the surrounding oleander and rosemary bushes so prevalent at that time of year. The aromatic coffee and meal prepared by the robot chef smelled great, but no scent compared to her sweetness. In the deafening silence, my mind wandered down passageways that lay deep in my sub-conscience with sweet and sour melancholy. Inevitably, I thought about how much I missed her.

The moon's reflection nestled itself upon the shimmering water of the small pond just below the top of the mountain, where my house sat quietly. Reflected moonlight had a funny way of dancing on water one instant, then disappearing the next. Earth's moon was never still.

A few years earlier, the moon had been one of the battlegrounds of the Third World War, and I had been front and center to witness the carnage. It was a gruesome thing to watch a human being's blood boil, their eyes bursting as the pressurization left their spacesuit. I would never forget just how fragile life was. The peaceful celestial body that ruled the night had been turned into a place of violence, especially by the battles on the dark side. At least the Martian base had seen no violence during the Third Great War.

There were active programs to begin the colonization of Jupiter's moon Europa and other celestial bodies. The technological advances of ultralight carbon nanotube construction materials and artificially intelligent robots made space travel and long-term colonization a reality. Earthlings were destined to leave Earth on pathways to the stars.

All seemed peaceful and quiet, almost too perfect. Peaceful nights were to be cherished since the end of the war. The amount of death and destruction I'd experienced was enough for many lifetimes. I guessed it had made me who I was, forged in the fire of violence and bloodshed, forever damaged by the same. We humans sure liked our violence, yet there was a fragility to being human.

The North Atlantic Treaty Organization, or NATO, was the predecessor to the Global League of Nations, also called the Global League, which was formed shortly after the Third Great War, replacing what had once been known as the United Nations. They headquartered in the same building on New York City's East Side. The secretary-general of the Global League of Nations was freely elected to four-year terms by the 193 nations on

Earth that belonged to the Global League and had voting rights. Hideki Yamamoto had served well. Serving well was characterized mostly as scandal-free since Earth had experienced several years of peace. In many ways, the secretary-general of the Global League of Nations was simply a symbolic figurehead. No real teeth to their bite.

The post-war peace had made the planet somewhat soft on military defense. After all, there was no longer a need for it. The nations of Earth focused on policing local crime rather than fighting one another. Even the weather was mitigated through the use of geocentric orbiting weather control satellites. It made people like me somewhat obsolete, really. I had, however, assembled quite an array of abilities in killing the enemy and leading troops to do the same. My medals indicated that much. It had been a hell of a ride.

Planet Earth had become soft, yet peace was precisely what Earth craved after thousands of years of war and violence between its nations, kingdoms, and religions. Human beings could finally be at peace with one another. No country invaded their neighbor, or any other country, for that matter. Nations' borders had become symbolic geographic lines. The global dollar was the common currency used by all nations.

Human thirst for violence had been quenched by the destruction of substantial areas in cities around the world. The devastation caused by the Third World War had been globally catastrophic. WWIII had led to famine, pestilence, and death. War had a way of stealing lives and dignity with calculated cruelty.

Once NATO had implemented Article 5, ninety-two countries had joined the fight in a catastrophic war that had lasted just one year, from which the world would never truly recuperate. All this destruction had been on the road I'd taken to find myself where I was at that moment and place in time.

Then the boom and the flash happened.

They arrived as I sat on the back porch of my retirement home. It was the kind of boom that shook the Earth, sending animals scurrying in all directions for safety. It felt like it could wake the dead from restful slumber. And the flash was blinding. It was as if a giant had stomped their heavy foot upon the hilly land in anger and released the brightness of the sun. My immediate thought was that something had exploded nearby. I instinctively ensured I had my pistol on my hip holster, which was almost always on me. It was there.

This was my standard reaction whenever I heard gunshots near my home. People often hunted in the area surrounding the Timberwood Park neighborhood, which was home to many wild deer. The fact that I lived in a house where the entire side facing the city was made of glass made me react that much more aggressively to loud and violent sounds. When seconds counted, the police were minutes away.

I didn't immediately see anything out of order. The boom was followed by the sounds of cars crashing, metal crushing, and glass shattering as if the electric cars, at least those not on autopilot, were no longer being operated by their drivers. I could hear car horns blaring in the distance. This confirmed to me that this was no ordinary boom. My initial thought was that one of the many geocentric weather control satellites that focused solar light on command to heat or cool areas of the planet had come crashing down through the atmosphere.

I entered my house, crossed to the front door on the opposite side of it, and exited to scan the horizon and neighborhood below. A bright, steady diamond-shaped light appeared over the western sky. The light was suspended just above the clouds and due west. The boom seemed to have originated from somewhere over Camp Bullis, a 28,000-acre army training camp in San Antonio, just west of the neighborhood. Camp Bullis was a somewhat creepy place to people who weren't accustomed to military facilities. The signs posted every few feet on the high perimeter fence made it expressly clear that you were cordially invited to stay out.

Although the people living in the vicinity of Camp Bullis were accustomed to hearing loud noises coming from the military base where no one was welcome, this sound was particularly loud and was accompanied by the blinding flash. What went on behind that fence was anyone's guess. The compound was densely wooded with oak and cedar trees, and the activity occurring in the deep interior of the base seemed to always be secret. Strange lights and aircraft flew in and out of the base at night under the cover of darkness.

It seemed people in the United States had a fascination with the secret military installation in Nevada known as Area 51 and with the likes of Roswell, New Mexico. The United States Government didn't seem to mind all the attention paid to Area 51 and Roswell; they were doing clandestine operations and test flights at Camp Bullis. It paid to operate in secret, but there was no way to hide that boom or the steady light above the camp.

This time, shit really had hit the fan, and everybody knew it.

# CHAPTER 2: LOST TIME

Warfare had changed. Most every sailor fighting in World War III had received extensive special operations training. We were experts in amphibious and outer space warfare. A new breed of warrior had been born out of necessity and the attrition of the war. The United States military branches had been blended into the existing United States Space Force to become the Naval and Space Force under one central command, ruling the seas of Earth and the seas of outer space. The USNSF was all the United States needed.

Many years before, when I'd been a junior commissioned officer and had not yet transitioned to special warfare, I had experienced the same loud boom and bright flash in the sky. That occurrence had also been followed by a brilliant diamond-shaped light. It had happened while I'd served aboard a USNSF warship transiting the Bermuda Triangle in the deepest part of the Atlantic Ocean. In my military career, I had experienced several hard-to-explain sightings in oceans the world over, on land, and in outer space. But this sighting had been particularly unnerving because of a lost-time effect.

It had been a clear and humid night in the Caribbean Sea, immediately north of a part of the ocean known as the Puerto Rico Trench. From the pilot house of the warship with hull number 136 at the time of 2311, we'd heard a tremendous boom, followed by that same bright diamond light. The light had been suspended directly above the sea a few miles in front of the ship's bow as the ship headed west. We hadn't had enough time to react before the next thing had happened.

Time had frozen in a way that would haunt me for the rest of my life. A significant block of time had simply disappeared from our lives, taken without our permission. From one second to the next, our clocks on the warship had advanced seven hours and eleven minutes. No one could explain it. Had the entire crew disappeared for that time? Had the ship disappeared with us? If we had indeed disappeared, where had we reappeared after that missing time? Were we in another dimension? Had time simply frozen for us? Why didn't we remember anything of the hours we'd lost?

The chronometers and even the mechanical wristwatches onboard had indicated the seven-hour, eleven-minute time jump. That block of time had passed as normal for the rest of the world but not for our ship. No one onboard had felt that a single instant had transpired, at least not that we could remember. Our lives had simply marched on from the darkness of night to the light of sunrise, one second to the next. It had absolutely baffled and terrified us that the sky could go from dark to light in the span of a moment, or so we'd thought.

The Atlantic Fleet's commander-in-chief had ordered a thorough investigation on the matter, and the investigation had confirmed that American warship 136 had indeed gone off the satellite grid for precisely seven hours and eleven minutes. But the investigation could not explain what had happened to one of the warships considered a crown jewel in the United States' fleet.

Since that experience, I'd had many dreams and nightmares about what had actually happened to me during that lost time. Some of these were difficult to explain, but the detail in them was simply too vivid to dismiss as an overactive imagination. Often, I woke up in a cold sweat, my heart racing and images and sounds running through my brain like a freight train. What I saw was a place unlike Earth, and the words spoken there were unrecognizable to me, though they seemed coherent.

I'd been convinced I was leaving these experiences behind for good when I'd retired from naval and space service the summer before the boom in Texas. After retiring, I'd moved to that quaint home with its great view, where I could feed the wild deer every night from my back porch, which faced southeast toward San Antonio. There, I'd planned to enjoy the peace and quiet of an uneventful retired life. I'd looked forward to some well-deserved boredom.

The deer came up to the back porch every night for their apple-scented dry corn and just about anything else I would feed them. Foxes, skunks, armadillos, and a variety of other animals came too. Since I had grown up in a large city, feeding pigeons and visiting the zoo once every five years or so were as close as I'd ever gotten to interacting with animals. It was wonderful to sit on the back porch, enjoying the spectacular moonlight and cool evening breeze while feeding the wild animals. I had always felt a spiritual connection to our animal brethren, feeling we were created by the same hand. I also helped the plants and trees grow. People thought I was crazy when I told them you could send positive thoughts of energy to all living matter. Those nights feeding the flora and fauna only reinforced my beliefs.

So that was my quaint retirement home, where the boom in the sky shook the ground below. In my personal life, I was the only son of two wonderful parents who'd adopted me when I was three years old. They'd taken me from an orphanage in the country of Honduras to the United States of America, where I'd been raised.

It was a beautiful thing to retire with a full pension from a military career at a relatively young age and in the prime of your life. There were quite a few major league baseball players who'd hit home runs who were older than I was before they retired. Many players played well into their fifties with advances in genetic and anti-aging technology available. Human umpires had been replaced by sensitive cameras that called plays, balls, and strikes.

One thing I wished I could have changed about my military career, however, was to be home more with my now ex-wife. She had finally reached her limit on just how much she could stand being a navy wife and being alone for most of our marriage. She'd broken the news to me as I'd stood on the pier in Guantanamo Bay, Cuba, while deployed for an intense training session called refresher training. Cuba had once been a foe of the United States before becoming one of its most important trading partners and a popular vacation spot for people from all over the globe.

The end of my marriage had been an awful time in my life, and for years, I'd still smelled her sweet perfume wafting through the house when I'd missed her most. I still felt the oppressive loneliness of continuing to sleep alone even after leaving the service.

How ironic it was that while serving at sea I'd assured myself that I would not sleep alone ever again after I retired. Now here I was, retired and still sleeping alone. The difference was that this time, I had no illusions that I would snuggle with my wife, the first and only woman I'd ever truly loved. You could say it was one of the prices I'd had to pay for a decorated naval and space career. It was an expensive price and one my ex-wife had paid also. Regardless, I knew I would pay it again if I had to.

Retirement meant that I could spend time doing some of the things I hadn't gotten to do as often in the USNSF since the deployment schedule of a naval officer on a combatant ship was so heavy. Some of the activities in retirement I enjoyed most included shooting my firearms, continuing my martial arts and weapons training, doing yoga, and going on silent spiritual retreats. I had been bitten by a crazy bug to become a doctor and start medical school way later than the average doctor. I was already enrolled in the pre-medical program at the local university. I was ready to risk papercuts instead of explosions at sea, in space, and on land.

I had decided to become a doctor after my military career on the day my wife had miscarried our baby. The pain a parent feels at losing a child is unbearable. Once you hear your child's heartbeat, you are hooked. My wife would have given birth to a baby girl had she made it to full term. We had already picked out a name. I was convinced that losing this baby was just one more reason our marriage hadn't made it, but who knew, really? I thought about what looking into my own eyes would feel like and even had dreams of interacting with my daughter as she became a woman. I knew the day would come when I would meet her, either in this life or the next. It had been eleven years since the day the Great Creator had reclaimed her soul.

I often wanted to kick myself for being so weak as to allow myself to miss my ex-wife so darn much. Only time would heal this awful plowing through my heart. You know that feeling when you hurt so bad you forget to breathe? We've all been there, and it's an awful way to feel. I needed to fall back in love with myself before falling in love with anyone else. After all, I would always be there for myself, for richer or for poorer, in sickness and in health . . . until death.

My late grandmother had used to say that you really knew you loved someone when the passage of time made your heart hurt more and not less. If you had ever met my ex-wife, you would understand. Anyway, it was no use fretting about it. I'd been okay before she'd entered my life, and I would be okay after she was gone. I told myself this regularly, declaring my own self-healing of sorts. She had recently gotten engaged to marry some chemist with green eyes who worked for an oil company in Houston. How lame.

# CHAPTER 3: THE LIGHT MAKES ITS MOVE

The only thing I figured it could have been was a sonic boom, the result of a flying object moving faster than the speed of sound traveling overhead. The sound was very similar to the sound jets made when they flew overhead in inner space at supersonic speeds. The boom had an incredibly ominous effect as it shook the windows of the house and shattered those of many surrounding homes. I'd requested that the home builder install shatterproof windows at my house because of the high winds at its altitude. This, it turned out, had been a good call.

At that point, I deduced the diamond-shaped light was traveling faster than sound, headed in a westerly direction toward Camp Bullis. That would explain it soaring right over the house. In the distance, I could still hear the car alarms sounding and the chaos as people stepped out of their homes to look at the sky and all around for any evidence of what had happened. I could hear my neighbors discussing whether the boom could have been an electrical transformer exploding or an airplane crashing at Camp Bullis.

The truth was that no one knew what had made the sound, but everyone knew it was something big and powerful. Just how powerful, we would soon find out. The first clue that something spectacular was happening was when all the deer in the vicinity ran frantically away from the diamond light in the sky and headed east, past my property and further into the city. Deer only headed into the city when they were in search of food or running away from what they perceived as life-threatening danger. Nothing was changing their minds about it; pretty instinctively smart, if you asked me. I should have done the same. Running, however, was never my way. In other words, my animal brethren were smarter than me.

I quickly realized that whatever had made the boom was far too large a threat to neutralize with small firearms. I stepped out into the front driveway, which faced west, and I saw it much clearer: the light I had seen before and had thought I would never see again, from the Bermuda Triangle to South Texas. I felt at that moment that my peaceful retirement plan of riding off quietly into the sunset was dashed. There, in front of me again, was the light and sound from that warm summer night when I'd transitioned to the ship's homeport in Mayport, Florida, many years before.

Some folks blamed the activity in the Bermuda Triangle on magnetic concentrations, methane hydrate, the powerful effects of the Gulf Stream, and other more mysterious theories. Still others were convinced that the lost city of Atlantis was underwater there. Others were sure there was a secret extraterrestrial base somewhere in the Sohm Abyssal Plain, which covered over 350,000 square miles of ocean floor. The depth of the ocean there exceeded five miles in places. Strange things happened there all the time. Strange lights, rogue waves, a green haze of electrical activity, wind and sound anomalies, electronic equipment failures, loss of compass directions, and then some. I'd seen many of these hard-to-explain anomalies with my own eyes. It was a place where you never quite felt comfortable in your own skin. It was something you simply came to accept as a part of sailing the Bermuda Triangle, something you had to experience yourself to fully understand. This happening in Texas felt completely different. It was too close to home.

I realized that the city lights were out in every direction from my home's elevated position, as far the eye could see. I hadn't noticed it before because of the brightness of the diamond light and the moon. It seemed strange and eerie that there was no road noise present. No vehicles moving along the roads in the distance. I stood in complete silence. I stepped out of my home under the cover of darkness and the few cedar trees that lined the edge of the mountain's small plateau, where my house was built. The only lights in the sky were the moonlight from the east and the bright diamond light from the west. The moon was not particularly threatening, so I focused my attention on the diamond light over the western sky that had once before made me disappear for almost a third of a day with no explanation whatsoever.

Since I felt the handgun on my hip wasn't of much use, I began the process of retreating into the house for some cover. Suddenly, before I could make it back inside, the diamond-shaped light became larger. It moved steadily and judiciously toward my elevated house. There was no sound coming from the direction of the light, but its size and brightness were increasing with every second elapsed. As I ran back toward the house, I began second-guessing just how smart it was to have a home high in the sky with great penthouse windows that stretched from the floor to the ceiling.

Those were my tactical circumstances, and I knew where everything was, including the best points from which to engage an enemy from inside the home. I could feel adrenaline shoot into my bloodstream and my heartbeat hasten in fight-or-flight preparation. I had been there before and knew the feeling well. I wasn't quite sure of the better of the two options, but I decided I would fly to take cover and then fight for my life. I ran through the front door and shut it behind me with a slam. I quickly turned over the sofa and pushed it across the tile floor to the front door, which was made of glass and was all that stood between the light and me. The light arrived and stopped directly over my house, blinding me with the most intense illumination I had ever seen. It seemed to penetrate every window at the same time, as though bending to reach more intensely into the house. Then all hell broke loose.

Remember my shatterproof windows? They weren't. Every window and anything made of glass shattered in that split-second. Luckily for me, I was using the overturned sofa as a shield, and it protected me for the most part from the flying broken glass, so I wasn't injured by it. The water from the large glass fish tank drenched my belly as I lay on the floor. Some glass rained into the house, while some glass fell away. This was frightening for me. It told me that this gigantic flying light was able to exert a force from the inside of the house, where I'd hoped to have some small measure of safety.

Then I froze. Literally. I was completely unable to move. I could breathe and see, and I could hear sound, but I could not produce it, no matter how hard I fought. Every effort I made was futile and terrifying. How could I fight without moving? I was stuck on the floor behind the sofa with my handgun, and I was completely helpless. I could feel the cold water of the fish tank crawling across the floor and wetting my upper body, a reminder that I was still alive and in serious trouble. I could see my cichlid fish flopping on the ground and could do nothing about it. Another victim.

A high-pitched electronic sound began to pierce the house, faint at first but growing louder and louder until it was deafening. I could only describe it as a sound like a house alarm going off, only much, much louder. At the same time, the bright light became even more intense. It entered in the form of a humanoid entity bathed in an ultra-brilliant glow. It stepped into the house and toward me through the blown-out front door. I was being hunted. The being had to be at least nine feet tall and was twice as wide as an average-sized human. This was not going to end well.

I could only lay there in terror, feeling the evil run through me until the dark entity decided it was done with me and had heard enough of my prayers for salvation and strength. I was helpless. The deafening high-pitched sound continued, and some type of craft moved silently at a speed not achievable by humanmade aircraft. The other sound I recalled hearing was, ironically enough, what sounded like horse hooves striking and shaking the ground. It must have been my mind playing tricks on me, assaulted as it was by pure terror.

I wondered how I could regain control of my body, and that was my final thought before I lost consciousness. The sound, light, and terror left. So did I.

The time was 11:11.

# CHAPTER 4: THE DRY LAND

Far away from Earth, the dry wind howled as it denuded the prominent rocks of a barren landscape. Shrah was the third of four circumbinary planets in the system of binary stars known as Kinich Ahau. Kinich Ahau was the name given by the people of Shrah to the binary stars that rose and set in their skies every day. As such, there were two suns in their sky.

The solar duo warmed the skies of the planets that orbited them. They were both at the center of the system, but they were different from one another. The main-sequence star was much like Sol, which warmed the skies of Earth in the Milky Way galaxy. It was comparable in size, intensity, and age. Its counterpart star, the smaller one, was a sub-stellar brown dwarf, no longer massive enough to maintain the hydrogen-1 fusion necessary to be a main-sequence star that burned hot like Earth's sun.

Shrah was a relatively small planet that

rotated on its axis every twenty-five hours and took 360 solar days to orbit Kinich Ahau, like many other planets in Andromeda and other galaxies in the universe. It contained water in deep underground aquifers but not on its surface; the radiation of light from the binary star system, Kinich Ahau, was direct and intense. Some of the underground aquifers were as deep as 5,000 feet.

The vast majority of the population lived in the poles of the small planet, where starlight was less direct and, thus, less severe. Temperatures at the poles weren't cold or wet enough for snow. The logistics of drawing underground water was a skill well known to the people of Shrah. The air always felt quite dry, making the skin of the planet's inhabitants leathery and rough to the touch.

Plants on Shrah had small leaves or none at all, reducing transpiration and preserving water. These plants were few and far between and were survivors in every sense of the word. On Shrah, the two choices were to store water or perish. The plants that survived were able to store and conserve water in accordance with the living conditions of the extreme desert. Others simply remained dormant in periods when it did not rain and woke when water became available. Life found a way.

Animals were no different. They too had the choice of storing water or dying. Life for animals on Shrah was greatly complicated by their need to preserve the very small amount of water they were exposed to during the planet's yearly orbit. For that reason, mammals, amphibians, and birds were few. It was far easier for reptiles and insects to survive in the dry climate. Most animals found ways to reclaim their own water to stay hydrated. They burrowed in the cooler underground and hunted at night. Still others manufactured water through their own metabolic digestive systems.

Shrah had no enemies and existed independently from the Empire of Tai-Anh, which had its headquarters on the fourth planet in the Kinich Ahau system. Shrah had once been a commonwealth of the empire. It was this relationship that had led many of Shrah's bravest young soldiers to fight for the Tai-Anh Empire in the Mine War. The empire was particularly fond of warriors from Shrah, as they inherently had the ability and will to fight far above any others known to the empire's leadership. It was as if those born on Shrah were ingrained with the fighting spirit of generations, centuries-old warrior ancestry buried deep within them. In keeping, warriors from Shrah were the most decorated of all warriors in the empire; they were intelligent and lethal. Shrah recruits and veterans were often the first to go into hostile combat environments, and many were killed or maimed. The survivors were battle-hardened for the rest of their lives.

Many of Shrah's surviving interplanetary warriors had returned home to join the leadership ranks and form the military forces of the planet. These were in place to protect the planet from any and all threats posed to them at any point in their existence. In addition to the veterans of war were Shrah's homegrown and highly trained templar knights and special forces operatives, who were trained to maintain the sovereignty of the planet. Shrah knew that its existence could be threatened at any time from places far beyond the galactic borders. It wouldn't be the first time.

With time to kill, Seth Alom sat atop the Great Pyramid, which reached high above the land without obstruction. The pyramid was his favorite meditation spot, as it towered high into the desert sky. The structure had been built by builders unknown to the present residents of Shrah before Seth's people had relocated from the distant stars in centuries past. He often wondered who had transported them and why his people had no knowledge of those who'd come before them. All Seth knew was that his ancestors had once lived and thrived in another land before a bright light in the sky had relocated them to this planet.

The bright light in the sky seemed to be a common appearance all across the universe when beings and entire civilizations were transported, sometimes against their will, to alien planets. The people of Shrah had been relocated to a desert with existing stone structures that closely resembled the structures found in many areas of Earth, millions of miles away in a distant galaxy.

Similar structures to the Great Pyramid of Shrah existed on Earth in North Africa, Mesoamerica, South America, North America, Asia, Europe, Australia, Africa, and even hidden deep in the snow in both the Arctic and Antarctic regions. Ironically, inhabitants of both Shrah and Earth were baffled by how or why these structures had been built and by whom. They could only speculate and hypothesize.

The young ruler-in-training was enjoying the view of the barren landscape created by the Great Creator, shadows cast by the high mountains and deep canyons bathed in sunlight and dust devils dancing over the dry terrain. He was also enjoying the smell of the few desert plants that surrounded the Great Pyramid. Nights on Shrah were especially cold, as the planet had very little cloud cover to trap the day's warmth inside its atmosphere. Shrah was a harsh planet, but it was also one full of harmony, beautifully stark landscapes, and brilliant starry skies. There was a certain clarity to the sky on Shrah. The little vegetation that existed there was brilliant and exploding in color, set into a golden and jagged landscape of rock and soft sand.

Shrah was Seth's home, and his soul felt at peace there, though deep inside, he knew he wasn't from there originally. He was of average height for his age, and he had exotic lines to his face. His mother had dark skin, and his father was of lighter coloring. Seth had sharp, strong muscles that were still developing to their full potential. His athleticism, sharp eye, and mind for combat were proof that some were born to survive over others. He was a specimen of sorts among a people who were bred for combat as it was. Eventually, Seth would assume the title held by his father and mother, Ajaw or Ruler of the Land. The title had been brought to Shrah by the planet's first inhabitants.

Listening to the spirits of ancestors had been an important part of the Alom family legacy for many generations. Sometimes, the spirits spoke to Seth in his dreams. Ancestors no longer physically alive, who had passed onto another dimension, communicated with him through a medium created by Seth himself in a connective trance. This was a dangerous way to communicate; it could have led to evil or occult entities passing through the medium and into the present dimension or even to spiritual possession. But these trans-dimensional meditative trances were a spiritual staple for the people of Shrah. They were called Atsalat meditations.

Through Atsalat, there had been plenty of cases of possessions by occult entities. Occult entities with physical or spiritual life prevailed in the universe, and Shrah was no exception. When portals to other dimensions were opened, both the enlightened and the occult became aware of a bridge connecting their dimension to the dimension of the physically living, the dimension where they had once found themselves before transitioning to life after physical death. Being connected to another dimension and having a sense of predestined purpose in the future was a part of Seth's daily life. He was connected to the past, present, and future.

Seth felt the need for Atsalat meditation at that moment, high above the desert. He craved the peace that came with the ancient practice of connecting with the Eleventh Dimension of spiritual existence. He looked up into the sky, took a deep breath, and closed his eyes. With his eyes closed and his lungs full of air, he brought his head back to level, exhaling slowly. Seth's breathing slowed, and he took in his surroundings with all of his senses. He knew well that the Great Creator's energy surrounded all creation and that energy spoke to all living creatures. The problem had always been that creatures did much asking of the Great Creator but not much listening to the responses provided. Seth listened.

He had received the message from his enlightened spiritual ancestors that the universe contained many inhabitable planets with living beings who were brothers and sisters of Shrah's citizens. Many of his sisters and brothers had been relocated throughout the universe by unknown entities, settling on other planets to preserve the continued existence of the original beings. In his dreams and visions, Seth often saw a male and a female. He knew their names to be Votan and Ixchel.

They appeared to him dressed in a way quite foreign to the people of Shrah. They were scantily clad and not dressed for the climate of Shrah, where the light from the stars shone without mercy. Shrah's inhabitants had to wear light-colored loose clothing to keep cool.

Who were these two ancestors, Votan and Ixchel? Did they come from a distant time and a distant land? What did they mean in his life? Were they to be feared, loved, or revered? Seth pondered these questions endlessly. One thing was certain: Votan and Ixchel were important to his existence, his past, and his future. Seth's mother and father had told him the origin of these two beings, and the universal plan would eventually be revealed to him, along with his role in carrying it out. Votan and Ixchel . . .

# CHAPTER 5: UNWELCOME VISITORS

Seth often visited the Great Pyramid, either climbing to the top on the outside or venturing into the labyrinths deep within. He spent days there, often sleeping inside and receiving energy and information he hadn't put together in his mind yet. He dreamed vividly. These dreams and visions were pieces of a grand puzzle that slowly but surely was completing itself deep in his psyche, to be fully revealed to his consciousness someday, as if being assembled in the Eleventh Dimension for delivery in the present.

Seth wondered who had built the pyramid. Who'd had the technology, engineering prowess, drive, and equipment to cut stone and limestone with precision far beyond that achievable by the present inhabitants of Shrah? Who'd had the means to lift and move millions of stones, some weighing as much as 100,000 pounds? Why had the pyramid been built in the first place? What had happened to the builders of the pyramid? Seth couldn't wait to have answers to all these questions that haunted him. The answers felt so very close and yet so out of reach.

As a teenager, Seth had already received much of his basic education and extensive hand-to-hand combat training. He was already very skilled in the ancient and deadly martial art of Ch'o'Jonik, lethal even to most adult warriors. But he still lacked training and real-life combat experience. What he lacked in experience, he made up for in guts and fury. Seth was the son of one of the most revered and respected warriors in Shrah's history, Ajaw Michael Alom. The ajaw was also the supreme teacher of Ch'o'Jonik, an art that had been developed and implemented long ago by the ancestors of the people of Shrah on a distant planet. Ch'o'Jonik had transcended space and time with his people. The leaders of Temple Alom were extensively trained in the fighting art.

Michael and his wife, Maya, had a simple policy: treat all living beings with love first. Force, they believed, was to be used only to prevent the loss of life. When force was used, it was to be used with lethality. This policy had been part of Seth's upbringing from day one. Michael had always made it clear that he was raising an adult, not a child. He loved Seth very much—too much to coddle him.

Colonel Buluc Hix was Seth's primary trainer in the art of lethality. Buluc had been trained at Tai-Anh's headquarters and had served on several combat expeditions for the empire. He'd also had extensive training in Ch'o'Jonik on Shrah. Buluc often worried that Seth had far too explosive a temper, even at his young age. Buluc knew that anger often allowed the intrusion of occult entities upon the soul. Much carnage throughout the history of the universe had come this wrathful way. Buluc wanted his ajaw-in-training to be more even-tempered and to understand that gentleness was sometimes more powerful than severity. Everyone was a work in progress.

Michael had tasked Buluc with mentoring Seth, teaching him to kill swiftly but only when deadly force was the only solution and always remaining in complete control. Michael remembered himself when he'd first served in combat for the empire at a much younger age, and he knew just how much maturity had corrected many of his temperamental flaws. Michael had learned much about life from his ancestors during his own Atsalat meditations.

Buluc was responsible for the development of Seth's fighting skills, but primary responsibility for Seth's spiritual development belonged to Temple Alom's reverend, Kabel Luu. Kabel was, to many, the most perfect creature the Great Creator could have created. She had flowing light-brown hair and large, expressive brown eyes and was just as beautiful outside as she was inside. Males, females, and non-binary people on Shrah and Tai-Anh lamented that she was not interested in physical relationships but was madly in love with the Shrah Philosophy and her service to Temple Alom. The priests taught directly out of the Sacred Codices and through oral tradition kept alive throughout the generations, passed from priest to priest.

Kabel was second-in-command to the ajaw and was high priest of the Shrah Philosophy. Michael was the sovereign of the Kingdom of Shrah. The Sacred Codices were expressly clear that the ruler of the land was to have special communication directly from the spirits of the ancestors and from the Great Creator. The Sacred Codices and the Shrah Philosophy prophesized that there was a spirit from beyond who would unify and bring peace to the universe. This peace would come after great strife in the form of war, famine, pestilence, and death. The people of Shrah were all aware of the prophecy and believed it. The Sacred Codices did not speak of when or whom.

Several missionaries and Shrah youth in service of the empire had taken a liking to the teachings of the Shrah Philosophy. They had taken it back to Tai-Anh and spoken about the wonders of it. The philosophy had continued to gain momentum within the empire. Emperor Herod Exelcior had forbidden the teachings and all practices and temples dedicated to what he called the Shrah religion. The people of Shrah never considered the Sacred Codices or their oral tradition as their way of life. Regardless, the Shrah tradition, or religion, as the emperor would have it, was outlawed and its practice made punishable by incarceration until full "correction" was achieved or, if correction failed, death. Those who practiced Shrah traditions, philosophies, and "religious" practices did so at great risk of persecution, arrest, or worse.

On Shrah, however, the philosophy could be practiced at will and with much freedom. Although Seth was surrounded by people who not only felt a responsibility for his development but also loved him deeply, he often felt he had a strong relationship with and much to learn from his spiritual ancestors in the Eleventh Dimension and from the Great Creator directly. This influenced how much time he spent alone in meditation, elevating his consciousness to a higher spiritual dimension. For Seth, the Shrah Philosophy was simply the only way to live.

Seth returned to the present dimension atop the Great Pyramid and ended his visit with his spiritual ancestors, Votan and Ixchel. They were a staple in his visits during Atsalat. He gathered his senses anew in the physical realm and breathed in the hot desert breeze. Something was off about it. There was an ever-so-slight difference in the scent of the air, caused by the charged particles of another body's presence. He scanned his vision over the vast and desolate gold land from the top of the towering stone pyramid. He became aware that he was not alone but didn't immediately react. Seth found that the universe spoke to him at a cellular level as if injecting information into his consciousness. He felt more aware and complete every time he visited the Great Pyramid. The ajaw-to-be was hyper-conscious.

Seth continued to feel that the energy flow of the cosmos was turbulent in his vicinity. High altitudes had a way of calming the soul. He focused his eyes to see what he felt on the ground from a height of nearly 500 feet above the dry desert sands. He saw movement on the ground below and heard a noise from the side of the Great Pyramid, close to him and facing south.

A voice within him told him to run. He quickly moved into a heightened state of readiness as he recognized the grave danger and listened intently for the repetition of noises from the pyramid's south face while keeping out of sight by beginning to descend from the pyramid on the north face. Seth knew he had a little over 200 steps to get to the bottom of the pyramid and to the sand below. He made the decision that he would rather fight on the ground than on the Great Pyramid at that height. He would have to fight. Although he didn't know whom he would fight or even why, he knew his life depended on it.

As he rapidly climbed down the north face of the pyramid, Seth saw two completely covered figures with blades already exposed coming over the top of the pyramid and after him from above. Seth noticed that the blades were made of metal and were not the typical obsidian knives, made of volcanic rock from the mountains high above the desert, used by the people of Shrah. He quickened his pace, knowing, in his youth and with the training he'd had with Buluc, he could outrun most men. He would fight only if cornered or engaged in combat directly.

Seth kept his obsidian fighting knife sheathed as Buluc had taught him so as to retain the element of surprise. The two attackers were matching their pace with his as they climbed down on the north face. Seth could feel his heart pumping blood through his entire body.

As he leapt from the final step and onto the dry sand at the base of the pyramid, Seth knew he had enough athleticism and a head start to outrun his attackers, but instead, he found strength. He stopped to face his attackers and neutralize the threat right there and then. Then he saw them. Two more were approaching him from behind. He was now surrounded by four attackers, all intent on bringing about his end. They were dressed in black outfits, and their faces were covered to hide their identities. They were competent assassins with strength and training. Their blades were unsheathed and ready as they approached. The metal of the knives shone in the light of Kinich Ahau, which hung high above the planet.

Seth unsheathed his knife and prepared for a deadly battle, slowing his breathing and heart rate down, increasing the oxygen flowing to his brain and muscles, and commanding his veins to recede to minimize blood loss. Buluc's training would soon be put to the test. He didn't have enough time to enter a trance and allow his ancestors to guide him. This fight, Seth would fight alone.

Before Seth could turn around, the tip of a blade at his back punctured his skin. He spun quickly, forcing the blade to slice open his back. The knife had been thrown at him. Seth realized that these were not attackers trained in Ch'o'Jonik. His training did not encourage separation between a blade and a fighter. Seth's quick reaction had saved his life for the time being. The metal blade had severely gauged the skin on his back, and blood began to drip in puddles onto the sand. All four attackers now advanced on him, moving their knives in trained and deadly strikes and swoops.

Seth assumed a modified front fighting stance and quickly hastened the closing of distance between him and one of the attackers. He slashed across the attacker's jugular artery, dropping him to the ground instantly. A second attacker moved in with a lunging knife strike. Seth blocked the strike with his empty fist, sidestepped at a forty-five-degree angle, and swept his obsidian blade in a calculated strike, cutting through the tendons of the arm with which the attacker was holding the knife, forcing the attacker to drop it.

Seth came back around in a fluid motion, decapitating the second attacker. The attacker's head thumped as it hit the sandy ground. Before Seth could do anything further, he realized he was beginning to lose consciousness from the blood loss caused by the wound on his back. As Seth kicked away the second attacker's head, sending it rolling in the sand with its eyes and mouth still open, the third attacker managed to stab Seth, creating a deep chest injury that left a sucking wound in its wake. As Seth dropped to the ground, he severed the third attacker's femoral artery, spilling blood into a bright red pool, which both Seth and his attacker fell into.

Seth and the third attacker rolled around in the blood. As the fourth and final attacker turned and ran, Seth saw a squad of templar knights headed his way from a distance.

One member of the six-person squad of templar knights was Buluc himself. Buluc did not stop to give assistance to Seth, instead leaving the other five templar knights to attend to him. Buluc continued his chase of the fourth attacker. The pair fled from sight on foot with Buluc in hot pursuit as his ruler-to-be was left behind to die slowly in agony.

# CHAPTER 6: THE LONG TRIP HOME

Far away from Planet Shrah, my nausea was so strong it made me miserable. Feeling nauseous is one of the worst experiences there is. The most nauseous I had ever felt before had been during hurricanes aboard surface warships at sea. Hurricanes had a way of turning sailors into vomit artists.

I had been taken, quite rudely, if I might add, from my home several months before and had been in what seemed like a dream state ever since. I had been slipping in and out of consciousness for days on end and had no way of measuring time because I hadn't been outdoors to see the sun. Instinctively, I looked for my wristwatch. The last time I'd seen it had been the night of the big boom in the Texas sky. I felt as if I had been drugged for months on end.

I could feel a slight sense of motion of the room I was in. Was I in a vehicle, or was I under the influence of a narcotic? Was I traveling on a ship, an airplane, or something else? To make matters worse, I found myself on a bed in a white room with white plastic-like walls and no windows. I was wearing a slip-on outfit, white in color, and no shoes. The temperature in the room was comfortable, dry and sufficiently warm. I didn't feel injury or pain.

As Pink Floyd would have said, I was comfortably numb. What bothered me most were the nausea and the immobility. I was just as frozen as I had been when the bright diamond light had pinned me down and brought me here to this room. This had to be part of what had happened to me at my home. Perhaps it was a continuation of those events. I must have been being held prisoner, but why and by whom?

The first thing I needed to do was figure out where my pistol was and break out. My immobility couldn't possibly be good, at least not for me. Since my last night of freedom, I had been having a long and vivid dream that had seemed to never end. The dream had felt so real I'd thought I had been killed, that I lived in a new dimension or parallel universe, or that I was in a coma.

But I felt just as alive as I had before my abduction. I felt that way mostly because I had the physical discomfort of the nausea to remind me of it. However, since I had no prior experience with being dead, I had no basis to prove that I wasn't. It was all one big nightmare, and I felt absolutely helpless and completely motionless. Oh, the vulnerability of being human.

What was happening to me? Why hadn't I woken up for so long? How had I eaten or pooped? Had I? I must have carried out bodily functions if I had lived as long as it seemed I had. Was I dead and finding that this was what awaited us at death? Had the light in the sky been the one folks who'd gone through near-death experiences spoke of? Where exactly was I? How long had I been there? How long would they keep me in this condition? What did the folks who had taken me want with me in the first place? Where was my damn pistol? Somebody needed shooting.

I was angry, for sure, but putting two rounds in the heart and one in the brain of my captor or captors was going to be tough to do when I couldn't move a single finger and had no pistol within my reach. I knew I was in a precarious situation. Then, as if out of nowhere, I heard a booming male voice.

The voice asked, "Is that better?"

It was the first audible sound I had heard in a very long time. How wonderful it was to finally hear a real voice. I looked around me.

"Your pistol is not here. Now, as I asked you before, is that better?" the voice reiterated.

This, whatever it was, somehow knew I was thinking of the whereabouts of my pistol. Was the voice only my imagination? It sure sounded real.

I decided to ask a few questions of my own in an attempt to further understand what was happening to me. I spoke from a dry throat that seemed not to have been used in months. "Who are you? How are you speaking to me? How do you seem to know my thoughts? Where am I? Let me see you!"

"Those are complicated questions, Captain Sauer. Sorry about your voice. It will come in fully soon enough. To answer one of your questions, your thoughts are a language we understand. From this moment forward, understand that none of your thoughts are private. Not to us. Your thoughts, as well as everyone else's, impact the universe in ways far deeper than you presently understand. Now, you never answered my question," the voice told me.

Although I was highly agitated, I knew I was powerless without being able to move a muscle. In fact, the more I thought, the more this voice would know what I was up to. I stopped thinking, or I tried to. I decided to play along with the voice for a bit. "What question are you referring to, and who wants to know?"

"Your nausea," the voice replied. "Is it better? You have a form of motion sickness, Captain Sauer. You Earthlings aren't physically accustomed to traveling at speeds approaching the speed of light."

"Approaching the speed of light! Bullshit! Who are you, and what do you want with me? What do you mean, 'you Earthlings'? What are YOU then?" I demanded.

"Captain Sauer, we are indeed traveling at such speeds. I will address your questions when you answer mine," the voice calmly explained.

I didn't have much choice but to comply, so I answered his question. "Yes, actually," I said. "It's gone! Just like that, gone. How did you do that? Am I dreaming?"

The voice replied, "You are not dreaming, Captain Sauer. We simply used what you would call osmosis to release the necessary drug into your bloodstream. No, I didn't use a needle. You have a vast array of drugs stored in pouches we have implanted in your body. There are three of them. We determine when and how much to release, and these drugs are released into your system. They are located adjacent to your anterior pituitary gland, between your liver and pancreas, and in your brain. Not to worry. You are in no danger. Quite the contrary," the voice said.

"Are you shitting me? I feel violated! Did you perform surgery on me while I was passed out?" I was completely beside myself. I made a mental note of the fact that the voice had used the term "we," not "I." There were more of them.

"Captain Sauer, you seem to have a fixation with using variations of the word shit. To answer your question, we didn't perform surgery on you. The technology we used is more advanced than you could possibly comprehend. We also implanted micro-stints in your brain to prevent the stroke you were going to have at age seventy-nine," the voice explained.

I reckoned shooting these pricks was of little use, not that I had my pistol or could move anyway. If we really were traveling fast, which I felt was most likely a bullshit game, where were we going at that speed? The statement about my medical condition struck me as somewhat probable since I'd never known my birth parents. I took a deep breath and decided to save my energy for the close-quarters battle I'd be instigating as soon as I could move again. "Did you otherwise determine I was in perfect health, Dr. Voice?" I asked sarcastically.

"I will address the questions you are thinking about in a while. You had a partially torn right bicep tendon, and your cardiovascular condition had you on your way to a stroke sooner rather than later," the voice told me.

I guessed that would explain the pain I had felt in my right bicep when I'd been at the gym. This whole experience was getting creepier and creepier.

"Not creepy, Captain. Science. We can interpret by your brain chemistry that you are surprised at your former health condition," the voice stated. "Not to worry. We corrected all of it. You are in peak condition now."

So this guy could read my chemistry. I couldn't help but feel violated. Given that he could also read my thoughts, I made sure to think about him kissing my ass. "Thank you for snatching me out of my home and forcibly 'fixing me.' You owe me new windows and the life of my fish, you destructive asshole. Who are you anyway? I'm sure that's a complicated question too," I snapped.

"Actually, not really. Your fish was within days of dying anyway. I will answer your question now. I am a traveler," answered the traveler formerly known as the voice.

"So you travel and abduct people from their homes?" I asked with obvious derision.

"Perhaps who I am is more complicated to explain to you than I initially thought," the traveler said. "I am a traveler. What you do often defines who you are. I have been called many names, but in reality, I am a traveler, a deliverer, and to some, a conqueror."

"Okay, fair enough. Where do you travel to, and what do you deliver, traveler?"

"The galaxy you call the Milky Way, the system of the star you call Sol and the planet you call

Terra, is one place I travel to. The places I travel to and from are too complicated for you to understand at this point. Captain Sauer, I am not being purposely deceitful or evasive. In your words, I am not shitting you. All four of us know who you are. We know where you've been, and we've told you what to dream. What you think and what you actually verbalize are one and the same. Language is just that: language. Your thoughts impose just as much energy on the universe around you as your words do. You know that, Captain Sauer. It's why you talk to animals and plants, one of the reasons we were drawn to you."

"All four of us? Who are the others? Let me guess, three more travelers. You will answer my questions at some point, correct?" I asked.

"That is correct, Captain Sauer."

"Well, then, the four of you should know I am no longer a captain. I'm a retired soon-to-be student again. Where are we traveling to at these high speeds you claim? When will you return me home?"

"I will answer these questions in due time," the traveler promised. "I can tell you, Captain Sauer, that you are no longer retired. You are a captain. A military leader is what you are, as well as who you are. You are not a medical student, nor will you ever be. That is not what is written for you in the stars. You will study and learn what we teach you. You have been our machine since the day you were born, but this particular trip has lasted seven months, seven days, and seven hours."

"You've kept me prisoner for seven months already and are just now communicating with me? Why? There are people on Earth who depend on me and miss me!"

"Name one."

He had a point there.

# CHAPTER 7: REALITY CHECK

I had no answer for the traveler, and that very thought made me feel quite alone in the universe.

The traveler continued, "Soon, you will learn how much more life there is in the universe and how important you are to many. You were in a sort of learning mode. When it's time, your learning will be unlocked, and you will have access to all of it. We have programmed your brain to store information confidentially from your own psyche."

"Do you mean to tell me that the long dream I thought I was having was a very long lesson you were teaching me?"

"Yes. It wasn't a dream, Captain Sauer," the traveler stated flatly. "Call it a private lesson. Dreams as you know them don't really exist. Dreams are your own existence in another dimension of your being. You will remember all the lessons when we unlock the part of your brain that stores this information."

This made me wonder if this was what happened when we died. It didn't make sense to me that we could only remember the physical life in which we lived presently. The sum of memories, consciousness, and experience couldn't just disappear. What about the concept of a soul? I didn't believe that my existence had begun with my physical birth and was set to end with my physical death. I was much more than flesh that grew old and then rotted. I snapped back to my present situation. "Why did you abduct me?"

"We did not abduct you, Captain Sauer. We simply gave you the means to travel elsewhere to complete the mission that was assigned to you long ago, before you were given a physical existence. These are things you presently cannot remember because they are locked in your brain until you transition spiritually or we unlock them. We are doing our service obligation, Captain. You appreciate service. We know you do."

"When did I choose this service again?" I asked, getting more irritated with the evasive answers I was being provided.

The traveler responded, "When you opted to add a physical dimension to your being."

"Are you saying it was my choice before I was born? Did I choose to be born an orphan?" I asked with obvious irritation in my voice.

"Yes," the traveler offered. "All beings

choose their way of entering the physical realm and having free will. Some choose suffering as a means to evolve spiritually. These things are beyond your understanding."

It seemed that a lot was. "This is giving me a headache now. I'm skeptical of what you're telling me. Changing the subject for a bit, when will I be able to move? Will you ever let me move again?" I asked. I was beginning to feel trapped, desperate, and vulnerable.

"Yes. We knew you would wake up ready to do whatever it took to break free and cause as much damage as possible. You have no other choice. It's how you were made, and therefore, it's who you are. You are a member of a highly destructive species: the human race," the traveler said. "I will let you move freely but will immobilize you if and when I deem necessary. Do you understand the terms of this agreement, Captain?"

"Yes," I agreed, as I didn't have much control or choice. The next instant, I was free to move. I sat up weakly and slowly. It took me a while to get my bearings and stability. I noticed my throat was very dry. As I thought about standing up, I remembered that I hadn't moved in a terribly long time. I began to stand and felt heaviness in my legs from the months of immobility, but I noticed I had not lost muscle mass in my legs. This made me very happy. I was afraid I would lose my footing if I took a step. It felt similar to when your legs fall asleep and you attempt to stand up too quickly.

It took me several minutes to regain my balance, bringing me flashbacks of learning to walk again in hydrotherapy after an injury I'd sustained during the war. That injury and the physical therapy afterward had been an experience I didn't want to re-live. It had taken me three months to learn how to walk again, only to walk on crutches for another six months. Fortunately for me, that wasn't the case this time around. I wondered why I felt normal gravity if I was really traveling through space but chose not to mess with my newly granted freedom to move by irritating the traveler.

As I walked slowly around the room, getting used to my bodyweight again, the voice I knew as the traveler began to materialize in front of my very eyes. What I assumed to be the materialization of the traveler was a being nine feet in height and twice the width of an average human. This must have been the entity that had entered my home on Earth, I figured. I noticed he was not imposing any weight on the soft floor under his feet. I wondered if the other travelers were also nine feet tall.

"We usually represent ourselves in our essential state, which, from your perspective, is nine feet tall. In response to a prior thought of yours, you are not weightless because this vessel creates an artificial gravity through centrifugal force equivalent to the weight you would have at sea level on Earth."

"You reading my mind has to go!" I said. "I have no privacy whatsoever with you inside my head!"

"Remember what I told you," the traveler replied. "Your thoughts are not private, and they exert a measurable force on others in the universe. Your thoughts make things happen. They cause harm or good. There is no privacy anywhere in the universe."

I searched for a weak spot where I could attack him and make my escape when the moment arrived. I figured the being that traveled wasn't human. "Is your goal to hold me hostage here and teach me stuff about thoughts and mindreading?" I asked with my usual sarcasm and increasing frustration. I approached the traveler, and we began to walk out of the room through a long walkway with a green room at the end.

The traveler was huge, but with two rounds in the heart and one in the brain, it wouldn't know what had hit it. I could see that it didn't seem to have weight, as the cushiony floor underneath our feet did not depress when it walked on it. Who or what was this thing? Was it even shoot-able? I figured it wouldn't be of much use anyway.

"Captain Sauer, I was hoping not to have to speak to you this way, but you have given me no choice. We are traveling at near the speed of light, heading away from your planet through a wormhole located along the underwater cliffs of the Puerto Rico Trench. They're miles deep in what you Earthlings call the Bermuda Triangle. We are deep in space already and entering a neighboring galaxy. We have artificial gravity technology on our vessel for your comfort and health. If you don't like it in the vessel, you are welcome to step outside of the hatch and out into negative 450 degrees Fahrenheit now. Forget about your gun. It is a waste of your time and only wastes your energy on futile activity. We know about your medals and commendations during the Third World War on your planet and in space. We commend you on your tactical training, leadership, and courage. However, your mind and spirit are the most powerful weapons you have and the ones we are most interested in. You are going to help ensure the survival of your species. The Great Creator has given you free will. We who travel, however, do not have free will and are faithful servants of the same Great Creator you know. We are here to help you save your own existence, and this responsibility has been preordained. Don't make us hurt you more than is necessary."

I listened carefully to every word the traveler told me, and for some reason, I felt the veracity of his words, although I didn't care much for his threatening tone. "Traveler, I understand that I can't help my present situation. I have no choice in the matter, just as you have stated. I don't know what you are. I know you are not human. I will listen to what you have to say." I continued, "With that, I have to share the following with you. If you ever threaten me with pain or otherwise, I will die if I have to, doing my best to knock your teeth down your throat."

The traveler turned to me and gave a genuine smile. "We knew you were the right person for this mission when we first abducted you from that warship in the Bermuda Triangle."

# CHAPTER 8: JUSTICE ACCORDING TO SHRAH

Michael Alom's favorite conference room overlooked the City of Nacaome on Shrah. The conference room was on the windward side of Temple Alom and was several thousand feet in altitude, overlooking the city from atop a rocky mountain. This was where the leaders of the golden planet had their most important meetings, encased by the large glass windows. The usual attendees were members of the ajaw's Security Council.

The view out the windows was striking. From there, one had the illusion of being on the gold planet alone. The windward side of the majestic mountain was not built on because it was steep, assaulted by the wind incessantly. That morning, the gold hue of the dry sky could be seen in all its splendor, shades of gold, yellow, and orange interweaving in the distance in the absence of clouds. Spectators could see the patterns on the sands left by the wind's overnight dance.

To the left in the distance below stood the Great Pyramid, a link to Shrah's past. To the right were the training and research engineering facilities that were linked to Shrah's future. From the conference room, Shrah's leaders could look forward and backward in time with great pride.

Present at that morning's Security Council meeting were Maya Alom, General Isaiah Gabriel, Reverend and Colonel Kabel Luu, Dr. and Colonel Noah Mandel, Captain Danli Itzamna, Lieutenant Yoro Copan, and Lieutenant Obasi Sabina. Danli, Yoro, and Obasi were representing the Shrah Special Forces.

All present at the meeting had already completed their early morning runs and showers and were wearing their peridot rings, made from pieces cut from the massive meteorite that had fallen from the sky and landed near the base of the Great Pyramid centuries before. The leaders of the Shrah people did not know where the peridot had come from exactly, but they knew that this gemstone had traveled among the stars and chosen to land on their planet. That was a good enough reason to wear a piece of it.

Absent from the meeting were Michael and

Buluc. The ajaw was away, sitting at his son's bedside while he fought an uphill battle for his life after the vicious attack on him. Buluc was somewhere out in the desert, hunting down Seth's single surviving attacker.

Michael's seat was at the head of the table next to his wife. Maya sat alone in their spot in her husband's absence. She could feel the pain in her husband's and her own heart, and she knew how hard Michael was suppressing his anger at the perpetrators of Seth's suffering. Maya and Michael were connected on a deep spiritual level. She knew it was just a matter of time before her husband exploded into retaliatory action, but she also knew he would never release his rage upon anyone until he knew for sure who was responsible.

In Shrah society, both spouses, regardless of gender, ruled as one.

Michael sat at his son's bedside, knowing that Buluc was somewhere out in the desert, dead or alive, for the second day in pursuit of young Seth's fourth attacker. Buluc had a way of wanting to resolve matters with his own bare hands, and he was highly qualified for such tasks.

Buluc had slayed many an enemy with only a knife while fighting in the war for the empire's control of the mining facilities on one of Tai-Anh's two moons, Magna Hermopolis. It was the moon that orbited closest to Tai-Anh and the one that contained mineable raw materials.

The warrior most respected by the citizens of Tai-Anh was the Ajaw of Shrah, Michael Alom. The ajaws, Isaiah, Kabel, Noah, Danli, Yoro, Obasi, and Buluc had served together in the Mine War.

At the time of the Mine War, the empire had fought against a separatist faction from within Tai-Anh known as Lyndon. During one such battle, Buluc's legion had been ambushed and nearly extinguished. Michael was the supreme ruler of the land in Shrah, but to the empire, he was General Michael Alom, promoted to the full flag rank after the Mine War. This would be his title for as long he lived, anywhere within the reach of the empire. This title wasn't important to Michael. He simply wanted his people to be left alone in peace in the Kinich Ahau system.

In the meeting on Shrah, Kabel spoke first in the Shrah language of K'iché. "How is he doing, Ajaw?"

"Not well, Kabel. He's in a medically induced coma," responded Maya with dread in her voice, barely mustering the strength to speak.

Maya and Kabel were the closest of friends and had grown up together in Shrah's Nacaome City. They'd gone to school together and confided in each other those secrets hidden in a woman's secret garden, the one where men weren't allowed, only thought they were. Besides Michael, Kabel knew Maya more intimately than anyone and was her most trusted advisor.

"I will maintain an intense meditation schedule for the intercession of the Great Creator so that purified universal energy may flow to Seth and replace the spent particles in his body," responded Kabel.

Maya smiled and turned her attention to Noah. "Noah, would you please catch us up on Seth's medical condition?" The pain, anger, and fear for her son's life were evident in Maya's voice.

"Yes, my lady. Seth lost over forty percent of his birth blood and is presently being kept alive by mechanical means. I am sorry to say his chances of living are very poor, so we must prepare for any outcome at this point," reported Noah, holding back his emotions as he delivered the news. "Our ajaw is not leaving his son's side and has posted guards at every access point to the infirmary." Noah was Michael's trusted childhood friend, just like Kabel was for Maya. He was the only person, besides Isaiah and Buluc, Michael considered a brother.

"Thank you, Noah. I will be at my husband's side as soon as we finish this meeting." Maya then turned to Isaiah. "Any updates on Buluc or on the whereabouts of the fourth assassin? Have we located them?"

Isaiah answered with frustration lacing his voice. "No, my lady. We are working ceaselessly to locate them and render any necessary assistance, but we have been unable to find them. As you know, Buluc is a master in operating covertly. This is most likely keeping us from finding him. This is personal for him. It's personal for all of us. Buluc has always preferred one-on-one combat. If this assassin is worth anything, he or she is also trained in evading capture. We will only find them if they wish to be found. Seth successfully exterminated the other assassins singlehandedly, and we are aware of only this fourth assassin presently. We used all available night vision and infrared equipment last night in the desert area adjacent to the Great Pyramid. All indications are that this was orchestrated not from within the temple but by outsiders. The investigation is underway, and you will have a full report as soon as possible."

The satisfaction and pride in Isaiah's eyes at Seth's fighting ability was obvious. All people on Shrah knew that their future ajaw might have to lead them into battle at some point. The fighting ability of the Shrah people was a source of pride for all citizens. Fighting ran in their veins, and physical gore was not upsetting to them, not even to the very young. They were, in a way, created to be comfortable with killing.

"Thank you, Isaiah. I want my son's assassin thoroughly interrogated and brought to trial."

"My lady—"

Before the general could continue, Maya

interrupted respectfully. "I understand. Buluc has our full support in handling the matter as he wishes."

"Yes, my lady."

Isaiah grinned at the thought that Maya understood that Buluc was a free thinker and that he had the full trust of the temple to handle matters such as this as he deemed necessary. Buluc just might perform the necessary interrogation of the assassin out in the field when he came face to face with the attacker alone in the desert. Both the assassin's and Buluc's lives were in peril.

Maya proceeded to close the meeting. "We will meet again to discuss the details we discover from the interrogation of the assassin when they are caught and put through the subsequent trial that will be necessary."

Maya stood to leave, on her way to Michael and Seth in the infirmary, when the conference room's door opened. All present saw who had opened it.

"Buluc!" Maya exclaimed with great relief that her grand knight was safe at home.

Buluc entered the room, holding a red rag in his hand, the hand that bore his peridot ring. He bowed to his ajaw, then placed the rag open on the conference table.

Maya looked down at the heart that had once pumped the blood of an enemy and stated flatly, "Looks like there will be no need for a trial after all."

# CHAPTER 9: THE WET LAND

One orbiting planet away from Shrah, on a wet and blue planet, there was an altar. Directly behind the altar was a black, white, and gold symbol. The symbol was that of a movement, both spiritual and physical. Below the symbol read the words, "School of the Eleventh Dimension." The altar itself was in an obscure building in the dark recesses of the metal city on Tai-Anh.

A group of 100 known as believers sat in Atsalat meditative trances in a large, dark, quiet room. Many were still wet from walking in the steady rain outside on their way to the meditation. The believers had been indoctrinated into the School of the Eleventh Dimension and had begun their path to becoming elevated and, eventually, enlightened. They were the first members of an extended spiritual family with origins from far beyond the Andromeda galaxy that connected to galaxies across the universe. The family of the Eleventh Dimension was one that projected its spiritual influence throughout the cosmos like an interstellar beacon carrying messages from anyone able to tap into the energy of a cosmic superhighway to anyone who had the ability and willingness to listen. The primary method for doing this was the Atsalat meditative trance that the inhabitants of Shrah employed one planet away. Tai-Anh was learning the ways of the dry golden planet.

The leader of that particular Atsalat meditation was Hamilton Nile, a doctor who performed surgeries on sick children during the day and was a self-proclaimed enlightened spiritual leader by night. Hamilton had a persuasiveness found only in the greatest and the most dangerous. He had traveled to Shrah on medical missions, where he'd discovered the Shrah Philosophy. Hamilton was thin with dark skin, sharp features, and piercing brown eyes, which gave the impression he could see deep into the soul.

To permit their connective trance, as Seth had done on Shrah, the believers inhaled oxygen and raised their eyes high above them, up into the heavens. The next step was to close their eyes while still gazing high above, then to exhale slowly, bringing their heads back to a relaxed position, keeping their eyes closed and slowing their heart rates. These steps allowed them to tap into the cosmic superhighway, where communication and light energy flowed like a wellspring throughout the universe. The cosmic superhighway was a pipeline where information, energy, and communication flowed freely, and anyone anywhere in the universe could tap into that pipeline and access the light and dark energy within it.

The initiated believers were on a listen-only mode. The elevated were those who readily received information from the cosmic superhighway they sought. The enlightened could send and receive information and communication at will anywhere and at any time.

Hamilton had been on a medical mission to the motherland of the Eleventh Dimension believers, and he'd been inside the Great Pyramid. He was the greatest of the Eleventh Dimension believers of the Shrah Philosophy on Tai-Anh and was the known leader of the philosophy's spread. The Shrah Philosophy and the Eleventh Dimension belief system were one and the same.

Hamilton had helped design the symbol of the motherland's philosophy, which represented all he believed in. The symbol was the white Great Pyramid with the number eleven superimposed on the gold planet Shrah. In the Eleventh Dimension, Hamilton was able to receive and send communication from and to ancient ancestors. Many of his followers on Tai-Anh believed and loved him, while others, especially those in power, despised and even feared him. Regardless of how people felt about him, they all knew of Hamilton Nile and his adherence to the philosophies expounded on distant Shrah, where one of the greatest military leaders in interplanetary history ruled as ajaw of his people in peace and harmony.

The group of Eleventh Dimension believers finished the meditation and were sent home by Hamilton to think about the message they'd received from the cosmic superhighway and what they thought it meant.

Hamilton and Janina Preston, a young and impressionable believer with deep-green eyes, remained in the room after all the others had returned to their respective homes.

Janina spoke first. "I'm troubled by what I saw during my meditation, Hamilton."

"Before we start, Janina, please take this envelope and open it when it is time. I need your promise that you will open it no sooner."

Janina took the envelope in her hand, wondering why Hamilton was giving it to her without much anticipation or explanation. "Time for what? I don't under—"

"You will know when the time comes. Now, tell me about what you saw tonight. You know beings in higher states of existence communicate important lessons to us during Atsalat," continued Hamilton with a warm smile.

Janina placed the envelope in her jacket

pocket. "Hamilton, I saw you and me standing at a high precipice, overlooking a very large body of water. The water extended as far as the eye could see, all the way to where it met the sky."

Hamilton smiled. "Where do you presume this body of water is, Janina?"

"I don't know. I have never seen this place before, and it felt very foreign yet very real to me. Do you understand, Hamilton?"

"Yes, I do. Tell me more. What else did you see?"

"I began to see ships on the water, coming toward the shore, where you and I were standing, looking out," Janina said. "They weren't ships like ours. These ships couldn't fly. They floated on the water's surface and didn't seem to have propulsion other than the wind."

"What were the ships doing?" asked Hamilton with a growing smile on his face that seemed to indicate he already knew Janina's story.

"They arrived on the shore, and when they touched the ground . . . the sky . . . the sky became very dark as if night had fallen. Then you grabbed my hand and told me to run and not to look back," Janina managed to say, her throat dry and her voice raspy. She was visibly shaken by her vision. "I ran as fast as I could, gripped by a terrible fear. That was where my communication ended, and I returned to the present dimension with my heart beating out of my chest. I don't understand what this means or if I simply made it up inside my head. Do you believe me?"

"Of course I do!" Hamilton promised. "What you see with your mind's eye is a very personal communication intended for you and you alone. I have seen the same. Some communications come from mistaken spirits, and they are not of the light. They are deceptive and very dangerous. It's important that you learn to recognize the difference between the two. Your life depends on it. When you raise your consciousness into the cosmos, you must do so with love. Love attracts light and keeps away the dark."

"The fear I felt was just so real," said Janina as she looked deeply at the peridot stone on Hamilton's ring.

"I'm afraid what you saw is very real, Janina. It won't be the last time you find yourself there. Always remember to let love and light flow through you when you are in the Eleventh Dimension."

"How amazing that you have been there, Hamilton! I'm glad I'm not making things up inside my head. What do you . . . ?"

Janina stopped speaking as Hamilton closed his eyes and put up his hand as if listening to a voice inside his head. "Janina, I'm sorry, but I need to be alone. Please leave now," stated Hamilton with a sense of urgency.

"But I don't understand—"

"Now! Janina, please!"

Janina knew the conversation was over. "Yes. I'm sorry, Hamilton," she said, turning to go.

"Don't be sorry, Janina. We will continue this conversation soon. You have my word," said Hamilton. He turned away from her and kneeled at the altar in front of the school's symbol.

Janina proceeded to exit the room and the building, somewhat bewildered by Hamilton's abrupt change in attitude but relieved that what her mind's eye had seen wasn't a figment of her imagination. She stepped out of the metallic building and onto the streets of the rainy city. She was about twenty steps away from the building already when she heard the loud bang in the sky, which broke all the windows in the building. A bright white light came down from a yellow diamond in the night sky and fell directly on the windowless building.

Janina froze, unable to move, and just as quickly as it had arrived, the diamond light shot away into the darkness of the night sky. A few seconds later, a massive explosion knocked Janina to the ground. When she was finally able to stand and focus her eyes, she noticed that the building, with Hamilton inside it, was now a pile of burning metal, completely erased from existence.

The time was 11:11.

# CHAPTER 10: DEADLY ENVY

The Emperor of Tai-Anh, Herod Exelcior, sat in Imperial Headquarters with the Head of the Imperial Third Realm, General Joram Antipas. The two men had history together. Exelcior had hand-selected Antipas for the position. Antipas was the only one who could match his cruelty. He made sure Antipas had plenty of opportunities to employ it.

Rain fell upon the windows in a steady beat, dropping from the sky and onto the metal streets and buildings of Gandolim. The emperor was in a particularly foul mood after the fiasco of the night before.

"Congratulations, General. Your forces destroyed an entire building in the heart of the city and only managed to exterminate one pest. Our intelligence forces informed me the entire group had been holding one of their rituals minutes before the disaster and escaped without a scratch. You missed your mark, General," stated Exelcior with bitterness on his tongue.

"I accept full responsibility, Your Majesty," responded Antipas, knowing full well that there was nothing he could say that would appease the emperor at that moment.

"You are correct. It is entirely your responsibility," rebuffed Exelcior. "Tell me, what exactly did we accomplish last night?"

"We created a martyr, Your Majesty," answered Antipas. He knew precisely where the emperor was heading with his questions and hoped he wouldn't think the response was sarcastic.

"Congratulations, General. You figured it out all on your own. Not only did we create a martyr, but we turned the attention of the entire Imperium to, shall we call them, last night's activities. This makes it much more difficult to accomplish the task of quieting the free thoughts of these Shrah fanatical religious imbeciles," spat the emperor as if describing something vile.

Antipas knew that it was a dangerous thing when Exelcior used his rank of general to address him so emphatically. He had to tread lightly. "I did receive some information, Your Majesty, that Hamilton Nile had been alone with a woman in the moments before the explosion. Her name is Janina Preston, and she is uneducated and young. I understand that she is a bastard child from Lyndon who was left orphaned by the deaths of her incompetent parents, who fought in the war on

Magna. They were exterminated by Noumeroi."

The Third Realm had fought against the forces of the separatists from Lyndon in what had come to be known as the Mine War.

Antipas continued, "I sent you the files with details about her. It is my understanding that she is homeless and bounces between the homes of other followers of that damn religion. Our intelligence reports also show that Hamilton Nile was quite fond of her, and she is fully aware of who the other members are and where we could locate them for a final solution to the Shrah problem."

Antipas knew this would please the emperor some. He knew he was as replaceable as the last five of his predecessors. They'd all been "removed" from their positions by Exelcior himself and had never been heard from again. The emperor was a trained assassin and the former highest-ranking officer of Tai-Anh's Third Realm Noumeroi Special Forces. He knew how to make someone disappear for good.

Exelcior had fought alongside Ajaws Michael and Maya Alom and the likes of Isaiah Gabriel, Buluc Hix, Noah Mandel, and Kabel Luu. He knew how dangerous a threat they were to his imperial rule. They were a problem that needed solving. "Have your forces arrest the girl and bring her to me for interrogation. The School of the Eleventh Dimension has been allowed to exist for long enough. What they are teaching is much too dangerous to leave unattended. At least we don't have to deal with that pest, Hamilton Nile, any longer. Although, I did order his arrest, hoping I could see to his death personally."

Antipas bowed his head and disappeared as quickly as possible, before the emperor changed his mind about his next step. He walked the dark passageways of the Imperial Headquarters, realizing that he had to find this young girl and be rid of everyone else who followed the dangerous Shrah religion they claimed to be no more than a philosophy. The rain continued to roll steadily down the windows of the metal building.

Antipas pondered the possibility that Michael Alom would find out that people who followed his philosophy of love were being exterminated on Tai-Anh. He knew it would cause a reaction they would have to squash swiftly. Temple Alom was loyal to its people, no matter what planet they were on. Antipas had a strong dislike of his counterpart, General Isaiah Gabriel. Isaiah was the epitome of a military leader. His exploits in the Mine War were well known by Imperial forces. Antipas was positive his own troops admired Isaiah Gabriel more than they did him. The very thought of it infuriated him.

He rode the elevator to the roof of the Imperial building, where a pilot awaited him in the rotorcraft that idled inside the see-through, semispherical canopy, high above the city of metal. It was a sort of bubble that kept the rain out and allowed the imperial craft to pass through its membrane. The canopy deactivated, allowing the rotorcraft to pass through it while continuing to keep the rain out. Antipas took off on his mission to find Janina Preston for arrest and interrogation. The general almost felt sorry for what was in store for her. *That poor bastard*, he thought briefly, but he didn't feel empathy for more than a few seconds.

Antipas arrived at the Gandolim City Police Precinct. He gave his orders to the commander there in his typical fashion: with a threat of consequences to her life should she fail to find and arrest Janina Preston.

At Imperial Headquarters, Exelcior seethed. He had just learned that the assassins had failed to kill the ajaw's son. It would be close to impossible to kill him after the failed attempt. Seth Alom was to have been killed and disposed of in the deep aquifers of a nearby mountain range without giving away the source of the attack. Exelcior awaited the full intelligence report from the operatives. The report would detail the information necessary for the main operation.

Exelcior walked over to the large window and looked out into the driving rain. He thought about how much he despised Michael Alom. The former emperor had hand-picked Michael to be his successor as Emperor of Tai-Anh. Michael had turned down the offer, returning to Shrah as ajaw, as he had no interest in Imperial expansion. Exelcior had been a second choice for the late emperor.

Exelcior had made certain that the former emperor had met his end forcibly, long before a natural death had had time to take its course. The former emperor had isolated himself when the Mine War had ended. He'd only trusted Exelcior, with whom he'd shared what he'd perceived as a friendship, along with his hopes and fears for the empire's future. Exelcior had used this trust and the emperor's advancing age to be alone with him and to kill him. Exelcior had strangled the emperor in his sleeping quarters and gained full control of the empire.

As emperor, Exelcior found himself living in the shadow of Michael Alom. The citizens of Tai-Anh had respect for the Aloms. No matter how hard he'd tried, Exelcior had been unable to tarnish the reputation of Temple Alom. He'd also failed to earn the love of the empire's citizens. Love would help ensure adherence to his rules. He needed absolute control. Since love wasn't free-flowing, he'd resorted to fear. Fear was the way of the empire.

Exelcior had then had to deal with the spread of Michael's religion on his own planet.

The very thought of it made his blood boil. It had been brought to his attention that a book they followed had a prophecy written within it that could be interpreted as Michael's son unifying the empire.

Exelcior had no intention to live the rest of his life in Michael Alom's shadow. The Shrah religion was spreading with a speed that greatly threatened his ultimate rule. More and more of his people were reading the book and believing that Seth Alom was the one in the prophecy who would assume control of the empire. The prophecy had to be mistaken. Seth Alom needed to be exterminated, along with his father. The risk of any Alom living was too great. This was personal.

# CHAPTER 11: OPPRESSIVE LONELINESS

Janina found herself walking aimlessly through the City of Gandolim for hours into the night, mourning the death of her spiritual leader. She sobbed at the mere thought of Hamilton telling her to leave immediately to save her life so he could bear the brunt of the attack. Hamilton must have seen with his mind's eye that a flash of light in the night sky would take his existence from the present dimension. For Janina, it was as if the hovercraft traveling at high speeds above the magnetized metal streets weren't even present. She was consumed by despair. She felt so very alone in the universe.

Janina thought about her final look at Hamilton's peridot ring. Ajaw Michael Alom had given it to Hamilton as a gift when he'd visited on a mission that had turned into a pilgrimage. The ring was an honorary gesture for the work Hamilton had done operating on some of Shrah's sickest children. Hamilton had trained at the Imperial Medical School in Tai-Anh. The stone had been cut from a meteor that had arrived on Shrah from the stars in the night sky, and it had been the most valuable thing he'd owned. It had been his connection to something far greater than himself.

Janina remembered the envelope Hamilton had given her shortly before the explosion. Surely, now was the time to open it. She opened the envelope to find a note with Hamilton's apartment address and a key, which she assumed was to the front door. Janina figured Hamilton had had a premonition of the danger he was in and had left something important for Janina to find in his apartment. She was on her way to discover what that may have been.

Unintentionally, almost automatically, Janina found herself back at the site of the blast. The only source of light was Kinich Ahau, its rays reflecting off the two moons in the night sky and casting a gray glow over the metallic city. The rain had let up for a few minutes. Magna Hermopolis was almost full and provided most of the moonlight. The scene seemed almost dignified under the bright light.

Janina found herself on her knees, weeping. "Oh, Hamilton, I am so sorry I wasn't there when you crossed over!" she said aloud through her sobs. She hurt so badly that her entire body shook and ached as tears rolled down her cheeks. A part of her wished death had taken her with him.

She felt the urge to enter into Atsalat. She knelt right there and then. She looked up into the sky and drew in a deep breath, keeping her eyes open. She then closed her eyes, lowered her head to eye-level, and began the process of slowing down her breathing and elevating herself into the cosmic superhighway.

With her mind's eye, she saw herself flying over a grassy windswept field that she did not recognize. Tai-Anh did not have fields like this. She felt at home over the grassy fields, though she had never seen them before. As she flew, her spirit came upon a city made entirely of crystal. Janina soon arrived at the crystal city and walked around the translucent buildings that towered into the sky like gigantic angels holding up the clouds on the tips of their wings.

She entered one of the buildings and saw what seemed to be classrooms full of people dressed in all white. Lecturers stood at the front of the rooms, pointing to boards. The writing on the boards was blurry, so Janina wasn't able to read it. As she turned the corner of the passageway, she came upon a classroom where Hamilton was teaching a class to a full room of white-clothed students.

Hamilton looked up to make eye contact with her, stepped out of the classroom, and gave her a tight hug. It all felt so real to Janina. This didn't feel like a dream. It wasn't a dream. They embraced silently for what seemed like a long time, and then he pulled back and looked at her with a smile. He took her hand, and together, they stepped onto an escalator that seemed to have magically appeared, traveling to the floor above them. She let him lead since this seemed like it was his world to show to her.

He turned to her. "This is our world, Janina. It doesn't belong to just me, you know."

Janina was taken aback that Hamilton knew what she was thinking. It had to be a form of spiritual telepathy, she reckoned. "Hamilton," she asked, "is it really you?"

"Yes, it's really me. We are all spirits, after all. Our existence does not depend on our physical bodies. We simply leave our bodies and continue existing in the Eleventh Dimension. You are here with me now in reality. There is no death, Janina. The law of conservation of energy assures us our continued existence."

As they walked on, Janina peered into a room where a strikingly beautiful dark-haired woman kneeled, sobbing in deep sorrow. The woman was wearing a purple outfit and a peridot necklace. She had a strong, powerful build, yet there was gentleness about her beautiful body's lines. Janina was mesmerized by her.

The woman looked up at Janina and managed to smile through her tears. Janina felt an instant connection with the woman and began to ask Hamilton about her, but Hamilton shook his head, letting her know that it wasn't time yet for her to know the woman's identity.

Hamilton continued his walk, and Janina followed, knowing she would never forget the sobbing woman in the purple outfit with the special peridot necklace.

He led her into another room with white walls. There, two men, one of whom was around Janina's age, sat, listening to a lecture from four teachers. The men were normal in size, but they had features like no one she knew. The four standing teachers were massive. They were approximately nine feet in height and of dense builds.

"Who are they, Hamilton?" Janina whispered. "They look like us but different at the same time."

"You will know them when it's time. All intelligent life in the universe was created in the Great Creator's image. All living beings throughout the universe look much like one another," responded Hamilton.

Janina knew that Hamilton provided information no sooner than when it was needed. It was futile to continue her inquiry.

Hamilton hugged her. "Janina, remember

not to lose hope." He gently pushed her shoulders, sending her flying backward and returning her to the site of the explosion. She came to full consciousness and could still feel Hamilton's lingering touch, confirming the intense reality of their time together.

As her senses settled fully on Gandolim again, Janina felt certain that she was being watched from an elevated position in an adjacent building. Immediate fear surged through her body as she quickly felt that she was being targeted. She had raised herself in the dark, wet, and metallic world and knew how to survive when in danger.

Janina also knew that hesitating to act could be just as bad as not acting at all. She quickly searched for, found, and moved on the quickest exit plan possible. She ran in between two of the buildings still standing next to ground zero, hurrying into an alley. It was dark, and the light of Tai-Anh's moons didn't penetrate there. She continued to run, keeping herself out of sight of any possible hunters and hoping that she wasn't being followed.

She was.

# CHAPTER 12: THE MOVEMENT SPREADS

The enlightened communicated without making audible sounds. There was no need for verbal communication. They often used their voices out of courtesy for those around them, though, allowing them to be part of the conversation. The elevated perceived the communications of the enlightened but were not yet able to send their own communication through the energy superhighway. Michael, Maya, Isaiah, Kabel, and Noah were enlightened and able to communicate using their spiritual access to the Eleventh Dimension. They weren't the only ones. There were others in other parts of the universe. Hamilton Nile was an example.

Michael stood looking into the Nacaome City night through the large penthouse-type window in the Temple Alom infirmary room, where

Seth was fighting a seemingly impossible battle to live. Michael ran his fingers along the prominent battle scar across the left side of his face, a reminder of violent days on celestial bodies that seemed so far away now. He was all too aware of the irony that his son would have the same scar on the left side of his face if he were to live after the vicious attack on his life. Michael had not left Seth's side since he'd been attacked two days prior. Noah had just left the room, leaving Michael with the dreadful realization that he just might lose his son.

Maya sat next to Seth, holding his hand and asking the Great Creator for intervention. Maya asked that the universe's purified particles replace her son's wasted and injured particles and that his body be restored to the perfect working order for which it had been created. Maya seemed millions of miles away, somewhere deep in the cosmos, collecting all the light she could from the energy superhighway and directing it toward her son. Maya was comforted by the friendship and guidance of Kabel, who stood by her side in good times and in bad. Kabel was never far away from Maya and never had been, not even when they'd both fought in the Mine War on Magna Hermopolis.

They'd fought the empire's greatest enemy of that time, although that enemy had actually been a subsection of the empire's own population on Tai-Anh known as the Lyndonites. The

Lyndonites of Tai-Anh were the empire's own citizens who'd separated from their neighbors and relocated to a subsection of the City of Gandolim, positioning their military headquarters on Magna Hermopolis, one of Tai-Anh's moons. On Magna Hermopolis, the Lyndonites had mined resources to build their own military to challenge the Tai-Anh Empire's rule of the solar system. Both sides, Tai-Anh and the Lyndonite separatists, had been involved in a bloody two-year war that had cost the lives of tens of thousands of warriors from Tai-Anh, Lyndon, and Shrah.

In essence, the Independent Republic of Lyndon was a self-proclaimed independent state relocated from Tai-Anh that challenged the empire by building metal warships for the vast oceans and space and metal buildings on land. The abundance of metal ore allowed for these metallic constructions of buildings, bridges, and warships.

Metals were abundant, but quality rock quarries were predominantly found deep below the oceans at depths of 40,000 feet and deeper. Excavating them wasn't very feasible due to the extreme depths, pressures, and logistical concerns. This meant that most building and manufacturing on Tai-Anh relied on more readily available metals. The empire controlled mining commodities in an attempt to prevent the Lyndon rebels from manufacturing an effective military force or substantial infrastructure.

The separatists from Lyndon held clandestine mining operations on Magna Hermopolis. Iron ore quarries were common on the moon, along with mines for gold, uranium, iridium, silver, copper, osmium, palladium, platinum, rhenium, rhodium, ruthenium, tungsten, cobalt, manganese, molybdenum, nickel, aluminum, and titanium. Helium-3, hydrogen, peridot gemstones, rock, and ammonia were also mined.

War had broken out when the Tai-Anh Empire had gathered intelligence that Lyndon was mining metals to build a fleet. The Lyndonites had challenged the empire in war and construction prowess by continuing to mine Magna Hermopolis despite repeated ultimatums from the empire trying to force them to cease mining on the moon. The Lyndonites had refused to comply, and war had erupted. The Mine War had drawn thousands of warriors from Shrah as volunteers, and Imperial propaganda had portrayed the Lyndonites as savages who threatened the very existence and freedom of the entire Kinich Ahau star system. Warriors from Shrah had fought, and many had died valiantly in the minefields and battlegrounds of the relatively small moon.

The brutality of the Mine War, however, had begun to change the hearts of many warriors who'd survived the war and returned to Shrah to lead in Shrah society. They'd returned disenchanted with the Tai-Anh Empire for fighting a war against a so-called enemy that they deemed, after the war, to simply have opposed the oppressive and evil empire.

Young Janina's parents had been veterans who'd never returned from Magna Hermopolis. Their remains lay silently on the moon's surface, which had once been used as a battlefield. They'd fought for Lyndon, and after the war, Janina had been relocated from Lyndon and placed in foster centers of Tai-Anh, from which she'd continually escaped abuse to raise herself in the streets of the cold and unloving metal city. The combined forces of Tai-Anh's Third Realm's Noumeroi and Shrah combatants had simply been too strong, and Janina's parents had paid with their lives.

Two leaders on Tai-Anh who'd survived the war were Emperor Exelcior and General Antipas. Lyndon had been defeated and had signed a peace treaty with Tai-Anh and Shrah.

Since the end of the war, Lyndon and Shrah had engaged in trade, and the Lyndonites had become very fond of Michael and the people of Shrah. The Shrah Philosophy of Love and War had spread rapidly in Tai-Anh, and this was of great concern to the emperor and Antipas. They knew the power of the philosophy, and they greatly feared it. They feared it enough to exterminate anyone following it.

Shrah, Tai-Anh, and Lyndon had lost too many of their finest in the brutal and senseless war on Magna Hermopolis. War had changed them. It had changed the leaders of Tai-Anh for the worse. It had made them that much more bloodthirsty and dark-souled. It had changed the people of Shrah for the better. It had made them that much more bathed in spiritual light. And the Lyndonites had become fascinated with Shrah's Philosophy of Love and War. The movement was spreading.

The brutality of the war had brought the people of Shrah close together, and they all now felt the anger and upset at the life-threatening attack on their ajaw-to-be. This was personal. They were in search of answers and anyone responsible for this act of brutality against the very heart of Shrah leadership. They worried for Seth and for Michael and Maya. They connected with the Great Creator spiritually to ask for intervention, and all accessed as much light energy as they could capture from the Eleventh Dimension's energy superhighway, sending it to young Seth, who was still fighting for his life. Positive light energy flowed through people to others in the universe the way heat and light flowed through space and warmed the planets and the moons that orbited them.

Michael turned to Maya. "I'm angry," he said. "I'm overwhelmed by pure anger."

Maya could see that her husband was clenching his jaw, which made his temple pulse. She saw his muscles tightening the way they did when he was infuriated. It was only natural that he felt that way. His son was fighting for his life, and he was powerless over the fate of his legacy on Shrah. Maya felt a pang of empathy for her life partner. She shared the anger he felt. After all, it was her son lying on that infirmary bed as well.

"I am too, my love," Maya whispered. "But our people need us not to be." Her spirit returned to the present dimension. "Kabel reminds us all the time that anger opens a medium for darkness to enter our hearts and minds. We can't allow it."

"I can't help it. Our son is fighting for his life before he's even reached manhood, and this was at the hands of others," stated Michael. His temples pulsated, and his nostrils flared. "I will find those who did this if it is the last thing I do in the present dimension."

Maya knew her soulmate better than anyone else on the planet and understood what was on its way: action. Michael was a tolerant leader, but he was also an intensely protective one. He protected the ones he loved with a conviction as strong as the most powerful sandstorm winds of the deepest desert. Action was inevitable. Maya asked the Great Creator to oversee the events when the time came.

"You have my word," Michael swore. "I will

find who was behind this, and I will execute justice for the innocent, especially for our son and our people."

"I know," responded Maya simply as she stood to walk over to her lover's embrace. Maya had deep love but also deep respect for Michael. She nestled in his arms and enjoyed his sweet scent, feeling the warmth of tender love move through her body and soul with a calming yet passionate force.

Michael held Maya tightly and said nothing as he embraced her. Michael always said that people no longer hugged with their entire bodies, only giving up their upper chest and shoulders to each other in quick, insincere gestures. Michael was not a victim to this. He loved and hugged with passion and conviction.

Michael took the lives of those he deemed unfit to live with the same passion. He was revered by his followers and friends and feared by his enemies. There was no better friend. There was no worse enemy. It was these qualities that had earned him the Tai-Anh Empire's Third Realm's Medal of Honor, Legion of Merit, and many other combat medals from the Mine War.

The former emperor of Tai-Anh had asked Michael to stay in Tai-Anh and head the entire military for him as heir apparent of the Imperial reign. Michael had turned the opportunity down, stating that his place was in the service of his people on Shrah. The emperor had then offered the opportunity to a general named Herod Exelcior. Once installed to head the military, Exelcior had replaced the emperor in a mutinous overthrow of central power. The former emperor had had his throat slit. That was how he'd been rewarded for appointing the bloodthirsty Exelcior to command his military forces: with betrayal and murder. This was the way of the current empire.

# CHAPTER 13: THE SAFEST PLACE IN THE UNIVERSE

Maya enjoyed the physical and spiritual strength of her life partner. She bathed in the muscularity of his arms as he embraced her tightly while she rested her head on his chest. Maya found respite from the fear and anxiety of watching her son struggle for his life at such a young age. But the pang in her heart returned as she refocused on what was happening in the room.

Then her heart was overcome by anger. Maya pulled herself away from her husband just far enough to look up into his deep-brown eyes. "You find who is responsible for this and bring our son justice."

It was obvious to Michael that his wife

wasn't requesting his consideration in the matter. He knew he had just been given a direct order. That was all he needed. The great Ajaw of Shrah looked into his wife's eyes, communicating his acceptance of her request.

The intense moment was interrupted by a gentle knock on the door of the hospital room. The ajaw turned to look at the door and verbally approved the entrance of the knocker.

The door cracked open, and the solicitor peered inside the room. It was Buluc Hix. Buluc stepped inside with a bow of his head. He could tell his ajaw had tears in his eyes, and that brought the same to his own. Buluc was the finest of trained fighters, but he was made of flesh and bone. He was a passionate man who loved and respected the Alom family.

Buluc was having a hard time coping with the attack on his mentee. He felt great disappointment in himself for not having discovered and prevented the attack before it had happened. Since, he had been quite upset, conducting a thorough investigation to get to the bottom of who was responsible for the attack. But Buluc knew that no coordinated action could take place against the perpetrators without Michael and Maya's approval. They would let him know when it was time to retaliate, and he awaited the order with great anxiety.

Michael noticed the sadness and regret in

his friend's eyes and stepped up to him, pulling him into a strong embrace. Buluc let out a painful sob he had been holding in for the three days since the attack. It shook the room, and his body trembled. Michael was the only person on Shrah at that very instant with the physical strength and credibility to offer Buluc a comforting embrace. He held Buluc until he felt he was ready to be let go. Not a single word was exchanged between the two. There was no need for words between them. Words ran the risk of getting in the way of pure communication and understanding. They had stared death in the face on another world, where the odds had been stacked against them. They had history.

After they parted, Buluc went over to the bed to look at Seth, who was still clinging to life. His face was grossly swollen and bandaged. His skin was ashen with the loss of so much blood. The sight horrified and saddened Buluc. He felt the strong hand of his ajaw on his shoulder and knew they needed to talk alone.

Michael turned to Maya, gave her a nod, and proceeded out of the room. Buluc instinctively followed. The two men walked down the infirmary passageway, turning personnel heads as they walked. They were war heroes and at the cusp of governmental leadership in the temple. They were both muscular and attractive men who instantly commanded attention. Buluc had darker skin than Michael and a completely shaved head. Across his face, Buluc bore a scar from an injury he'd received during an attack on Lyndonite forces on Magna Hermopolis. His scar was on the right side of his face, while Michael's cut across the left side. Buluc walked to the left of Michael, allowing his ajaw the honorary position of being on the right. They would never lose sight of their fellowship and all they had experienced together.

The two men rounded the corner, passing the tall windows. Temple Alom was bathed in soft gray moonlight. The passageway led to a large lobby, where they were alone at last.

Suddenly, with a swift and powerful movement, Michael kicked over a quarter-ton clay sculpture of a desert scene that stood in the middle of the room. The sculpture came crashing down loudly on the stone floor of the lobby. The racket was tremendous. Michael then picked up the largest piece of the broken structure, held it over his head, and threw it to the ground with an even louder crash. Pieces of the sculpture flew everywhere, many of them pelting Buluc's body and face.

What was left was an unrecognizable array of shattered cement in the middle of the damaged lobby floor. Buluc, unfrazzled by the violent scene, simply closed his eyes to protect them from injury and didn't flinch a muscle as all hell broke loose around him. When all the pieces settled back to the ground, spread throughout the entire lobby, Buluc opened his eyes and simply stated, "I never really liked that sculpture anyway."

Isaiah and several templar knights came running from different directions with weapons drawn, ready for action. They quickly discovered that their ajaw and grand knight were safe from what had sounded like an explosion. All who arrived on the scene realized that their ajaw had been relieving great stress. They understood, and no one said a word about the incident.

As the orderlies began the massive task of picking up all the pieces, Michael apologized to them for the extra work they now had and attempted to help in the cleanup. His apology was unnecessary. His assistance was not accepted. They understood.

The ajaw, general, and colonel stepped aside in a private conversation.

Isaiah was the highest-ranking officer on the planet and considered one of the most brilliant and effectively lethal combatants and leaders to have come from Shrah. He was a combination of soldier and leader. The two functions used similar yet different skillsets, and the general had them both. "Gentlemen, let's continue walking. I have some information for you," he said.

Michael broke the silence in their walk

down the temple's passages. "What have you found so far, Isaiah?"

"All four attackers were killed, so they were not available for questioning. Noah autopsied the bodies and found some interesting things. He looked at genetics, plants, and other microscopic evidence on their clothing to determine where they were from or where they had been. He found evidence that they were not from this planet but had been around Shrah plant life that he believes is from the Tela Mountain Range.

"The second thing we found is that their tongues were missing," Isaiah continued. "We studied the insides of their mouths carefully and determined that they had been surgically removed based on the infection-free incisions and sutures present. Whoever made this attempt on Temple Alom was serious about maintaining the secrecy of the attack. They did not want to risk the attackers being tortured into speaking truths about where they'd received their orders."

"This screams of Imperial tactics," stated Buluc.

"Yes, but there's more," continued Isaiah. "One of the attackers was female. She happened to be the second attacker, the one Seth decapitated, which may have been a favor to her, as she was actually very sick with desert fever."

Michael processed. "Desert fever from the fungus?"

"That's correct, sire. According to Noah, the spore is found in alkaline soil and sand below the surface. It's a fungus that grows more aggressively in wet weather and is spread by the wind during the following dry season. It seems she had accumulated an infection in her lungs, spine, and meninges. She was ill and was, most certainly, already feeling death's grasp."

"Regardless, she was able to function and carry out this attack against Seth," interjected Buluc.

"That's precisely why I believe this female was the toughest of the four," asserted Isaiah.

"We have tough fighters ourselves. She tried to take my son's life and could have succeeded." Michael shook off another fit of rage at the thought of his son clinging to life.

"If we believe this attack was carried out by the empire, is it time to retaliate?" asked Buluc hopefully.

"No, it is not time. I will let you know when it is time."

Both Buluc and Isaiah seemed dejected by the ajaw's response. They were born warriors, after all. Buluc had expected a negative response, but he'd felt he had to try. The people of Shrah had brought the tradition of removing the hearts of those they sent to the darkest recesses of the Eleventh Dimension with them to their new home planet.

"General, can we locate the area on the planet where these attackers are from?" asked Michael.

Isaiah responded, "Noah thinks he can narrow the location down to several square miles within the range. It would be our responsibility to hunt them down. So long as they are on Shrah, they can run, but they cannot hide forever."

Michael gave the information Isaiah had provided him a brief moment of thought. "Gentlemen, locate, investigate, and eliminate this threat. Let me know what resources you will need."

Isaiah and Buluc bowed their heads to their ajaw and no longer spoke. With these three men, words were simply used for memorializing dramatics, as their understanding of each other transcended eleven dimensions. They had history, deep history.

# CHAPTER 14: THE ART OF OPPRESSION

Janina walked down the metal streets under the glow of Tai-Anh's moons. The dual light source in the night sky created a strange and magnificent array of shadows, casting over the city streets under a light rain. Reflected starlight was magnificent anywhere in the universe. The gray glow of the moon reflected the light of the planetary system's binary stars.

Janina walked past some of the poorest and most oppressed neighborhoods in Gandolim. This area was known as Red City because of the rust on the metal of its structures. These buildings were much older than those in the rest of the city and contained more iron than steel. Red City's occupants battled extreme poverty and violence. Although the empire was a wealthy enterprise, controlling all aspects of socio-economic importance on the planet, the people of Gandolim were not so fortunate.

Those not closely associated with the empire lived in downright misery. The empire paid a miserable salary that wasn't nearly enough to feed one person, let alone an entire family. Citizens were forbidden from having more than one child. Subsequent pregnancies were forcibly terminated.

The poor neighborhoods of Tai-Anh were essentially falling apart. They smelled like sewage and rotting garbage in the parts where the most vulnerable lived. The saddest of all conditions were those of the children and the elderly. Janina redirected some universal light energy from the Eleventh Dimension to the poor and suffering of Tai-Anh. The people in Red City were hardened by adversity and oppression, which made for strong citizens. Living in Gandolim was living without dignity. Undignified or not, it was dangerous to threaten the ways of the empire. Hamilton's life had been taken for this very reason.

Janina decided she would stay clear of the area of Hamilton's murder. The magnitude and savagery of the attack pointed squarely to the empire, specifically to Emperor Exelcior and General Antipas. The spiritual movement behind the School of the Eleventh Dimension had picked up some popularity lately. Janina gathered that the rule of the empire was threatened by the rapid growth of the movement.

The thought was upsetting to Janina. The School of the Eleventh Dimension practiced drawing good energy and purified particles from the universe's energy superhighway in the Eleventh Dimension and redirecting it to all living things in acts of love. Hamilton had always spoken of the impact positive thoughts had on the world at large. He'd taught that love was a verb, not a noun. It wasn't a thing but an action. He'd loved to death.

Hamilton had taught that energy could not be destroyed. This law was universal, and it made valid the reality that there was really no death but simply a transcendence from one dimension to the next. One lived both before physical birth and after physical death. This gave Janina solace.

Regardless, Hamilton wasn't there in physical form anymore, and this filled Janina with nostalgic longing to have him next to her once more. She quickened her pace on her way to Hamilton's apartment. She felt like there were eyes hiding in the shadows of every corner of the metal city. She wasn't sure if it was her developing sensitivity to the energies of the world around her or simply her imagination playing tricks on her. It didn't matter; the anxiety she felt was as real as it got. Janina could feel her heart pounding inside her chest.

Janina decided to run to Hamilton's apartment to avoid being followed through the streets of the city. She came over a hill and picked up speed, preserving some of her energy. She breathed deeply and in rhythm to ensure maximum oxygenation of her strong leg muscles. Youth had its advantages. She ran with the deliberateness of prey being hunted. The street leveled out and overpassed the expressway, where magnetized passenger cars flew at great speeds over a network of rails. She continued to run as she approached the intersection one block below the street where Hamilton had lived. She continued to pick up pace as she raced up the city steps until she arrived at the top and stopped in front of a forty-story building. The address matched.

Janina entered the building. She could feel blood engorging her thighs and calves as she walked. The locked door to the front lobby denied her access. Janina was thinking about what to do when she heard the voices of a young mother and a child, about seven years old, who were walking up to the building. The mother stopped and smiled at Janina before proceeding to open the hatch. Janina followed them inside.

They waited at the elevator tube, the child keeping his eyes on Janina. She figured he thought her strange looking, as she was sweaty and dirty from the events of the past two days.

When they entered the tube and pressed the numbers for the respective floors to which they were headed, the little boy spoke to Janina. "Do you know how beautiful you are? You look like the angel that visits me in my dreams."

Janina's eyes welled up with tears at the surprising and very welcome kindness and sincerity of the child's powerful words. She blushed but felt the powerful light energy the boy had sent her way. She perceived the charged particles.

The elevator approached the twenty-first floor, and Janina began to exit. Upon stepping out, she couldn't help but stop to give the little boy a kiss on the cheek.

He opened his mouth wide in amazement and put his little hand on his cheek as if to keep the lingering kiss pressed against it for just a few seconds longer.

The child's mother smiled and said, "Well, don't just stand there, Max. Tell the beautiful girl thank you."

"Thank you, angel from my dreams," said Max.

As Janina stepped out of the elevator tube and into the hallway of the twenty-first floor, she bathed in the positive energy that engulfed her like a gift from another dimension. She was astounded by how powerful the energy produced by such a small child was. The little boy's kindness overwhelmed Janina for a moment, and she struggled to refocus her attention on the task at hand.

Janina found Hamilton's living quarters and unlocked the door. It took a few seconds for her eyes to adjust to the low light inside. She locked the door behind her and leaned against it. She could smell the lingering sweet scent that had often wafted from Hamilton when he'd entered a room.

Immediately to her right was a food preparation and storage area. A sitting area opened up straight ahead from the door. Janina stepped into the room and saw sleeping quarters on her left. She could sense that this was where Hamilton had entered powerful Atsalat trances.

Janina opened her mind's eye and found a box on Hamilton's sleeping cot that immediately attracted her attention because it seemed so out of place. She opened the box and began sifting through its contents. The first item that caught her eye was a book bound in animal skin. "The Sacred Codices," Janina whispered, reading the title. She knew this book would be important. Hamilton had made reference to it on several occasions, telling his followers that the great book's content would be revealed to them all in due time.

She found a picture of a younger Hamilton being awarded the peridot gem. The picture showed a strange stone room with large windows on what she assumed to be Shrah. The other person in the picture was the woman Janina had seen wearing purple and the peridot necklace in the

Eleventh Dimension, the striking brunette. Janina knew at that moment that she needed to find her, that she was important somehow. Otherwise, she wouldn't have seen her in the Eleventh Dimension with Hamilton.

Hamilton had told Janina the peridot ring had been a gift from Shrah, given to him in recognition of his service as a young doctor to the children there. Perhaps the person in the picture knew something important. Janina put the picture in her pocket.

She then found a list of over 100 names and addresses of the members of the School of the Eleventh Dimension. The list also contained status categories, which ranged from believer to elevated. The enlightened list had no names on it. Janina put the list in her pocket as well.

Finally, Janina found a knife made of obsidian. It was a beautiful knife with a handle of jade, sheathed in a type of animal skin that was foreign to her. She remembered Hamilton speaking of the long tradition on Shrah of keeping obsidian knives with jade handles. This was a special knife, as it had belonged to Hamilton, and she was honored to keep and protect it. She felt, somehow, that Hamilton would provide her instructions on what to do with the list. The believers on the list included some of the original practitioners of the Shrah Philosophy, and they would be hunted aggressively if the empire learned their identities.

Janina felt a great sense of honor coupled with a great wash of fear come over her. With these items in her possession, she knew she had to move forward with the teachings of the great Hamilton Nile. The obsidian knife in the box impressed her most, leaving no doubt that she would have to defend herself and her fellow believers to protect the teachings of the School of the Eleventh Dimension and the Sacred Codices. Just holding the obsidian knife sent chills up her spine.

With those chills came the exhaustion that Janina had been shutting off from her thoughts. She lay on the cot and fell asleep instantly. When she awoke a few hours later, she entered the bathroom and showered. After showering, she ate until her belly was ready to burst. Revitalized and with a full stomach, she took advantage of Hamilton's residual energy in a quiet and private place where he had dwelled, and she settled in for an Atsalat meditation.

Janina sat up comfortably and drew in a deep breath, leaning her head back and looking up into the heavens with her eyes open. She closed her eyes and slowly brought her head to a forward-facing position, deepening and slowing down her breaths. With her physical eyes closed and her spiritual eyes wide open, Janina began to rise out of the present dimension and into the energy superhighway in the cosmos that transported her into the Eleventh Dimension. Her body was in Gandolim, but her spirit was connected to the entire cosmos, traveling through space and time.

Janina stepped into a tunnel bathed in a bright light that washed out everything at the end of it. She walked forward. An instant later, she found herself on a dirt path, stones on the ground marking a way forward. She came upon some winding stone steps, which were surrounded on either side by more stones and trees unlike any she had seen on Tai-Anh. These trees were very large and had thousands of leaves. She was completely covered by their shade.

She came upon a large triangular pyramid structure of five stories with eight doorways on the second level, four on the third level, two on the fourth level, and one at the top on the fifth. Janina continued to walk up the stone steps, climbing to the top of the pyramid. Once at the top, she walked through the doorway and was mesmerized by what she saw on the other side.

Janina was overlooking what appeared to be a large stone stadium that could have seated thousands of spectators. In the center of the stadium was a natural grass field, a place for fantastic sporting events. She could feel the warm sun on her face and body. Her head, shoulders, breasts, and thighs were covered, but the rest of her skin was exposed to the natural elements of a star that burned much hotter with less cloud cover than the suns of her native planet. She wore sandals on her feet and could feel a knife sheathed in animal skin at her side. She removed the knife from the sheath, revealing a jade-handled obsidian knife, an exact replica of the knife left by Hamilton.

Janina sheathed her knife once again and turned to walk through the doorway in the opposite direction. On the other side, she came upon a man and a woman. She was overcome with emotion. They were people she had seen in a picture once before. They were her parents, who had been killed on Magna Hermopolis in the Mine War. She couldn't help but run up to them, hugging them with all her might. The three of them embraced without saying a word, parents and daughter reunited. Love flowed all around them.

After a while, her father reached to his side and withdrew a small box, which he offered to Janina. "It's a gift for you," he said with a loving smile.

"What is it?" Janina asked.

"Hope."

# CHAPTER 15: THE RANGE'S OCCULT SECRETS

"It will soon be five days that my son has been in this condition," Michael told Noah. The ajaw sat next to his still comatose son's bed in the infirmary of Temple Alom. "I have sent Isaiah and Buluc with a select group of knights and special forces personnel to investigate the area where you indicated the assassins most likely staged their attack in the Tela Mountain Range," he continued.

According to Noah and his team, the spore that had caused the desert fever afflicting Seth's attacker was only found in the Tela Mountain Range. Temple Alom had no knowledge of anyone living in the area. It was believed to be uninhabited.

"It's reasonable to investigate the mountain

range for clues. If the assassin picked up the fungus on Shrah, they most certainly did so living and hiding close to the ground in the range," affirmed Noah.

"Since the attack on Seth, I've feared this was the work of Emperor Exelcior, but we need to confirm that he is responsible," said Michael. "This whole situation is senseless, and I have difficulty understanding why it happened."

Noah grew pensive as he listened to his friend speak. "You know, Michael, I was convinced we would live out our lives peacefully here. I thought we would concentrate on interplanetary trade and enjoy safety. We must find out where this darkness is coming from and neutralize the point of origin. We have the right people out there in the mountain range. We'll know something soon. You and I have seen firsthand the abilities of Isaiah, Buluc, Obasi, the knights, and the special forces."

Michael nodded his head in agreement. "I can't tell you how furious this attack on Seth makes me. It's so hard to see my son fighting for his life, unresponsive this long. He was so young —"

"He is still young, Michael!" Noah snapped. "Don't you dare give up on him! He is your son, and he will fight to the end as you would yourself. The power of your bloodline and the power of our people runs centuries deep. We are born warriors, and Seth is one of us. Don't ever doubt it."

Michael greatly appreciated the unwavering support of his lifelong friend. "I wish I could spare and have mercy on those who planned and carried out this attack, but—"

"But you can't and won't," Noah finished for him with satisfaction in his voice.

"I have looked for Seth in the Eleventh Dimension, but neither Maya nor I can see him. It's like the Great Creator has him in his grasp and away from us," said Michael.

"Really? What does Kabel say about you and Maya not seeing him there?"

"Kabel isn't able to see him either. The Great Creator's plan with Seth is a mystery to us all. It's a mystery that, unfortunately, is taking its toll on Maya and me."

Noah saw the immense despair and agony on his friend's face. He placed his hand on Michael's shoulder and squeezed it tightly, redirecting as much light energy to his friend as he could muster.

Michael could feel the purified light energy particles. The flow of light energy, which all living beings could transfer to the people they cared about, warmed him. "Thank you," he said. "You are a true friend."

Noah simply smiled. Deep down inside, he was overwhelmed by the powerlessness of not being able to save young Seth and having to submit himself to the plan of the Great Creator.

As the two men spoke in the infirmary at Temple Alom, forces led by Isaiah, Buluc, and Obasi traveled deep into the desert to the twenty-first-degree north latitude and thirty-third-degree east longitude in the Tela Mountain Range. The airborne survey of the area had already been performed, including night vision and heat signature searches, all to no avail. If someone was there, they were good at staying hidden.

The special forces were led by Obasi. She was a veteran of the Mine War, where she'd served as a sergeant in the Imperial Combined Special Forces Group with the Noumeroi of the empire's Third Realm. Obasi had been promoted by Isaiah to the rank of lieutenant upon returning from the war. She'd accepted a role on her home planet with the special forces.

The military on Shrah existed to maintain good order on the planet, as Temple Alom had no intention of finding itself in yet another bloody war. The people on Shrah had no interest in invading other planets or starting a conflict. Many veterans and citizens of Shrah resented that they'd been dragged into the Mine War against Lyndon. A great many of their veterans had lost life and limb in the war. Ironically, since the war, Lyndon had become a trading partner of Shrah as the true imperialistic intentions of the Tai-Anh Empire had become apparent.

Obasi led a force of twenty-two, who traveled via rotary craft through the warm Shrah air, straight up to the top of the mountain range, which rose 8,000 feet above ground level. The temperature dropped as the rotary craft gained altitude. The special forces officers wore dark beige fatigues and carried CO2 pulsating laser rifles and handguns known to them simply as PLRs and PLHs. They also carried night vision and diving equipment to use if necessary. They were prepared for anything and only wondered what or who they might find in the mountains or in the aquifers.

In addition to the weapons, Temple Alom issued all citizens of Shrah an obsidian fighting knife with a triangular-edged blade and a jade handle when they reached the age of thirteen orbits. The serrated design of the blades provided rigidity when cutting through flesh, internal organs, muscles, cartilage, tendons, and bones. The obsidian came from the highlands of Shrah, where volcanic activity was present. Training in lethal arts was provided to all citizens.

Ch'o'Jonik was the fighting style of the people of Shrah and had been with them since their creation. The warrior spirit ran through the veins of the people of Shrah as it had for centuries and across multiple galaxies. They were comfortable with killing, though they preferred to love. The members of this highly-trained special forces team were on a mission. They knew well of the vicious attack on young Seth Alom's life. This was personal.

From the bottom of the mountain, traveling on foot, were seventy-five similarly outfitted templar knights, who were operating under the leadership of Buluc.

The special forces team secured the top of the mountain range to ensure the most elevated positions were scrubbed clean of possible enemies well before Buluc's forces moved in to begin the swirl around the mountain range. The overall forces commander was Isaiah, who had traveled to an observation spot in the mountains, where he could keep command and control. He had with him a long-distance sniping rifle that he very much liked to use.

Several hours into the search, Buluc's templar knights were under observation on the south side of the range. They were in the sights of the enemy. A group of deadly para-military mercenaries had been watching the movements of Buluc's forces and were waiting for the right moment to begin the carnage. The mercenaries were in fatigues that made them virtually imperceptible against the contour of the barren mountains. Buluc's forces approached from below at 7,000 feet of elevation, where there was a large aquifer recharge zone.

The little rain that fell in the area would be

reclaimed in the recharge zone. There were only twelve enemy combatants present, and they had the element of surprise on their side. The templar knights climbing the mountain were easy targets for slaughter. The mercenaries didn't move a muscle. They each slowed their breathing to maintain the utmost imperceptibility. They had long-range and powerful CO2 rifles ready to begin the massacre. As the knights came into sight, the mercenaries opened fire with the excruciatingly loud noise of simultaneous discharge of high-potency rifles.

None of the knights were dropping. The mercenaries continued firing at the easy targets without success. The vicious laser fire failed to injure a single knight. The smell of discharged CO2 and burned sand and rock was pungent in the mountain air. By the time the mercenaries realized that they had opened fire on deceptive holograms of the knights and not the knights themselves, it was too late.

From higher ground, like wild animals attacking their prey from above, Obasi's special forces officers rained down on them instantly. In the span of no more than a few seconds, eleven of the twelve mercenaries had their throats slit from ear to ear, with four of them completely decapitated. There was almost silence on the mountain, with the exception of the massive amount of blood spattering the ground and mountain rocks.

Two of the four bodiless heads slipped from the hands of the Shrah special forces fighters, slick with blood, and began to roll down the mountain-side, slapping onto rocks on the way down. It was a special sound that a skull, jaw, and nose made as bones and teeth broke in high-speed collisions, thudding on impact. Only one mercenary was knocked unconscious. He needed to be interrogated as to the identities of those responsible for the attempt on the life of Seth Alom.

The remainder of the templar knights, who were further down the mountain, came up to find the blood and tissue on the rocks. They stepped over the bodies of the eleven dead and the two separated heads. It was apparent which special forces operatives had executed the attack, as they were the ones with the bloody arterial spray on their Temple Alom uniforms. They were the ones wetted by enemy blood.

The dead were six males and five females. The mercenary who'd been spared from death had no markings other than the camouflage that allowed him to blend into the mountainside.

Buluc ordered the knights to begin placing the dead bodies and their heads into body bags to be returned to Temple Alom for investigation and funeral services. Obasi began searching the area of water reclamation for the aquifer recharge zone.

The captured mercenary fully awoke and

could not speak. Like the four attackers who'd led the attempt on Seth's life, he'd had his tongue surgically removed to prevent him from talking to Shrah forces if apprehended. The brutality behind this act of amputation was shocking. Michael Alom strictly forbade the mistreatment of captured combatants. His forces were always to treat prisoners and all living beings with dignity, even those possessed with dark energy. With this in mind, none of the operatives present at the Tela Mountain Range wanted anything to do with the prisoner missing his tongue. Buluc ordered the transport of the prisoner to Temple Alom for disposition there, knowing that strongly 'encouraging' the prisoner to talk would lead his operatives to engage in motivation tactics that Michael wouldn't approve of.

Next, they investigated the area surrounding the aquifer recharge zone. They arrived at an opening to a large cavern, which was filled with dark, cold water commonly found under the surface of the planet. They proceeded to investigate the aquifer's close vicinity to the recharge opening. The mercenaries had hidden somewhere in the area and had not appeared in night vision or infrared searches. It only made sense to search beneath the rock and underwater.

Isaiah gave Obasi the order to have her operatives gear up in compressed breathing and rebreathing gas gear, tanks, powerful waterproof lights, fins, bodysuits, and rifles. The Temple Alom officers present decided it was most likely that the mercenaries had found refuge somewhere inside the aquifer.

By order of the general, it was time for the special operatives to suit up, enter the underground aquifer opening, and begin their dive into the deep, dark abyss. It was a good thing the CO2 laser rifles worked underwater. Diving among the winding deep and jagged rocks of the aquifer was unnerving at best. It was a pitch-black world that was totally unexplored. The mouth of the underwater cave known as the Blue Hole opened up into a sinkhole that dropped underwater to 800 feet, offering a scary beginning to the exploration. There wasn't much a CO2 laser rifle could do against the crushing depth of a dark underworld of winding canals and caves. A rifle couldn't guide one to safety and didn't help keep one from panicking.

Obasi's divers entered a long tunnel at a depth of fifty meters, where the water temperature sat at an even fifty-five degrees. The tunnel was just a couple feet more than shoulder-width for 500 meters. This trek took nerves of steel and great mind control. At the other end of the underwater canal was an opening that funneled out into an area cavernous enough to fit a large living structure. The water there was crystal clear and icy cold. It became obvious to Obasi that they could travel upward quite a way since there seemed to be fifty meters of water above her head. She even thought she could see the waterline, as though the cave was only partially filled with water and they would soon arrive at an air bubble inside it. Once all her divers came through the canal opening, they began the ascent to the waterline, chasing their air bubble.

Then Obasi saw them through her night vision goggles in the dark underground abyss. They were swimming around them with massive bodies, no eyes in their heads, and no artificial breathing equipment. Her forces were completely surrounded.

# CHAPTER 16: SEEING IN THE DARKNESS

The Shrah special forces operatives were in a precarious situation. They were underwater in complete darkness, completely surrounded by humanoid creatures with gills and no eyes.

Obasi was face to face with the largest of the creatures, which appeared to be the leader. There were nine creatures in total, and Obasi knew exactly where each of them was swimming. She hesitated to pull the trigger because Michael had made it clear that all creatures belonged to the Great Creator and were not to be killed unless life was in immediate danger. She worked through the mental process of determining whether the creatures were a threat.

Obasi knew instinctively when she was facing a born fighter. This creature treading water in front of her was lethal. She sensed that one wrong move would drive the creature to kill her on the spot. But as much as this monstrous figure sent shivers through the special forces soldiers' spines, they didn't appear to be an immediate threat. The operatives were cognizant of the fact that if these creatures so wished, they would have killed them a long time ago. This was a species completely alien to them. They seemed to be tailormade for engaging enemies underwater.

Obasi waited for their next move with her finger on the trigger of her gun. The leader of the creatures gestured for her to follow it to what appeared to be the surface of the water. She complied, and the entire special forces team followed her up to the waterline with their fingers on triggers and safety switches off. They were ready for any surprises that might await them, knowing well that the odds were stacked against them.

The team of twenty-one heavily armed special forces divers followed the nine creatures upward until they surfaced to see that the inside of the gargantuan cave was full of dripstone mineral structures. Stalactites hung from the ceiling like icicles, and stalagmites rose from the ground like liquid rock that had frozen in place.

They then saw hundreds of creatures similar in length to the height of a full-grown Shrah male. They had thick-finned tails that were four or five feet long. More to add to the initial nine. The creatures observed them not in a threatening way but with fascination and curiosity. But they had no eyes.

Instead, there were fleshy black knobs of skin that seemed to have replaced eyes that had previously been present. Obasi assumed that the creatures had adapted after hundreds, or perhaps thousands, of years living in absolute darkness. The creatures were a translucent white color due to the lack of light. They had flattened heads and two arms and two legs with webbed digits, and their elongated bodies acted as tails, assisting them with swimming. They had blood-colored gills for breathing underwater.

Obasi took a look at the overwhelming group of creatures, which together made up an entire civilization deep underground, and she couldn't help but think that she was glad she hadn't shot the ones in the water. If she had, she was almost certain none of her subordinates would have made it out alive. Now she wondered what the creatures intended with them. So far, they didn't seem aggressive, but perhaps they were awaiting orders to attack. Obasi and her team were ready, as always. She noticed that the original leader of the creatures kept a striking distance from her at all times. She respected the instinctive combat posture of her counterpart.

Suddenly, the creatures began to move apart as if a giant were spreading them with enormous arms. In the background, Obasi could see that one of the creatures was approaching them, and all the others were moving out of the way to let it through, doing so with an apparent reverence. This creature was the largest of them all, standing at a height just above seven feet, with thick muscles under its translucent white skin. It stopped just in front of her.

Obasi reassured her team without looking at them that they were to stand down and not shoot unless lives were in danger. She gave this order by speaking into a small microphone in front of her mouth that transmitted via the interconnected communication system.

The team complied.

Without explanation or reason, a voice was heard by all the special forces operatives over the communication system. It appeared to be the voice of the head amphibian creature and came through in the language of K'iché. "Welcome to our home, people of the light. My name is Eurycea. We mean you no harm. It is not in our nature to compete for resources or power with our cohabitants on this planet. What brings you so deep into our domain?"

The operatives were beside themselves that thoughts could be projected through their communications system.

"Your domain will stay your domain, Eurycea. I am Lieutenant Obasi Sabina, and these are my people. We are being assisted by specialized systems for underwater breathing and swimming, as these capabilities are not part of our bodies. We serve Temple Alom, the temple of Michael and Maya Alom, and are gathering information about an attempt on the life of our leaders' son, Seth Alom. We mean your people no harm and wish to peacefully coexist, provided that you did not assist the mercenary forces that brought such unprovoked violence to our temple. Please share with us any information you might have regarding the mercenary forces we found at the entrance to your domain."

"We assure you, Obasi Sabina, that our people were not involved in the attempt on any life from your temple," Eurycea replied. "These dark energy beings, the ones you call mercenaries, have been operating here recently, and we have been observing them. We have no reason to assist them. We do not assist anyone bringing unprovoked violence to a peaceful people. We, like you, were relocated here centuries ago. Your people and mine come from the same planet in a distant galaxy. These dark energy beings killed three of our young children who strayed away from here innocently. I am afraid they have consumed their flesh after adding fire to it. We know there are twelve of them living. They will not live for long if they enter these waters again. We will end their lives."

Obasi quickly explained, "You will have no

need to do so, Eurycea. We have killed eleven of them already and transported one survivor back to our temple for questioning."

"Are you certain they are dead, Obasi Sabina?" asked Eurycea.

"They are very dead, Eurycea," Obasi confirmed. "I personally made sure of it. There is only one exception. That mercenary is our prisoner and will face justice. You have my word of honor."

"Then you are our friends, Obasi Sabina. What do you require from us?"

"We will go in peace. I will report your interest in friendship to our leaders. Do we have your permission to return to your domain?"

"Our friends are welcome here at their desire."

"Thank you, Eurycea," said Obasi. "I do have one question before we depart. It's a simple question resulting from my own curiosity about the leader of the underwater team. I am greatly impressed by their disposition as a combatant and thank the Great Creator that I wasn't a victim of it. I wish to know their name."

"That is my daughter, Ruby," Eurycea told Obasi. "I must say you are very perceptive and accurate in your estimation, Obasi Sabina."

With that, Obasi smiled and ordered her team to don their diving equipment once again and begin their descent into the depths of the aquifer to return to the templar knights who awaited their safe return above ground.

As the special forces group exited the aquifer, Obasi removed her facial breathing apparatus and drew a deep breath of fresh air into her lungs. Isaiah and Buluc each extended a hand to her, helping pull her up and over the lip of the aquifer recharge entrance.

"Did you find anything interesting down there, Lieutenant?" asked Isaiah.

"You're not going to believe it."

"Very interesting, then?" said the general.

"General, have you ever seen a telepathic salamander larger than you who can see you while missing its eyes?" Obasi asked.

Isaiah smiled wildly. "Definitely interesting."

# CHAPTER 17: A RAY OF HOPE

Janina remained in Hamilton's apartment. This last Atsalat meditation was somewhat confusing to her. Spiritual trips to the Eleventh Dimension were often mysterious and only exposed partial elements of long stories. She felt, however, that the place where she had found herself this time was the same place where she had been with Hamilton in the meditation just before his murder. There had to be a connection. She hoped time would reveal it to her.

Janina stood up and looked for something she could use to carry the items from Hamilton's apartment. She found a backpack in a storage space. She placed the items inside it, left the apartment, and locked the door. She waited for the elevator tube and once again felt Hamilton's absence like an ache in her chest. She entered the tube, rode the lift down to street level, and left the building, stepping out into the metal city under falling rain. Janina couldn't help but feel a sense of sadness, as she was certain she would never return to Hamilton's living quarters; it simply wasn't smart for her to be there or anywhere close to the building.

As she walked away, Janina pulled out the list of the School of the Eleventh Dimension believers. The first name was Cedano Jole. The second name was Hope Zenobia. Janina focused on her, figured that another female was a good person to start with, given that Janina was quite young and all alone. She also recalled that the gift she'd been given in the Eleventh Dimension had been referred to as hope. With an address in hand, Janina quickened her pace and headed toward the train station. This would be a rapid transfer. She headed east on the magnetically levitating train, which traveled at speeds exceeding 300 miles per hour.

The train arrived at its destination station, and Janina got off. She took the lift down to street level and began to walk toward Hope's address. Janina had grown up in the streets of Tai-Anh and knew how to use public transportation to get around the city. She could smell the salt of Tai-Anh's Panthalassan Ocean in the cold air, and she could see the signs of oppression and suffering in the residents she passed by. Some things never changed. Suffering was a constant on Tai-Anh.

Janina's mind got to thinking about all that had happened to her over the last couple of days.

Her spiritual mentor, role model, and friend had been murdered by her own planet's leaders. And she had lost touch with over 100 fellow believers, not to mention those she hadn't met yet. What she didn't understand was why. What was it about the spiritual school that taught love and connection with a higher dimension that threatened the empire to the point of murdering its practicing members?

Hamilton had never criticized the empire, and he'd never spoken of any plans to challenge its power. It made no sense to Janina. She was a fugitive enemy being hunted down. She knew her life depended on her not being captured by Exelcior's forces. She had heard the stories of rape, torture, and execution by the empire's brutal forces.

As she walked under the elevated train tracks, Janina noticed a hovering patrol vehicle slowing down on the road as if its occupants were trying to get a better look at her. She was fairly certain this was a government hovercraft. The vehicle passed her once, then turned around to pass a second time. Janina tried to ignore it, avoiding making eye contact so as not to look suspicious. She quickened her step as her heart began to pound inside her chest. She began to wonder what the government agents might think of her carrying an obsidian knife and items belonging to a man they had recently blown out of existence. At this point, she couldn't ditch the knife anywhere to return and pick up later. She was being watched too closely already.

After the vehicle passed her a second time, it stopped just ahead, and two agents stepped out in front of her. Janina could hear her heart pounding but decided to continue walking past the agents. The male agent looked at the hologram produced by his wristband, and it was obvious to Janina that he was looking at a representation of her. He studied the hologram closely to confirm his suspicion. They were looking for her. She was sure of it.

*I really need to learn how to fight,* she thought. Unfortunately, there was no time to learn, which meant that running was her only option. She would have to depend on her physical fitness, intelligence, and youth. She began to run, and the two agents took off after her.

Conditions on the ground were treacherous, making a foot chase very difficult. Janina raced down a corridor between the fast-flowing Bructeri River, which hadn't frozen yet, and a tall glass and metal building. She came to an area where several roadways met. The area looked like a bowl of noodles, with several interchanges and levels of roads. Hovercraft moved rapidly on the roadways, traveling at minimum speeds of 100 miles per hour and up to 350 miles per hour, all under remote control from local stations to prevent collisions.

As she continued running as fast as she was able, Janina began to put distance between herself and the two agents chasing her. In the distance, she could hear the sirens of other government hovercraft responding to the chase. The sirens of emergency response vehicles were used not to alert civilians but to activate the systems that moved hovercraft out of the way for responding vehicles.

Janina ran down a steep hill toward the lowest of five roadways, cars moving at great speeds on levels overhead. She slipped on the wet street and lost her footing. Thinking this was the end of her escape plan, her heart sank. With the momentum she had built up, she slid at great speed and traveled a long distance. This loss of footing turned out to be a savior. Janina slid underneath the lowest roadway and continued to slide to the other side of it, where there was a steep drop-off into the Bructeri River.

One thing Janina had learned from her foster parents was how to swim. She was a strong swimmer and managed to keep her head underwater for a great deal of time as she traveled further and further away from the chase. After a while, she swam to the edge of the river. To her surprise, she'd ended up not too far from Hope's address. She thanked the Great Creator that she hadn't been caught with the list of believers and their addresses. This would have led to an immediate arrest order or worse for all the believers on the list. She carried all their fates with her. She considered dropping the list into the river, but that would mean losing it forever. Worse, it could be found by the empire's forces.

Janina climbed out of the river. A heavy cold started setting in, and her fingers and toes began to go numb, so she picked up pace and began to run again. As she approached a crowded street in the city, Janina slowed to a brisk walk so as not to attract unwanted attention. A soaked young woman running briskly through a city would definitely attract funny looks.

She walked a few more blocks before she arrived at her destination. Hope's residence was in the basement of a building. Janina walked down a flight of stairs and stepped into an open courtyard between two tall buildings. She shivered as she knocked on the door, feeling the cold in her bones now that she wasn't moving anymore. No one came to open the door, which was set at the top of a five-step staircase. The bottom of the door was at eye level, and Janina could see that someone silently approached the door and stood out of sight, listening, not saying a word.

Janina decided to say something, hoping it wasn't the last thing she would ever say. She took a deep breath. "Hello. I . . . I'm looking for Hope Zenobia."

No answer.

Janina tried once more. "My name is Janina Preston, and it's important that I find Hope Zenobia."

No response again.

Janina was sure there was someone behind the door, listening intently, so she continued to speak. "Dr. Hamilton Nile gave me—"

Before Janina could finish her sentence, the door opened swiftly, and a strong woman's hand reached for her, caught her wet jacket with a strong and heavy grip, and yanked her inside.

Janina almost let out a scream but quickly got her emotions under control. She looked into the eyes of a beautiful, strong woman, who pulled her close and seemed to peer into her soul without saying a word. Janina instantly knew that she was not going anywhere without doing as she was told.

"I am Hope," said the woman. "Were you followed here, Janina Preston?"

Janina was impressed that the woman had remembered her name. "No," she said. "I lost them at the river, and they didn't regain my trail. Do you know—?"

"Were you there when Hamilton was killed?" Hope interrupted.

"Yes, I was there."

"Did . . ." Hope's eyes suddenly became misty. "Did he suffer?"

"So—"

"I asked you if he suffered!"

"No!" Janina promised. "It was a quick, loud boom from the sky. It was over in a split-second."

Janina realized that Hope must have held Hamilton in high regard, and she felt empathy for Hope's sense of loss. She too missed Hamilton; she felt the same deep sense of loss. The two women shared mutual pain. "I was in Hamilton's living quarters this morning," said Janina, suddenly remembering the wonderful smile of the innocent little boy she'd met in Hamilton's building. "It's still hard to believe he's gone."

"Only Herod Exelcior could order this murder and get away with it," Hope said darkly. "His forces are most likely on direct orders to arrest you and bring you in for questioning so they can find the rest of the believers. Ever since the peace treaty with Lyndon was signed, he's been executing anyone or anything that threatens his power on this planet or elsewhere, relying on his elite forces, the Noumeroi. You were not chased tonight by them. You were chased by government policing agents."

"How do you know it wasn't the Noumeroi who chased me today?" Janina asked.

"I know because you are still alive. The Noumeroi are hardened veterans of the Mine War. I fought with them in that hell hole, and if they are hunting you . . ." Hope allowed a moment of silence for the harsh reality to sink in.

Janina felt overwhelmed by just how scary life had become and how alone she felt in the universe. Hope could tell and placed her hand on her shoulder, peering kindly into Janina's eyes without saying anything.

Janina broke the silence. "That's scary. Oh, you should know that I have a list of the believers and their addresses."

"You do?" Hope exclaimed. "Let me see it."

Janina handed Hope the list and watched as her eyes grew large.

"I know the people on this list. This is a dangerous thing to keep around. I'm meeting with most of these people tonight. We can make sure everyone on this list is contacted. Once we meet tonight, we will commit it to memory, and this list will need to be destroyed," said Hope. She gestured for Janina to step into the living area of her apartment. "Take off your clothes."

"What?" asked Janina, startled by the shocking request.

"Take off your clothes," Hope repeated. "You're shivering and will get sick if you don't get your body warm. Go in the closet of the next room and pick an outfit. We're about the same size, so you should find something there to fit you." Hope walked away to give her some privacy.

Janina watched as Hope retreated. She was impressed by how intimidating and physically fit Hope was, her legs strong and muscular. Janina proceeded to the room and the closet. She changed clothes and walked over to a frame on the wall that held several combat medals for valor, most likely from the Mine War. Among the medals was a picture of Hope standing with a group of three males and four females, all holding CO2 pulsating laser rifles. "Is this you in the picture here?" asked Janina.

"Yes."

"Who are the others? Do you still talk to them?"

"Yes, in a way," said Hope. "I see them in the Eleventh Dimension. They were all killed by Lyndonite troops on Magna Hermopolis."

"I'm sorry," said Janina, suddenly uncomfortable and regretful for her ignorance. "My parents were killed there as well," she offered empathetically.

Hope realized she had fought against Janina's parents and very well may have contributed to making Janina an orphan, a revelation that hit her like an explosive blow to her chest.

Janina saw the effect the realization had on Hope. "Are you okay?" she asked.

"Yes. Sorry. Just remembering some old friends is all," stated Hope, returning to the present situation.

Hope was relieved when Janina did not attempt to continue the conversation about her parents. Regret was one of the most powerful universal emotions.

Janina had already made the connection that Hope may have known how her parents had been killed, but she had noticed the effect the discussion had already had on her. *Another time, perhaps*, she thought. "Hope, will you teach me how to fight?" asked Janina, surprised at herself for asking such a random and direct question to someone she hardly knew.

"I'll do better than that, Janina. I'll teach you to kill. Killing is the most effective form of self-defense," said Hope with a matter-of-fact expression on her face. "Tonight, we're meeting several believers at a studio where I teach an ancient fighting art called Ch'o'Jonik. I learned it after the Mine War but saw its effectiveness from the warriors from Shrah during combat. The master teacher of the art, Michael Alom, is the ruler of Shrah. Unfortunately, Exelcior and his general, Antipas, are two others here on Tai-Anh who are experts in fighting arts, and they are obviously not on our side. Your training starts tonight. Get your backpack ready, and let's go."

"How will we get there?" asked Janina, reluctant to leave Hope's apartment and expose herself again to Exelcior's agents.

"We'll take my hover car."

The two women, one beginning her life as a woman and the other a battle-hardened war veteran, headed out into the night.

As they sat in Hope's car, Janina asked, "Where are we going to meet the other believers?"

"Where Exelcior's Noumeroi won't think of looking for you," Hope replied.

"Where is that?"

"Lyndon."

# CHAPTER 18: INSIDE MY HEAD

Today, I have decided to work much harder at no longer feeling sorry for myself and getting over the fact that my ex-wife walked out on me. Easier said than done.

"That is a great idea, Captain Sauer," said the traveler, reading my mind again.

I remembered that I could hold no secrets from my fellow spaceman, and it irritated me. Regardless, that was my new normal, and I gave up fighting for my inner privacy. "Thank you, Traveler. I appreciate your confirmation that not feeling sorry for myself is a great idea. Now, do you have any suggestions for me as to how I can do that? Maybe you can squeeze one of my new glands? It's the least you could do since you insist on invading my private thoughts."

"One cannot erase memories once they have been memorialized in your conscious mind, Captain Sauer," said the traveler. "Strong memories can only be blocked for a limited time. It's much like locking them up in what you would call a bank. Many will be erased when you reincarnate. Unfortunately for you, you still love her. Love is a complicated thing that can't be simply erased. It can only be mitigated by new love and the passage of time. My suggestion is that you fall back in love with yourself. You must conquer loving yourself. I know about conquest. Conquest is my specialty."

"Conquer loving myself, huh?"

"Conquer yourself, Captain Sauer."

"Let me get to work on that," I said with obvious sarcasm. "Traveler, I've learned much from you since I woke up from the deep seven-month sleep you had me in. I have a few questions for you about that."

"I will try to answer what I can to the extent that you are able to understand my answers," the traveler told me.

"Great. Where are we headed?"

"The galaxy is known to the people of Earth as Andromeda. There is a planet there where you will be reunited with your people."

That statement took me a second to digest. "My people? You mean I'm not from Earth?"

"You are from Earth, Captain Sauer, and so are the rest of your people. Your true origin will be revealed to you in time. I can tell you that your people were relocated away from Earth many centuries ago and are presently located on the planet to which we are traveling. In effect, you are a universal citizen. The blood that runs through your veins today is the same blood that ran through your people's veins centuries ago in the geographic region Earthlings call Mesoamerica. Your people on this planet, new to you, need you to help them survive. This time, we will not relocate your people. This time, you must fight for your people's survival. We have no way of knowing the outcome. This is part of the free will given to living beings by the Great Creator."

"Mesoamerica is my birth place, Traveler," I said. "Obviously, you know that I was adopted by an American couple, but I was born there. My parents weren't very young when they adopted me, and I buried both of them."

"Yes, we know everything about you, Captain Sauer," the traveler confirmed. "You will be reunited with your parents when the Great Creator calls you home to the Eleventh Dimension."

The traveler's statement overwhelmed me with happiness. Being reunited with my parents would be a dream come true. They were and would always be my true parents. "Is this the same Eleventh Dimension where I was for over seven months?" I asked.

"There are different realms within the Eleventh Dimension," explained the traveler. "You were not in the realm where your parents are. You see, Captain Sauer, you are a direct descendant of the Maya of Copán. Your soul has lived many physical lives. One of these lives will be revealed to you when we unlock the hidden memories stored in your consciousness. When you leave the spiritual realm in the Eleventh Dimension and reincarnate, your memories of your past lives are temporarily locked away from you to protect you from the traumas of them. All your lives come to reality when you return to the Eleventh Dimension between incarnations."

"This feels like a really bad dream," I grumbled. "It almost feels as if I'm in a coma in a hospital and am imagining all this. It also feels as if I'm dead and this is what dead people experience but don't return to life to describe. Am I still alive, Traveler?"

"You are always alive. There is no death. If you want to know if you have physical life, the answer is yes. You are still physically alive and traveling close to the speed of light away from Earth, heading to the Andromeda galaxy. We, the travelers, can travel without physically relocating ourselves. We are traveling through a wormhole because you are physically alive. This craft is for you, not us. Due to relativity, time on Earth has greatly accelerated for you. Earth as you know it is changing dramatically into a distant future."

This was simply too fantastic to fathom all at once. Truth be told, there was nothing left for me on Earth. It saddened me to think it really was over with my ex-wife. She would be long gone in history if I were to ever return. Although the answers were mind-boggling and painful, they were answers, and I needed answers. I took some time to let it all sink in. I then said, "So we're bending the fabric of space, then."

"We are traveling through a tunnel that connects one point in space with another and requires less time to travel," the traveler replied. "We have to resort to physical technology we borrowed from other civilizations related to yours. Some of these civilizations are scattered far away from Earth. There is intelligent life all over the cosmos at different stages of development. By all measures, Earth is still in its infancy. We are being propelled by an antimatter engine that is of a technology not dominated in the galaxy we are leaving or in the galaxy we are traveling to, at least not yet."

"I don't understand much of the science, Traveler," I admitted. "I know how to win in war. It's about all I really know, to tell you the truth."

"We are well aware of this, Captain, and this is the reason we are transporting you."

That actually made some sense to me. "Are you physically alive, Traveler?"

"I am alive, Captain Sauer. I am not alive in a biological sense. In a spiritual sense, I am more alive than you because I am never separated from the Great Creator and have no free will. The time of great uncovering approaches us. We ensured the continued existence of several civilizations from Earth by relocating them to other planets among the stars at other points in history."

"Are you a spirit or something like that?"

"I am a spiritual being," the traveler said. "I am also a warrior myself. The closest definition on Earth is that I am an entity. I have had many interactions with civilizations throughout the universes, of which there are multiple. You live in one and are going from one place in your universe to another point in the same universe. Technology in your universe has not advanced enough for intergalactic communication or travel."

This was even more fantastic. My response was laced with my usual sarcasm. "So I can't shoot you for taking me away from my home in Texas and taking my gun away, huh?"

"You could try, Captain Sauer, but my sword could cut you into pieces physically and spiritually. I suggest you listen carefully to me and realize that this is your destiny," the traveler said. "You will soon have weapons far stronger than the metal slugthrower you wore on your hip on Earth."

"Slugthrower?" I demanded. "I'm offended."

"Captain Sauer, you will meet another young temporary visitor we have with us presently. We will enter a separate realm of the Eleventh Dimension now. Through those doors, we will pass into Crystal City. Follow me."

I followed the traveler, noticing yet again that the soft floor did not sag underneath his feet. Considering the height and weight of this bearded and muscular behemoth—he must have weighed 400 pounds or more—this seemed very unsettling. I also noticed that his skin gave off a white glow like an aura radiating from beneath his tunic.

We proceeded down a long corridor that led to a white-walled room, where there were three larger-than-human beings standing in front of a seated human-sized young man. The standing entities, who I assumed were the three other travelers, gave off three different-colored glows; one was reddish, another almost black, and the third a pale grayish color. I couldn't help but notice that the reddish entity had no beard, the dark entity seemed thin and emaciated, and the pale gray one looked almost skeletal.

The three of them looked at me with deft attention. The young man stood and turned to look at me too. He seemed strong. He had the look in his eye that I had seen in some of the finest warriors on Earth. This young man was a fighter. I knew a fighter when I saw one, no matter where we were in the universe.

The original traveler turned to me and stated, "Captain Sauer, the time to unlock the language you once spoke in biological life on Earth many centuries ago has come." He placed his massive hand on my forehead, and vibrations flooded from his palm into my brain's frontal lobe with a wave of heat and what felt like an electric current. This went on for about a minute. I was again immobilized. I hated that feeling.

He removed his palm from my forehead, and I was able to speak with the young man in his native tongue, which was apparently mine as well. Without missing a beat, we were speaking K'iché. It was like I was thinking and speaking in English, only for my words to be magically translated before they were heard by others. There were at least two planets in two different galaxies in the universe where K'iché was spoken.

The traveler also unlocked my memories of my past twenty-one biological lives. I now had access to my entire repertoire of past lives. I'd reigned in the Yucatán Peninsula centuries before, and my name had been Kinich Ahau.

The traveler explained that from now on, I would be known by both my names. I was the living person the people of Yucatán, the people to whom I was returning, associated with their two-starred sun. I finally also recognized the four travelers present, and this chilled me to my core. In addition, I recognized the young man in the crystal room. He was now Seth Alom, but I had once known him as B'alam Nehn.

Seth had not reached full enlightenment yet, and I was certain he felt the instant connection to me but did not know of our association in our past lives. He simply knew we were connected in a deep and powerful way.

Soon, I was to be known as Kinich Ahau once again, bearing the same name as the binary stars the planet I was traveling to orbited. I once had been associated with the god in the sky, who rose every day to bring warmth and life, and I was returning to my people in a galaxy millions of miles away. I was still Andy, but I had memories of my time as Kinich Ahau.

From that day forward and for the remainder of the flight, I became well acquainted with my mission, with the four travelers, and with Seth. I prepared for "the great uncovering" and the fact that my people's existence could very well have come to an end after being uprooted and relocated from Earth to Shrah. I learned that the four travelers had also uprooted some of the greats of Ancient Egyptian civilization, including Osiris, Isis, Akhenaten, Nefertiti, and Imhotep.

Imhotep had been the polymath who'd served in the third Egyptian dynasty and who'd been responsible for the construction of Shrah's Great Pyramid, among other monumental structures throughout the universe. Imhotep had been designing and sharing anti-gravity technology eons before the first human being had walked on

Earth.

Earth was not the first and would certainly not be the last. All the great civilizations on Earth and throughout the cosmos were interconnected by the same intelligent beings responsible for erecting structures of stone to remind future civilizations that they had been created and were not the first to exist in their planetary domains.

Seth and I, two aliens in the same dimension, trained together. I had been a lifelong student of martial arts and close-quarters hand-to-hand combat on Earth and was excited to share this knowledge and experience with the ajaw-to-be of a great civilization on Shrah. I was a practitioner of Earth-based martial arts like Brazilian jiu-jitsu, taekwondo, karate, Muay Thai, boxing, and more. The traveler had also unlocked my ancient knowledge from past lives of lethal arts and killing enemies. Among these was Ch'o'Jonik.

Seth explained, "I have received extensive training in Ch'o'Jonik from my father and the grand knight of the temple, Sir Buluc Hix."

I was impressed by Seth's understanding of lethal martial arts and by his ability to implement them in a battle to the death. Seth and I also received extensive teachings regarding Atsalat, the Sacred Codices, and the spirituality of our people. Seth and I were decades apart in biological age, but spiritually, we were old souls tied together by the binding forces of destiny and brotherhood. I knew it would soon be time for young Seth to depart, so I spent as much time teaching the young man as I could, helping him become that much more lethal a fighter.

What would happen to Seth's spirit was a mystery only the Great Creator knew, and all waited patiently for when it would be revealed. He might decide to take Seth to another dimension, forcing him to face biological death on Shrah. The Great Creator even kept the enlightened and the travelers in the dark regarding this mystery.

In the Crystal City in the Eleventh Dimension, Seth's spirit and I trained together and learned from each other. Seth was proficient in Ch'o'Jonik, and I was proficient in a mix of fighting disciplines, as well as having recently unlocked centuries worth of ancient Ch'o'Jonik knowledge. I explained to Seth that what he practiced was a hybrid of fighting styles I had learned from all over my planet as I'd traveled and been stationed in land formations surrounded by oceans.

One day, a man Seth knew from his days on Shrah entered the white teaching room, where we were discussing the Sacred Codices with the travelers. Seth knew him as Dr. Hamilton Nile, and I knew him as Ahau Chamahez from ancient Earth. Apparently, he'd been created to care for the health of our people, one life after another.

He was allowed to recognize me in the Eleventh Dimension. I was thankful for that and gave the great spirit a long hug. After all, it had been centuries since I had been with him. Out of respect for the present, I addressed him as Hamilton Nile. "It is so wonderful to see you again! What brings you here, my old friend?" I asked.

"Kinich Ahau, it is great to see you as well. I am here to take Seth Alom with me. His time here has been brought to an end by the Great Creator," responded Hamilton. When we interacted, the travelers faded away as if disappearing from existence.

"Where are we going?" asked Seth.

"We are going to see an old friend," Hamilton told him. "And you are going where you belong."

# CHAPTER 19: A HEALING ART

Michael received word that his special forces and templar knights had found mercenaries at the Tela Mountain Range. He learned of the neutralization of eleven combatants. “Are the bodies here and whole?” he asked Noah.

“The bodies are here, and their hearts weren’t removed by our forces. However, their tongues had been surgically removed in keeping with our findings with Seth’s attackers. Two of the bodies were decapitated, and those two heads are also here. We have one combatant who was left alive here with us. He was transported here, and other than having all of his companions killed in front of him, he seems to be fine. We have begun the interrogation process. I assume you want us to refrain from torture,” stated Noah.

“Yes, we will preserve his dignity, as it seems it may be all he has left.”

“Do you wish to participate in the interrogation, Ajaw?”

Michael shook his head. "No. I will not leave Seth's side. Please see what can be done. See if he will write down what he knows. Maya might be of little use to you. The fury of a mother when her child was almost killed is very powerful and raw. She is getting some much-needed rest, thanks to the sedative you gave her. She will return at any moment. It might be a good idea not to let our prisoner know that we will treat him decently. Deception of an enemy combatant is fine. Just don't hurt him physically," asserted Michael in a tone that let Noah know he was only convincing himself again to fight the temptation of ripping the enemy combatant's heart out of his body with his bare hands while it was still beating.

Noah understood. "Michael, you should consider teaching Ch'o'Jonik class tonight. It would help you with the pain you are feeling, and the people could use seeing their ajaw. They're worried about you. They've seen Maya, but they haven't seen you lately. Besides, class is best taught by the best teacher and fighter we have."

"Thank you. I'm afraid of the hand-to-hand combat practices right now, though. I might use excessive force with all the emotions running through my consciousness presently. I'm very angry."

"And that is precisely why you should train," Noah argued. "I know you won't hurt anyone. Please think about it, old friend. I'm worried about you." Noah placed his hand on Michael's shoulder and looked into his eyes. No more words were necessary between them.

That night, Michael stepped out of his son's infirmary room while Maya stayed at their son's bedside. He donned his ceremonial training uniform, made of animal skin, and proceeded to the Nacaome city center, where Ch'o'Jonik class was being held that evening.

Hundreds of fighters were there training. There was instant silence in the city center as Michael stepped into the arena. All eyes fixed on him—his muscular structure, broad shoulders, and defined physique. He truly was the most lethal and beloved man on the planet. This was their leader, who understood that gentleness had far more power than severity. This was the man who could snap a neck with little effort but managed to teach the masses how to be precise in their executions, approaching situations with patience and understanding. He was a father figure to them, and they loved him and protected him with their lives. All heads in the arena bowed.

Michael smiled with his people, who he loved and respected as though they were his own flesh and blood. He approached the center of the arena and bowed his head to the large flag above, which bore a graphic of the white pyramid on the gold planet with the number eleven superimposed over it. It was the same symbol that had appeared at the altar where Hamilton had been killed.

That night, Michael decided he would teach the Nacaome youth how to defend against a four-person knife attack in honor of his son's battle for his life. He taught one-step, three-step, and side-step attacks, slashing, stabbing, and thrusting. He also taught defensive moves, head movements, forty-five-degree-angle movements, slipping, rolling, pulling, and blocking. It felt wonderful to be back on the arena floor, teaching the ancient art of lethality taught to him as passed down by generations of his people from distant galaxies. He remembered when he'd taught Buluc and the rest of his forces, who were now putting into practice these ancient movements that proved time and again to be effective.

At the same time, in an abandoned building in Lyndon, Hope, Janina, and over 100 believers also trained in Ch'o'Jonik. They reviewed weaponless hand-to-hand striking, footwork, takedown techniques, and large-joint grappling tactics. They had a removable flag given to them by Hamilton. The flag was the same that flew at Temple Alom and had hung in the School of the Eleventh Dimension before its destruction.

Believers from the school had found refuge in Lyndon with some of their counterparts there.

The Shrah Philosophy had infiltrated the ranks of the people in Lyndon just as it had in neighboring Gandolim. The total number of believers had already grown to several hundred, and some estimated that the philosophy was attracting youths and adults from all over the planet by their thousands. The message of an ancient civilization from a distant galaxy had been heard throughout the vast open spaces of the universe.

When the group of believers at Shrah's Temple Alom and the group of believers a planet away in the abandoned building in Lyndon finished their training, they began mass Atsalat meditations.

In Lyndon, Hope led the way, and Janina's wish of learning to fight began to be realized. Although Hope was not enlightened yet, she had learned from Hamilton how to lead an Atsalat meditation. The spirits in Nacaome and the spirits in Lyndon entered Atsalat meditative trances almost simultaneously. While alive, Hamilton had led meditations in Lyndon and in Gandolim. This could have been a primary reason why he was targeted by the empire.

Michael led the meditations on Shrah. Hope picked up where Hamilton had left off. Every believer who entered the Eleventh Dimension had a personal experience. This mass mediation showed them parts of the great uncovering that was soon to arrive. They saw the fire from the heavens raining down, the destruction and the bloodshed.

Later that evening, five spirits entered At-salat meditative trances and left the physical realm, traveling to Crystal City in the Eleventh Dimension. They flew past vast windswept green pastures and arrived simultaneously to be received by Hamilton Nile himself. This was a meeting of the leaders of the Shrah Philosophy of Love and War. Hamilton, Michael, Maya, Isaiah, and Kabel found themselves together in the highest realm.

A new addition to the group arrived: Janina. This wasn't the first time she had met Hamilton in the Eleventh Dimension, but it was the first time she had met the representatives from Shrah. Janina was introduced to the group and immediately recognized Maya. She recognized the beautiful dark-skinned woman in purple she had seen in the city of crystal before and in the picture in Hamilton's apartment.

Hope, Michael, Maya, Isaiah, and Kabel. The five of them had escaped biological death on Magna Hermopolis, although Hope had fought alongside the warriors from Shrah in the Combined Imperial Forces Command of the Third Realm. They were all operatives of the Noumeroi who'd fought together and become staunch believers and protectors of the Shrah Philosophy after the war. This was in spite of the differences that had existed between the empire and Shrah civilization in the post-war years. This was a reunion of great warriors from a common war, where their mettle had been tested to their cores.

Hamilton spoke first. "The great uncovering is quickly approaching. This is the only communication I will share with you as ordered by the messengers of the Great Creator. Free will must reign. Our people's destinies hang in the balance. Only time will tell what is to finally become of us. We have managed to escape many planets throughout the cosmos, but now the true moment of reckoning has arrived. The believers on Tai-Anh are in grave danger. So are all the believers in Lyndon. I cannot tell you who is responsible for this. Confirm it as you wish. You can find them hiding on Tai-Anh and Lyndon, with many others spread silently throughout Gandolim. Finding them is your duty. I love each of you."

With that and with no opportunity to respond or ask questions, all five spirits raced through the cosmic superhighway and returned to their bodies.

Michael found Maya, who found Isaiah, who found Kabel. They didn't say a word to each other until they were alone in the conference room, overlooking the valley.

Michael addressed Kabel directly. "Kabel, Isaiah and I have discussed who we would send on a mission such as this. You are to represent us on this important mission to Lyndon. Maya and I will assist you in preparing anything you need. We have space transports leaving for Lyndon on trade runs weekly. A transport ship leaves early tomorrow morning. Go undercover to Lyndon, and go immediately. Take whatever and whoever you need. Look for Hope and the young woman the empire is hunting. They are in grave danger. Bring our people home, and help spare them from slaughter. They are in need of our intervention."

Isaiah took over the briefing for the highly clandestine and dangerous mission to save lives.

The order had been given. The ajaw let his people own their actions and consequences. Michael had the utmost trust in them. When the briefing was done, Kabel turned and walked out of the room in double time, honored by the trust and ready to perform as ordered. None of this was new to her.

# CHAPTER 20: FRIENDLY VISITS

Kabel was enlightened. The enlightened were able to receive and transmit light energy via the cosmic superhighway. She, like Hamilton, was a key player in the spread of the Shrah Philosophy throughout the planetary system. These details were told in the Sacred Codices and in the teachings of Eleventh Dimension Atsalat meditations.

Seth's body fought for physical life in the infirmary of Temple Alom while his spirit sat in a room in Crystal City in the Eleventh Dimension, receiving invaluable lessons from the four travelers and Andy Sauer, the alien who was Kinich Ahau himself reincarnated.

In a past life, Kabel had known the alien under a different name and in a different galaxy. But he now lived in the galaxy where Kabel and her people had once lived and thrived before being uprooted. Beings often knew one another perpetually, as they co-existed in the Eleventh Dimension. Energy could not be created nor destroyed, and the soul was no different. Living energy could only be transformed from one form to another. Physical birth and death happened in a perpetual cycle of energy transformations.

Hamilton was a caring soul sent to Tai-Anh to be born and travel to Shrah to serve, learn the Shrah Philosophy, and return to Tai-Anh to spread the message of love and war to the believers there. That was precisely what he'd done. Emperor Exelcior had sent his forces to end his life because of it.

Kabel had been sent to help harvest the ancient philosophy from the relocated people of the desert in a distant galaxy. She'd done this in support of her ajaw and her people. The ajaw relied greatly on Kabel to be the premier spiritual leader of his people. She performed this duty in the same way Isaiah led the military and Buluc led the templar knights. They maintained the good order of Temple Alom and its people without resorting to heavy-handed tactics. These leaders of Shrah were descendants of warriors, reincarnated with the innate ability to defend their existence and that of their people through love, preferably, or violence if left with no choice.

As she rode a space transport belonging to Temple Alom, heading toward Tai-Anh, Kabel sat engaged in Atsalat. As her body hurtled through outer space, her spirit traveled through cosmic hyperspace, moving over the windswept green fields of the Eleventh Dimension, heading to Crystal City.

When she arrived, she was greeted by Hamilton, but he was not alone. The priestess couldn't tell who was standing next to Hamilton. She only knew that it was a male of a slight yet strong build. Kabel came face to face with Hamilton. He smiled with intense warmth, and she immediately felt just how much love flowed through him. She had known Hamilton when he'd visited Shrah and could tell there was a more powerful energy about him now.

"Welcome back to Crystal City, Kabel," Hamilton said. "Your presence here fills the entire city with happiness. You are one of the city's most precious daughters."

"Oh, Hamilton, it's been too long since you were with us on Shrah," Kabel replied. "Your service to the temple is always regarded as a priceless blessing to our people. It's wonderful to see that your mission of love continues here in the Eleventh Dimension. It flows through you."

Hamilton smiled. "Your prayers and intense light energy exchange here in the Eleventh Dimension have moved mountains of love and hope. The Great Creator has felt the flow of energy to and from you, Michael, Maya, and all the people of Shrah."

"It's been seven days now, and we are sick with worry. It's as if the Great Creator is keeping things a mystery from us," explained Kabel.

Hamilton nodded his understanding. "Kabel, Shrah and its people are in grave danger. The Great Creator will reveal the source of the danger soon. There is a woman on Tai-Anh who knows more. She is a believer on the verge of becoming elevated. She is quite young, scared, and in grave danger herself. She is with Hope Zenobia presently. You must listen to her story when it becomes available. It's critical that you do. She was my student, and her parents fought and died on Magna Hermopolis."

"I understand, Hamilton. I will find her. You have my word." After a brief pause, Kabel continued, "Who is the man with you, Hamilton? His aura seems so familiar to me. I'm sure I know him."

"The Great Creator has sent me here to return to you the spirit that belongs to the people of Shrah."

Without hesitation, Kabel bowed her head to the man standing next to Hamilton as a sign of respect. After a few seconds, Kabel looked into the eyes of Seth Alom. Tears began to well up and flow from her eyes at this wonderful realization. Seth embraced her without saying a word.

Within an instant and without warning, Kabel was traveling at great speed back to her body on the space transport bound for Lyndon. She came out of her Atsalat trance, overwhelmed with emotion.

At the same time, Seth's spirit returned to his body in the infirmary room. He moved the fingers on his right hand slowly.

Michael and Maya grabbed their son's cold hands, and Maya kissed them as Seth opened his eyes. Father, mother, and son all burst into tears. The Great Creator was indeed good, and his intention for Seth was no longer a mystery.

Michael stared for what seemed like a very long time, taking in the miracle of his son's life. He spoke first. "I love you, son. Welcome home. It will be a long recovery process, but we will bring you justice when it is time. I need to leave to see an old friend. I will return soon." He turned to Maya. "My love, I must go now. I can't wait any longer. You know where to. I will send Noah in to check on Seth."

Michael thanked the Great Creator for allowing his son to return to him in the physical dimension as he walked the passageways of Temple Alom, heading toward the remand center, where the surviving mercenary prisoner was being held. Joy flowed through his body. As he walked into the temple, workers and citizens bowed their heads to their leader. He smiled at everyone he encountered, and his people were filled with hope and joy at the sight of their ajaw in such positive spirits that he seemed to be glowing in white light. Michael always felt that his greatness was only in direct proportion to the respect with which he was treated, even by the lowest member of his society.

When he arrived at the temple's remand center, Michael was greeted by two templar knights, who stood on either side of the remand center custodian. The three men bowed their heads to their ajaw as he approached. They had been expecting him, knowing it was only a matter of time before he arrived.

"Thank you for being here," Michael said. "How is he?"

"He seems to be fine, sire. We understand his tongue was surgically removed, and he has made no attempt to communicate otherwise. He just finished eating. It was painful to see him chew food without a tongue."

"Compassion is an elevated emotion. Please let me in. I want to be alone with him," stated Michael.

The young custodian at arms was surprised. "Let you in there with him alone, sire? Are you armed? He could be danger—"

One of the templar knights placed his hand on the custodian's shoulder in an attempt to spare him the embarrassment of continuing to question if Michael would be safe. The custodian must have gotten the hint because he stopped his line of questioning, and his cheeks flushed bright red.

Michael placed his hand lightly on the

man's shoulder and smiled warmly at him. "Thank you for caring so much about my safety."

Michael did not mince words, and he absolutely meant to express his gratitude for the man's concern, no matter how absurd it may have seemed to the templar knights. The custodian unlocked the door, and Michael walked inside the room and waited to be left alone in the cell with the imprisoned mercenary. The door closed, and the three men stayed in front of it to unlock it when their ajaw was ready to leave.

Just a short time later, Michael called to the door in a soft voice. Michael issued no threats and never laid a hand on the prisoner. When the custodian unlocked the door, the prisoner was sobbing in Michael's arms, held and comforted by the man whose son he had plotted to have murdered. An instant later, Michael walked through the door, returned a bow to his men, and thanked them. As he left the remand center, he processed the fact that he now knew who had ordered his son's murder. It was time.

# CHAPTER 21: A MEETING BETWEEN NEIGHBORS

Michael, Maya, and Noah surrounded Seth's infirmary bed as a nurse removed his dressings to clean the wounds he'd incurred during the attempt on his life. Swelling and bruising spread across his face. Michael and Maya had to hold in gasps when they saw the depth and extent of the wounds and the beginnings of scarring on the left side of Seth's face. Ironically, the scar very closely matched the scar on his father's face; like father, like son. Regardless, no parent would ever wish to see that kind of scar on their child.

The nurse asked Seth if he wanted some time to let his wounds air before rewrapping them.

Seth responded in a forced, raspy voice,

"Thank you, but I don't need wraps. I can keep them clean going forward. Please give me the necessary items I will need when I clean my own wounds. I'm leaving in a few minutes."

The nurse balked. He looked at Michael as if to confirm that what Seth was suggesting was acceptable.

Michael nodded and said nothing.

The nurse understood. "I will return with the necessary supplies. Please excuse me. Sire. My lady." The nurse and Noah left the infirmary room and closed the door gently behind them to give the parents and their son a few moments of privacy.

Seth looked at his parents. "You both look so sad for me. There's no reason for sadness. I'm fine. I'm stronger than ever. Those assassins did me a favor. Do we know anything about them? I know three of them are certainly dead."

"Yes, you killed three of them, and Buluc killed the fourth," responded Maya.

Seth took a second to let the idea that he had taken the lives of three trained assassins sink in. It was big news to process, especially for a young man.

Michael could see this reality settling in on his son. "I'm sorry, son."

"I am too. I'm sorry I let the fourth one get away," Seth said with obvious cynicism.

Maya let out a short laugh but regained her

composure quickly. Maya always laughed when she was uncomfortable. She was not laughing because she found the situation amusing but because she knew, at long last, that her son would be okay. She now developed an even greater level of admiration for the man her son was fast becoming.

"Father, did Buluc obtain any useful information from the fourth attacker?" Seth asked.

"No," Michael told him. "I will share more about what I have discovered regarding the attack later. The attack on you was part of a much greater threat to our people. In my absence, Buluc will stay with you to help protect you and continue your training as you regain your strength. Son, I need you strong quickly. Do you understand?"

Seth smiled a knowing smile, and no more was said. Michael kissed his son on the forehead and his wife on the lips and left.

Michael stepped out the door and was greeted by Isaiah and Obasi. They both gave their ajaw hugs and looks that spoke a thousand words. The looks said that they loved him and would protect his son with their lives. They began walking together. Isaiah and Obasi had previously briefed their ajaw on what they had found in the Tela Mountain Range.

"Are the special forces, rotary craft, weapons, and dive gear ready?" Michael asked.

"Yes, sire," Isaiah and Obasi answered in unison.

"Then let's go see this salamander of yours."

The three laughed as they continued to walk out to the heliport, where both rotary craft and thirty-nine personnel were ready and waiting.

One of the special forces sergeants bowed to his ajaw and handed him his obsidian knife, CO2 rifle, and pistol. Michael returned the bow with a smile and a thank you. He took the front passenger seat, and they took off en route to the Tela aquifer. The ajaw was a pilot himself, but he chose to let someone else fly the craft so he could think through his upcoming meeting with the ruler of Shrah's watery underworld.

As the two rotary craft soared through the hot, dry, gold-bathed skies of Shrah, the space transport cut through the icy cold void of space, carrying Kabel Luu, Danli Itzamna, Yoro Copan, and three other hand-picked operatives.

They were traveling through outer space at a highly accelerated rate that used nuclear fusion as a means of propulsion. The troops in space were dealing with the monotony of long space flight. They were able to practice Ch'o'Jonik when Danli, the craft's captain, turned on the artificial gravity. They closely studied the maps and topography of Tai-Anh and Lyndon, entered Atsalat trances often, and reread the parts of the Sacred Codices that spoke of war. Kabel led them in meditations, beginning to prepare them for what they would find in Lyndon. They looked up above their heads with their eyes open, drawing in deep breaths. Then they closed their eyes and lowered their heads while slowly exhaling and eventually resting their heads at eye level, slowing their breathing down.

The special forces avoided contact with Gandolim. Lyndon was allowed to exist as an independent state, attached to Tai-Anh geographically but not politically. The relationship between the two was explosive, as Tai-Anh had declared war in Lyndon for their mining operation on Magna Hermopolis. Lyndon had continued to mine metals from Magna Hermopolis to build their infrastructure, military aircraft, and warships in spite of repeated warnings and threats from the Empire of Tai-Anh.

The leadership of Lyndon had always suspected that the peace agreement would end soon. Since the war, Lyndon and Shrah had become trading partners. The space transport carrying the six operatives from Shrah was on a weekly run between the neighboring planets.

Kabel was to inform the leadership in Lyndon that some of their citizens, those practicing the Shrah Philosophy, were in grave danger. She also planned to offer relocation assistance to help protect the lives of persecuted Lyndonites and return to Shrah with refugees and an assessment for Michael and Maya as to the situation in Lyndon.

During the trip from Shrah to Tai-Anh, Kabel entered several Atsalat trances. Once in the Eleventh Dimension, Kabel found herself in one of her past lives as Akna, an ancient incarnation of a distant planet. During another meditation, she led the group of special forces soldiers on an inside look at what they would encounter in the Republic of Lyndon. Under Kabel's enlightened guidance in the Eleventh Dimension, the five operatives saw what they were headed for; at least, they saw what the Great Creator allowed them to see.

One thing Shrah's special forces were known for was disguising themselves. They were already dressed in full Lyndonite garb and hoped to pass for ordinary citizens. It helped that the transport ship belonged to Shrah and had an authorized reason to enter Lyndon for trade.

Disguising Kabel was another story. Wherever she traveled, males, females, and non-binary alike were mesmerized by her physical beauty. When she looked at someone with her brilliant brown almond-shaped eyes, she sent her victims into a temporary stupor. They often rambled out nervous nonsense. It was quite amusing to Kabel, although she never made her admirers feel shame for it. She couldn't help the effect she had on people.

There was far more to Kabel than just physical beauty. She was an enlightened priestess and a decorated war veteran. She hadn't been operating as a priestess when she'd served in the Mine War, though. Kabel had served in a unit headed by none other than Buluc Hix in the Imperial Combined Armed Forces in Noumeroi. Kabel was well aware of their abilities. She hoped she wouldn't have to deal with them on this trip to Lyndon. If she did have to, she was ready. Kabel was always ready. Exelcior's forces did not know she was aboard the transport. Her military rank of colonel was active for the secret mission.

The pilot, Danli, and co-pilot, Yoro, were well aware of the secret mission. Yoro was to fly only in the event that Danli was incapacitated. He was a special forces pilot who could fly well enough but who fought far better. With the group were Sergeants Anayansi Sula, Areni Dayami, and Morazan Ceibo.

Once the transport reached Lyndon, Yoro, Anayansi, Areni, and Morazan would accompany Kabel into the teeth of the situation to inform, protect, and extract the followers of a philosophy of love and war. Danli would stay behind in the space transport, hidden and ready for an emergency extraction out of Tai-Anh if necessary.

Kabel had not been in a combat situation

since the Mine War, which now seemed a lifetime ago. The first part of their mission was to locate Hope and Janina. They had intelligence reports that showed them the location of an abandoned warehouse, where Eleventh Dimension believers were thought to meet regularly. Kabel couldn't help but think if she had this intelligence report, there was a strong possibility that Exelcior and Antipas were also aware of the location.

She asked Danli how much longer he thought it would be before they were in Lyndon. He confirmed their arrival time. Kabel read her copy of the Sacred Codices to help calm her anxiety. There were no messages or conversations coming in from Shrah. This lack of communication was needed to maintain information discipline and avoid compromising the mission.

Yoro ordered Morazan to inspect the CO2 laser rifles, pistols, dive gear, parachutes, and night vision goggles that were hidden in compartments in the craft for functionality and readiness. They were fully operational and ready to go. Each operative examined their equipment and prepared to use it.

On Shrah, Michael, Isaiah, Obasi, and the detachment were heading back to Temple Alom after Michael's visit with Eurycea in the Tela aquifer. The special forces troops had already named the amphibians salamanders. Michael thought about all Eurycea had said to him. He felt a strong connection to the aquifer salamanders; they too had once lived on the same planet and had been relocated together to another, although they had only just met in the brave new world.

Eurycea had explained that they once had had an entire civilization living on Earth in the adjacent galaxy. The same name that was mentioned in the Sacred Codices: Earth. Eurycea had said that her people had lived in a vast lake under the ice in a place Earthlings called Antarctica. She'd explained that after centuries of living undisturbed, exploration by Earthlings had driven violent and aggressive forces into the ice caps, jeopardizing their freshwater habitat. Before the Earthlings could find and extinguish them, a diamond-shaped light coupled with a loud boom and blinding light had appeared over the western sky and lifted them from the lake to relocate them to Shrah. She spoke of four beings inhabiting the vehicle that had transported them. They remained undetected, having left no tracks for others to find.

Michael was fascinated by the ties between what Eurycea had said and the story in the Sacred Codices, which told of his people being uprooted in much the same way from this planet called Earth. Eurycea had explained that the intergalactic transit had lasted many months and that the adult salamanders in her civilization had been taught the language of K'iché. Michael thought it was too much of a coincidence that both his people and the salamanders spoke the same language. There was a deep and significant connection, a shared destiny, between their civilizations. Michael thanked the Great Creator, who Eurycea referred to as the Star Maker, for the salamanders' arrival on Shrah and for allowing Seth to return from the Eleventh Dimension to once again walk among the living. He wondered what was in store for these creatures in regards to Exelcior's murderous actions. He would soon have his answer.

# CHAPTER 22: CHOICES

They were getting much closer to the blue marble in the dark, cold void of outer space. Soon, they would feel the full weight of their bodies, plus a few pounds under Tai-Anh's greater mass. Danli slowed the re-entry speed to lessen the glow of the superheated blanket of incandescent plasma at the transport's leading edge.

They entered through the day side of the planet, where it was still light, and soon went full-stealth into the dark side of the planet. They didn't have to go full-stealth since space transports from Shrah were normal on Tai-Anh, but they wished to take the extra precaution.

Water began to accumulate on the transport's blackened windows as they flew around the dark side of the planet toward the city of Gandolim.

The six uninvited aliens from Shrah could feel their adrenaline pumping for what appeared to them to be an excruciatingly long time, as

Danli wanted to make sure not to create a noticeable heat signature in the cold, wet night sky that hung over the metal city.

Danli confirmed they would be arriving just south of the spaceport on the surface of the Panthalassan Ocean. The surf was calm that evening, just as the meteorological intelligence reports had anticipated. The alighting on the ocean's surface was smooth with minimal noise or splash. The captain was a crack pilot. The only perceptible sound was the hum of the spacecraft's stealth engines winding down. Shortly after touchdown, Danli piloted what was then a surface ship on water as he approached the abandoned shipyard in Lyndon territory. He kicked on the engines to push toward the southernmost pier.

After anchoring the craft and before submerging it for cover underwater, the team of five exited onto the dark pier in individual stealth mode and spread out from each other for better cover, walking several miles to arrive at the industrial complex where the abandoned warehouse was.

Danli stayed aboard the transport to prepare for their departure when the moment arrived. As planned, they were arriving at the customary time for Hope to lead the Lyndon believers in Ch'o'Jonik training and Atsalat meditation, where Lyndonites learned the ancient art of lethality and connected with the Eleventh Dimension. They proceeded through the streets of Lyndon in a clandestine and careful fashion. They were well trained for these operations, but they were nevertheless very dangerous in nature.

Their intelligence information appeared accurate. The believers were meeting where the intelligence report had anticipated they would. The team of five decided to approach the group, who weren't expecting them, from an elevated position and observe them from hidden spots so as not to alert any empire forces that might be watching.

Kabel, Areni, and Morazan entered one building, and Yoro and Anayansi entered another. The buildings were adjacent to the structure where the believers were having their meeting in a complex of old, abandoned, rusted metal structures. Both teams proceeded to the roofs of their respective buildings for observation. They climbed the metal staircases silently.

As Yoro and Anayansi approached the rooftop, they noticed someone dressed in black on the edge of the roof, overlooking the group of believers several stories below. This someone seemed to be a prime candidate for an empire observer or sniper. In response and preparation for engagement, they initiated radio silence and approached the friend or foe stealthily from behind the exhaust vents on the roof. No use risking being noticed until it no longer mattered. The lieutenant and sergeant assumed the worst and unsheathed their obsidian knives in preparation to maintain silence if they had to kill. They could hear the Ch'o'Jonik class going on below. The rooftop observer had a great vantage point from which to watch the believers.

The observer held a long-distance laser pulse rifle with a long-range scope looking through a ceiling window directly down on the training session. Yoro assumed the observer was waiting for a specific person to appear where they could get a clear shot and snipe one or more of the believers. He knew he didn't have time to wait. His course of action was clear. Yoro began his silent but swift approach, knife in hand. When he was within a few feet, he noticed the sniper beginning to turn around to engage him. The sniper must have been warned by intruder detection gear.

It was too late. Yoro flew through the air, striking the sniper in his spine with his right knee, snapping their spine instantly as he simultaneously pulled their forehead back, exposing the throat for a deep ear-to-ear cut that nearly decapitated them. With the force of the momentum, the sniper fell five stories through the rooftop window and landed splat in the middle of the floor of the warehouse below, where the believers were training. Glass rained down.

Chaos ensued, and the believers spread out, taking cover and trying to see where the body had come from. Yoro and Anayansi began their sweep to clear the rooftop of any enemy combatants. They found none. It appeared the sniper had been operating alone.

The sniper's head had disconnected from the body when it had hit the ground. It rolled away, smacking into one of the warehouse walls.

Communications opened up with the three special forces operatives on the other rooftop, and Kabel began her quick descent, followed by Areni and Morazan. Kabel was at ground level in little time and took cover, scanning the area with infrared and night vision.

When Kabel determined all was under control, she called out to the believers who were still inside the warehouse, most likely ready to strike at the first person they saw enter. The arrival of the Shrah visitors was unannounced, after all. Kabel spoke from outside the building, undercover. "Bahlam Jol burned for the second time."

There was no response.

Kabel repeated, "Bahlam Jol burned for the second time."

"A conquest of the Queen of Naranjo," responded a female Lyndonite voice.

"I am Kabel Luu from Shrah, and I am looking for Hope Zenobia."

The challenge phrases were ones only believers in the Shrah Philosophy knew. These were the words they all pledged to take to their physical graves without sharing them with anyone. They were the affirmation that you were interacting with a fellow warrior who would lay down their life to save yours.

The believers who comprehended what had been said were stunned. This was precisely what they had asked the Great Creator for. They'd asked for a sign to tell them they were not alone. They had received the answer to their requests in the Eleventh Dimension via their Atsalat meditations. Regardless, they remained silent.

"I will set down my weapons and approach you through the door with my hands in the air."

Yoro, who had already caught up with the rest of the team, put a bloody hand on Kabel's arm and looked at her, unsure if this was a good idea.

Kabel looked at him and said, "Lieutenant, I have to do this."

Yoro let her arm go, understanding he was outranked by Kabel when she used his rank to address him. He gave the order to his special forces to cover her and not hesitate to shoot anyone who threatened her life.

Kabel stood up and walked through the door unarmed, her hands in the air as she had promised. The believers inside the warehouse who could see her were awestruck by the immense physical beauty of the high priestess from their homeland. Some began to shed tears of joy, but no one dared approach her. Kabel's deep-brown eyes radiated beauty as the light hit her face.

Hope recognized her from their interaction in the war. She knew that athletic and graceful gait from when she'd been a part of the Imperial Combined Armed Forces. Hope knew of Kabel's battle prowess and her reputation for taking lives. She stood up, sheathed her obsidian knife, and stepped out to meet Kabel.

The two women hugged without saying a word. The embrace was an emotional catharsis for Hope. The presence of the high priestess overwhelmed her with joy. Kabel held her tightly.

The rest of the believers slowly began to emerge from the places where they were hidden, led by their most faithful believer and trainee, Cedano Jole. Once all the believers had emerged and everything seemed peaceful and under control, the remaining four Shrah operatives emerged from their hiding spots. Kabel made all necessary introductions between people alien to each other.

Yoro walked over to the sniper's head and examined it. He grabbed the head by its bloody hair and, just as he'd thought, found that its tongue was missing from its mouth. This was the mark of the other assassins and enemy combatants on Shrah. The empire was to blame.

With that realization, Yoro advised that they break up and leave the warehouse immediately. More enemy forces would likely arrive soon. The special forces disposed of the body but kept DNA samples to return to Noah. The group of believers, now led in three separate groups by Hope, Kabel, and Yoro, agreed to meet at a specific time at a different location in a park just west of the spaceport. The area was heavily wooded and dark. There, they would be harder to detect. The special forces would lead the way with night vision and ensure the location was safe. They were to meet there in a half-hour, when Janina would call Hope to verify that all was clear. Janina was to go with Kabel's group. Hope knew Janina's greatest chance for survival rested with the high priestess, who was also an elite alien combatant.

# CHAPTER 23: A FORK IN THE ROAD

Janina walked along hidden alleys and past the endless rusted and abandoned buildings of the neighborhoods just west of the spaceport, accompanied by the new arrivals from Shrah. This was a predominantly industrial area that had been mostly abandoned when Lyndon had been given its status as an independent state after the peace treaty. Deep within, there was still manufacturing going on, but it was well hidden. Those who worked there risked their lives. Lyndon did not have permission from the empire to let this industrial part of the city thrive openly.

The special forces were vigilant, keeping their eyes peeled for snipers and ambushers. They altered their course regularly and kept their distance from each other so as not to lose many lives in single attacks.

Kabel and Janina advanced together, which gave them a little privacy for a low-voiced conversation while still protected by the other special forces operatives. Janina informed Kabel of all that had transpired so far. She told her about the details behind the killing of their mutual friend, Hamilton Nile. Kabel listened intently.

"It was the most horrifying thing I've ever seen," said Janina. "Hamilton knew something was about to happen. He saved my life by telling me to leave immediately. When I left the building, a bright light appeared over the school, and seconds later, the entire structure disappeared from the face of the planet. It was horrible! It had to have been ordered by Emperor Exelcior. Hope thinks it was carried out by the forces of General Antipas. They've been hunting me ever since. It's a miracle I'm still alive. I need to learn how to fight! Hope is teaching me already."

Kabel couldn't help but be impressed with Janina's willingness to learn and fight for what she believed in and for whom and what she loved. Janina couldn't help but be in awe that she was receiving such rapt attention from the most perfect woman she had ever met.

Kabel spoke, aiming to close the perceived social gap between them. "You know, I wasn't always a priestess, Janina. When I was in the Mine War, I served with what were some of the most elite forces from the Empire of Tai-Anh against the people of Lyndon. Those elite combatants are the Noumeroi. They are a force to be reckoned with, but we have no choice in the matter."

"Hope has spoken to me about the Noumeroi," replied Janina. "I figured it was why you and Hope seemed so familiar with each other. Almost in-step at whole other level."

Kabel smiled with inner satisfaction at just how sharp Janina was to have picked up on that subtlety. "I didn't know Hope very well, but I did know her reputation as a fighter."

"And I'm sure she knew of yours." Janina paused for a moment. "You don't look old enough to have fought in any war. You're so beautiful!"

"Oh, believe me, I'm definitely old enough. Thank you for the compliment," Kabel said with a smile.

Janina smiled in return. "Do you think it's the Noumeroi who are hunting me? Hope seems to think it's not."

"Hope is correct. It's not the Noumeroi," Kabel stated flatly.

"How do you know it's not them?" asked Janina. She figured the answer would be the same one Hope had given her.

"The Noumeroi don't take prisoners, and they don't fail very often," said Kabel. "They are formidable. The templar knights and Shrah Special Forces are also a force to be reckoned with. The Noumeroi are well aware of it. We are simply greatly outnumbered by them."

Janina's eyes teared up at the thought of her parents being killed by Noumeroi and Shrah forces on one of the moons in the night sky.

"I'm sorry, Janina. I shouldn't have—" Kabel started.

"No!" interrupted Janina. "Please continue. Hope and I had a discussion about them earlier. I feel it helps me keep them alive somehow. It's just that I wish I could have known them in physical form as an adult. That's all."

Kabel stopped walking to add emphasis to her words. "Janina, your parents are very much alive in the Eleventh Dimension, and you will know them very well if you continue your path toward enlightenment. I will show you how. In the meantime, you should know that when we meet with the Lyndon believers again, I will offer anyone who wishes to leave with us the opportunity to return to the motherland of Shrah and train there to continue evolving spiritually and physically. Our people are no longer enemies of the people of Lyndon. We never should have been in the first place."

"Will training include me, Reverend?" asked Janina.

"Absolutely! It includes you especially."

Both women smiled and focused again on their walk and the surrounding area. Janina's mind whirled with the excitement of possibly traveling to another planet to become what her parents had been, to do what they had died doing.

Kabel and Janina arrived at the meeting spot. All seemed to be safe for the meeting with the remainder of the believers, who were already growing in numbers as the Shrah Philosophy gained momentum in Lyndon. The park was within visible range of the spaceport. Janina called Hope and informed her that it was safe.

Moments later, the remainder of the believers arrived at the park and made a circle around Kabel.

Hope spoke first. "We are all present except four. A small detachment, led by Cedano Jole, has separated from us to scope out elevated ground for the enemy. Unfortunately, we lost contact with them. They are seasoned war veterans, and we pray the Great Creator will be with them."

Kabel took over. "We need to make this brief. Our forces are keeping guard around us. As you know by now, the forces of Herod Exelcior, under the command of General Joram Antipas, are looking for you as we speak. They will soon notice the loss of their sniper in the warehouse, no matter how well we cleaned up after him. They have already killed our friend, Dr. Hamilton Nile, and many others. Although the Independent State of Lyndon has graciously offered asylum, I am afraid it doesn't have the means to protect you. Many of us here fought with or against

Lyndon, and we can assure you that we are not safe. Exelcior will begin using the Noumeroi as his frustration mounts. Hope has already called to arrange a meeting for me with your Prime Minister, Broteas Ovidius, for tomorrow morning. For those of you who opt to stay here on Tai-Anh, I will ask for Prime Minister Ovidius's support in relocating you to a place where you can train and prepare to defend yourselves from Tai-Anh's aggression. At dusk, we will be leaving for Shrah by space transport that is presently anchored in the Panthalassan Ocean, not far from the spaceport. This is a plan we cannot change without arousing suspicion."

There was a low rumble as the believers digested just how quickly they had to decide on a course of action. They were well aware that staying behind was risky. The empire had killed most of their combatants from the Mine War. They needed updated training on weapons, tactics, and physical conditioning. The empire secretly hunted Mine War veterans and exterminated them under the guise of unfortunate accidents.

Kabel continued, "Our special forces operatives, Lieutenant Yoro Copan and Sergeants Anayansi Sula, Areni Dayami, and Morazan Ceibo, will be staying behind with you on this planet to begin your indoctrination and training in clandestine lethality. We will be in constant communication with you and our trainers here to coordinate future action. You are all welcome to leave for Shrah with us and continue your Ch'o'Jonik and Atsalat training there ahead of joining forces in defense of Lyndon and Shrah in the near future. You have been officially invited to your home on Shrah by the ajaws personally. You are already citizens of Shrah."

This last statement generated an excited response from the believers. They knew of the ajaws, having had to fight against them and their forces in the Mine War. Lyndonites were thankful to have them on their side. They knew of the Shrah people's reputation as born fighters. The Aloms were now their allies and leaders. They had issued a personal and open apologetic statement of deep regret to the people of Lyndon, who accepted and greatly respected them for it.

The next morning, Kabel, Yoro, Hope, and Prime Minister Ovidius met in the prime minister's quarters. The special forces sergeants remained with the believers in case any further attempts were made on their lives. On that day, Lyndon and Shrah united as one in secret. As leader of Lyndon, Broteas Ovidius explained to Kabel that the people of Lyndon would help protect anyone who was being persecuted by the Empire of Tai-Anh. He explained that Lyndon had secretly continued to build its military resources in preparation for someday defending their independence from Tai-Anh. He committed those resources to Temple Alom for their use. Economic conditions on both Tai-Anh and Lyndon had been terrible for a long time. The suffering of the poor in both societies was immense, and it was only beginning.

At dusk, the scheduled time of the spaceflight departure for Shrah, the believers had to move with extreme caution, as it had been many hours since the empire's sniper had been neutralized. The Shrah operatives and 137 believers met at the park to the west of the spaceport. Again, all seemed safe and secure. Kabel awaited the decisions of the believers to stay behind in Lyndon and relocate to train with the special forces or to leave for Shrah to continue their training there.

Hope spoke on behalf of the believers, noticing as she surveyed the area that Cedano Jole was not in attendance. "Believers, step forward if you wish to leave for Shrah with Reverend Kabel Luu."

Sixty-three believers stepped forward. Janina was one of them. She was leaving for Shrah to begin a new chapter in her young life.

Hope would stay behind and train with the special forces in a remote location. Hope was a war veteran, but it seemed like a lifetime since she'd fought in combat. All of those present at the park broke up into groups and began their careful movement toward the spaceport. The night was cold, and the stars seemed brighter than usual.

Oftentimes, weather marked an event. For a brief respite, the rain stopped, and this filled the believers with hope.

Kabel, Janina, and the other believers began to make their way to the abandoned pier, where Danli was waiting for them. At Kabel's request, Danli handed her copies of the Sacred Codices to be issued to the believers undergoing training on Tai-Anh and bid them good luck in their mission training the new forces of Lyndon.

Prime Minister Ovidius kept his promise and had three rotary craft fueled up and ready to transport the Shrah special forces and seventy-four remaining believers to a remote location for training. Training was to begin immediately. Time was short.

# CHAPTER 24: CRUEL INTENTIONS

The space transport piloted by Danli departed from Lyndon after egressing from Tai-Anh's Panthalassan Ocean in full-stealth mode. For the first time in their lives, many believers would experience space travel. They would experience weightlessness and the enchantment of visiting an alien planet. The trip would be relatively short, as the planets were quite close together.

In space flight, the sixty-three believers from Lyndon began their training in Atsalat meditation, readings of the Sacred Codices, and Ch'o'Jonik fighting. Exelcior began to tighten his iron grip on the people of Lyndon even further to punish and control them. His spies in Lyndon had informed him about the beheading of the sniper and the departure of Shrah Philosophy believers for Shrah. The escape of Janina Preston particularly infuriated him. This was an act of war.

Exelcior knew it was time for him to punish and destroy the believers and those who provided them shelter. He moved swiftly to extinguish any ideologies that threatened his power and control over his empire. The School of the Eleventh Dimension, the teachings of the Sacred Codices, and the Shrah Philosophy did just that. They threatened Exelcior's absolute rule in an indirect yet powerful way. The threat wasn't of violence but of justice, which made it that much more real and dangerous to him.

Exelcior had the imperial media announce the outlaw of Eleventh Dimension gatherings and practice as a threat to empire security. He made possession of the Sacred Codices grounds for immediate arrest, and he made it clear that his full intention was to make those possessing the book disappear permanently. Those who chose to practice the philosophy did so at the risk of their lives. Exelcior sent Antipas to Lyndon to meet with Prime Minister Ovidius, seven members of Lyndon Parliament, and three members of the High Court.

Antipas entered the elevator, heading up for the rotary transport vehicle that was waiting for him atop the metal building within the imperial complex. At the rooftop, he was met by the pilot, co-pilot, and three Noumeroi who would accompany him on his supposedly diplomatic trip to Lyndon. They boarded the craft, which soon proceeded to exit the bubble membrane into the dark, raining sky of the metal city. Minutes later, the craft had crossed the ceremonial border and was landing at the rotary port at Lyndon Headquarters.

"I will make this brief. This meeting is not officially taking place," began Antipas. "We are aware you have harbored and assisted criminals practicing the dangerous cult teachings of the Eleventh Dimension. Sanctions in Lyndon are in effect immediately as a result of your crimes against the people of Tai-Anh. These sanctions will include an increase in income and property taxes from fifty to seventy-five percent, the halt of all trading activities between Tai-Anh and Lyndon, and the immediate entrance of Noumeroi forces to Lyndon to sweep your no longer independent state for the criminals in question.

"From this point forward, the empire will take what it wishes from Lyndon, or Lyndon will cease to exist. Any resistance to these sanctions will be considered an act of outright war on your part and will result in immediate retaliation that will lead to your extermination."

"You can't do this! This will mean the starvation of thousands of Lyndon children and innocent people!" protested Ovidius.

"Wrong, Ovidius! We can and will! You,

your parliament, and your high court will implement these changes immediately. You can blame your lack of insight and failure to militarize further after the Mine War ended," responded Antipas with dire acidity.

"We have a treaty between our nations!" Ovidius argued.

"Silence, Ovidius! Lyndonites shouldn't die because of their leader's stupidity," stated Antipas, a smile on his face. "You never had a nation to begin with. We simply allowed you to exist in your fantasy world. You have been harboring dangerous criminals who threaten the safety of Tai-Anh's citizens. That ends now!"

Ovidius considered challenging this statement but quickly thought better of it. He knew his protests were of no use, and the thought of his people being killed terrified him into silence.

Antipas continued, "Let me assure you that the Mine War was over a long time ago, and we will move swiftly in Lyndon this time around. When you announce these sanctions to your people, you will tell them that they are your decision and are in the best interests of your independent state. You will also outlaw the Shrah Philosophy."

With that, Antipas left the meeting room, leaving Lyndon's leader in stunned silence. Ovidius had no choice but to be abusive to his own people and, even worse, make them believe the sanctions were his idea. There was already so much suffering in Lyndon. The announcement would surely anger Lyndon's citizens, but it also was the only way Ovidius could protect his people from being exterminated by Exelcior. He made his decision to make the announcement.

The people of Lyndon were not ready for another bloodbath like the Mine War. Ovidius knew they could not survive it. The other leaders of Lyndon wouldn't stand for it. Disclosing the meeting to anyone else in Lyndon would result in disaster for the people. Ovidius knew the empire was fully capable of it. His people would not be happy, but at least they would live to be unhappy. He would absorb the brunt of the citizens' anger. He knew he was going to pay the price of power.

The first action by Lyndon's leaders was to ensure the clandestine training of the Shrah special forces operatives and the remaining Lyndonite believers in the Shrah Philosophy. More trainees would be added soon enough. These forces were already being transported to the remote, rainy, and heavily wooded island of Choluteca for training. There was an old abandoned research installation there that had once belonged to the government of Tai-Anh and had long been uninhabited. The wind there blew with the sharpness of a surgical instrument, and it rained without mercy, as it did on the entire planet.

The northern coast of the island had high

peaks that rose several hundred feet above the windward end of the island. These elevated peaks provided a sort of cushion since they were the part of the island closest to the mainland, where Lyndon and Gandolim were. The southern and southwestern coasts were where amphibious training would occur. The focuses of the training would be urban, forest, mountain, and amphibious warfare. Food, water, ammunition, ropes, sleeping bags, and equipment were being provided via airdrop by Lyndon. Choluteca was one of the islands west of the mainland on the vast Panthalassan Ocean and had an extensive cave system and dense forest. It was a good place to hide and train.

Training began the morning after arrival on Choluteca Island. It rained every day. The trainees were awake before the binary suns of Kinich Ahau appeared over the horizon in the eastern sky. They began their day running on the sandy beach and swimming in the cold and murky Panthalassan Ocean. At first, they ran one mile before having breakfast and swam half a mile afterward. Within a few weeks, they increased their pre-breakfast run to three miles and their post-breakfast swim to two. This was just the beginning of their day. When they were done with their daily run and swim, they began physical training.

They deepened their learning in Atsalat

meditative trances and learned combat communications in their native language of K'iché, along with rappelling, combat swimming, diving, parachuting, shooting laser guns and rifles, Ch'o'Jonik combat fighting, sniping, applying first aid, operating at night, engaging in team urban warfare, and knife fighting. They studied the outlawed Sacred Codices at length. The only training they didn't undertake was the use of explosives. They couldn't risk making that much noise.

In the beginning, believers became nauseous as a side effect of the strenuous exercise regimes. The Panthalassan Ocean was cold and deep. The sand was unforgiving on the leg muscles and the heart and lungs. Some believers were physically unable to undergo the training regimen, either because of advanced age or physical incapacity. Regardless, no one quit of their own accord. Those who were unable to complete their training received the maximum training their bodies could endure and would be assigned non-combat roles.

The believers who did complete the rigorous training provided by Temple Alom's elite special forces would be assigned to special operations teams. The top graduates of the accelerated training program would be squad leaders. The believers of the Shrah Philosophy were thus changed from average citizens to military fighters. They knew they would eventually have to face enemies that greatly outnumbered them. The odds were stacked against them, but not fighting would lead to their enslavement or destruction.

# CHAPTER 25: NEWS FROM ABROAD

A few weeks into their training, the believers on Choluteca received visitors. They heard the distant chopping of air that came with rotary craft. The sounds grew stronger. Two dozen craft slowly but surely became visible on the horizon, appearing larger as they approached. The trainees knew they were receiving visitors but had not been told who their visitors were. They weren't sure what to expect. They could be friends or foes, and they were so many of them.

They prepared for deadly combat. Yoro could feel his heart rate hasten, so he began deep breathing exercises to calm his nerves and feed his brain extra oxygen for quick thinking. He was in charge. The level of tension rose immediately among the trainees. In an instant, they were no longer trainees but combatants. Things had just gotten very real.

The craft dropped off their passengers one craft at a time. Each craft carried twenty-five passengers who were citizens of Lyndon. There were over 600 in total. Recruits of varying ages emerged from the craft, ready to join a new class in the training ranks of the believers on Choluteca Island. Some believers had already seen the arrival of the new recruits during Atsalat meditative trances. Most had not seen details regarding the identities of the new arrivals but had known they were arriving soon.

Once Yoro felt comfortable enough with the new arrivals, he gave the order to stand down. Many of them were veterans who had fought valiantly in the bloody Mine War. They had once believed they would never fight again, but things in Lyndon were only getting worse, and the persecution of Shrah Philosophy believers was well underway. Some believers were arrested, tortured, or murdered without due processes, trials, or witnesses. There were never any surviving witnesses in the first place.

Hope had emerged as a leader during the training on Choluteca. War veterans had a way of doing so. They understood the importance of sweating more in peacetime to bleed less in wartime. Hope had also begun the process of ascending in her spiritual abilities from believer to elevated. She had begun to receive messages from the light energy superhighway.

Hope was aware that new recruits Candice Lucia and Quintus Salvius were war veterans who had once been her enemies. She also knew they were in charge of this class of new arrivals until they fell under the command of Yoro. Candice and Quintus would be aware of the affairs back in Lyndon and Tai-Anh's city of Gandolim.

As the believers watched the arrival of the rotary craft, Yoro approached Hope. "Sergeant, great job during Ch'o'Jonik training this morning. I can honestly say that you are ready for combat again. And for your promotion."

"Promotion?" asked Hope incredulously.

"Military units need a clear chain of command to maintain good order and discipline," said Yoro. "You will now hold the rank of sergeant in the joint special operations group. It's the rank you held during the Mine War and the rank you will hold on Shrah and any place in the universe where you defend our existence. Congratulations, Sergeant." *I hope she lives long enough to enjoy the rank*, he thought to himself. "All veterans of the Mine War will be reinstated to their wartime ranks when training has concluded, regardless of the side they fought for," he continued.

"Thank you, Lieutenant," said Hope, a chill creeping up her spine as she realized the increasing military responsibility her new rank gave her.

"No need to thank me. You earned it."

Yoro gave the first genuine smile Hope had seen on a man in a long time. The smile unveiled his military identity for a brief moment. It struck her violently just how attractive the alien from Shrah was. He'd served in another unit on Magna Hermopolis, but at that moment, he was her leader. She wondered why she had never noticed him that way before. *I must have been too busy killing and surviving, I guess*, she thought to herself.

Yoro continued, "Sergeant, we need you to join us in a meeting with two of the new arrivals today. They have told me that they know you and have a report to give us from the mainland in Lyndon."

"Yes, sir. I will join."

"Good. I'll send for you when it's time," responded Yoro.

A few hours later, Areni, Morazan, Anayansi, and newly promoted Hope waited for the arrival of the two new trainees in a room in Choluteca's southwest. Hope was already wearing her rank on her training uniform.

Candice and Quintus entered the room, escorted by Yoro. As the senior officer in the room, Yoro took charge of the meeting. "Sergeants, our new members from Lyndon are Candice Lucia and Quintus Salvius. Although we fought against each other during the Mine War, they are now our allies and, as our allies, warrant the same respect you have shown Sergeant Zenobia and the believers in our training classes. They will begin their training tomorrow morning with other recent arrivals and will start from the beginning as the first class did."

Yoro could see the awkwardness of the Shrah troops next to the former Lyndon warriors. Circumstances had turned enemies into allies. They needed one another to survive. He continued, "Sergeant Zenobia will finish her training with the first class as the military situation in Lyndon allows. Recruits Lucia and Salvius will be reappointed to the rank of sergeant when they finish training, as will the remainder of the veterans from the Mine War. If there are no questions, Lucia and Salvius can commence their report."

There were no questions about Yoro's instructions. The four sergeants and two recruits were very clear that the matter was not open for discussion. Yoro did not mince his words.

Candice began the briefing. "Thank you, Lieutenant. It's an honor to train here with you and fight alongside you when the day arrives. We were briefed by the Lyndon Parliament on some information they believed it important that we shared with you. Matters in Lyndon are desperate. Broteas Ovidius announced an increase in taxes, an embargo on trade, and the criminalization of the Shrah Philosophy. People took to the streets, rioting at the cost of their freedom and lives. As a result, martial law was imposed, resulting in more violence and destruction of property. The emperor had Ovidius incarcerated for imposing sanctions and punishing the people of Lyndon. As you know, it was not the decision of Ovidius to impose sanctions. The emperor sent General Antipas to secretly threaten Ovidius with military action against the people of Lyndon if he didn't announce the sanctions as coming from him. We have reason to believe the lives of the prime minister's children were also threatened, although the prime minister hasn't confirmed it."

Quintus took over. "Unfortunately, the people of Lyndon do not know details, and many were clamoring for the removal of Ovidius as prime minister. Exelcior has announced publicly that Michael Alom refuses to engage in trade with Lyndon and that Lyndonites can place full blame for the great suffering in Lyndon on the actions of Ovidius and Alom. Unbeknownst to the people of Lyndon, trade ships from Shrah attempting to dock in Lyndon had been intercepted and returned to Shrah, being told that Ovidius had ceased all trade between Lyndon and Shrah. We know this to be untrue, but the people in Lyndon and the rest of Tai-Anh do not. Exelcior has begun propaganda, spreading lies of Shrah's betrayal of all citizens of Tai-Anh."

Candice continued, "I'm afraid to say that it seems to be working, and the people of Lyndon are retaliating against their government and discussing joining forces against Shrah. Some in Lyndon have grown to distrust Shrah and believe they are enemies who are responsible for their suffering."

"The Shrah natives were incensed over the mass deception that put their leader's integrity and reputation in the darkest of positions," said Quintus.

Hope's heart broke for Ovidius because she knew him as compassionate and caring. Now he was being demonized by the darkest of all souls on the planet, the emperor.

"Is there anything that can be done to change that?" asked Anayansi.

Quintus responded, "There is one thing we can do. We have two clandestine operatives working deep within the City of Gandolim. They have been secretly recording conversations that point to the treachery of the empire and would show the public the true manipulations of Emperor Exelcior. They are part of our movement and can help us show the people of Tai-Anh what's really going on."

"Is there a plan to obtain those recordings?" asked Morazan.

Yoro nodded his approval of the question.

"The secret operatives have a specific location that they visit on a pre-arranged schedule to drop off these materials," Quintus replied. "They drop off the same items in two different locations in case one of the locations is found. That way, there are always two copies of the materials hidden. They have nothing in their possession that appears to be a calendar or schedule. There is no real way to communicate with them outside of these places and times. Otherwise, their cover might be blown. They operate in grave danger. Our challenge is to have someone retrieve these items and get out of there safely."

"We must figure out a way of retrieving the items sooner rather than later. Time is running short. Who knows these locations?" asked Yoro.

"The parliament's security council divulged the location to Quintus and me so that we could share it with you," responded Candice.

"Understood. I will use the secure interplanetary communications system and request permission for an operation. Once I receive approval, we will begin training a special detachment to plan and execute the retrieval of this material. What else do you have to share with us?" asked Yoro.

"As you know, Dr. Hamilton Nile was targeted by Emperor Exelcior, and recently, the building where Dr. Nile lived was bombed in the middle of the night, bringing the entire structure crashing down while hundreds of innocent residents slept in their beds," said Candice. "Gandolim's police inspectors stated that the explosion was the work of agents from Shrah attempting to hide evidence of their crimes against the people of Tai-Anh and Dr. Hamilton Nile's involvement in betraying them. Exelcior has publicly declared that a young woman named Janina Preston was Dr. Nile's accomplice and, as such, is wanted dead or alive for the crime of treason."

Yoro and the sergeants sat in horror as they thought about the hundreds of lives extinguished, the manipulation of public sentiment by Exelcior's evil rule, and the grave danger Janina was in.

"Janina Preston is safe on Shrah and is in training," assured Yoro.

"Thank you, Great Creator, for allowing matters to result in Janina being transported off the planet and to Shrah for training," said Hope with obvious relief in her voice.

"That's another thing," continued Candice. "Emperor Exelcior has announced publicly that Janina was believed to be hiding on Shrah, which further reinforces to the people of Tai-Anh that Shrah was involved in a cover-up and harboring of enemies of the State of Tai-Anh. Exelcior also has footage of Janina visiting the building where Dr. Nile lived just a few days before the massive blast that killed all the residents, insinuating that Janina had a hand in destroying evidence kept in Dr. Nile's building. Exelcior has publicly requested Janina's extradition from Shrah and her return to face justice for her crimes against the people of Tai-Anh. He has informed the public that further proof of Shrah's treachery is their refusal to return Janina to the people of Tai-Anh. The saddest thing is the emperor ordered the public execution of the Gandolim police commander for dereliction of duty and treason. Her wife and children were present to witness the execution. The empire later publicized that a copy of the Sacred Codices was found in her possession."

"We are convinced that Michael Alom isn't aware of any of this," stated Quintus.

"He will be aware of it now," offered Yoro. "The one thing that's for sure is that Shrah would never hand Janina to the empire willingly. They would have to strip her out of our ajaw's cold dead hands. Thank you, Lucia and Salvius. Sergeant Zenobia will show you to your barracks. Tomorrow at Kinich Ahau's rise, you will be running in the sand and swimming in the Panthalassan Ocean with us."

# CHAPTER 26: A PROMISE TO KEEP

As the believers who remained on Tai-Anh continued their training, so did the believers who'd departed for Shrah. The sixty-three believers from Lyndon had arrived in Shrah's Nacaome City and were under intense training provided by Shrah's elite military unit. As for Janina, she felt like she was finally home, although she had never set foot on Shrah before. This was something she had been searching for her entire life, and ironically, she found it as an alien on another planet.

Janina's militarization had begun, and she was thriving in her new home. Several hundred of Shrah's citizens who were of the appropriate age joined the believers from Lyndon in their training. Seth also trained with this class of recruits, as his health was returning, and he was getting stronger and stronger. All graduates of this training class would serve Shrah's military forces, led by Isaiah. The general had appointed Buluc as training facilitator and commanding officer.

The training was identical to the training received by the believers on Tai-Anh's Choluteca Island with the exceptions of the ocean training and their use of explosives. Water survival and dive training were being conducted in the absolute darkness of Shrah's aquifers in the Tela Mountain Range with the full permission of Eurycea.

The salamanders understood well the threat to the planet's peaceful existence. Ruby was instrumental in providing Buluc with layouts and guidance for places to train within the aquifer. She taught the officers more effective underwater swimming strokes and rotational kicking for underwater combat and survival. She stood by as a safety watch and saved the lives of three trainees who would otherwise have drowned.

Michael, Maya, Isaiah, Buluc, Noah, Kabel, and Obasi also joined the training class. Michael personally thanked Eurycea for Ruby's services. The two Shrah species became quite acquainted with each other.

As the recruits on Tai-Anh trained in the cold and rainy weather, the recruits on Shrah trained in the hot, dry desert. The classes of trainees on Choluteca Island had an amphibious focus, specializing in bringing war from the sea to land. The classes on Shrah specialized in desert and urban warfare. They all trained in mountainous and low-intensity warfare, including hand-to-hand and close-quarters combat. Michael's idea was to eventually have Shrah's special forces train on Tai-Anh and vice versa.

Like their counterparts on Choluteca, the believers training on Shrah were overwhelmed physically and psychologically in the beginning. They dealt with dizzy spells and nausea from overexertion, heat, and dangerous Eleventh Dimension visitations. They quickly became accustomed to the rigorous exercise regimen and great demand on their bodies, minds, and spirits. They became accustomed to pressing on without regard for pain or injury. They learned firsthand that the limits of the body extended far beyond those of self-doubt.

Janina was happy to continue her training in Atsalat meditation, combat communications in K'iché language, the Sacred Codices, and Ch'o'Jonik. She was learning to fight.

The believers also learned how to fight with knives and how to shoot laser pulse weapons tactically and with accuracy under duress. They learned to serve as special operations groups like their counterparts on Choluteca, a planet away.

Seth and Janina became fast friends. The

students knew that Seth was to be ajaw someday in place of his parents. This fact, however, did not lead to Seth receiving any form of favoritism during his training, nor did it intimidate or discourage Janina from seeking his friendship. He was expected to outperform everyone during training, and he did.

All the personal training Seth had already received from his father, mother, Isaiah, Buluc, and Kabel had prepared him to develop faster than the rest of his classmates on Shrah. Genetics helped him excel. After all, he was the son of ajaws. Seth had a more developed ability to use Atsalat. All of these advantages added up to one very capable and deadly combatant. He even had a thick scar across the left side of his face, just like his father. Their scars were visual reminders that the physical dimension practiced the art of brutality.

Janina was interested to learn that Seth was the son of the beautiful woman she had seen dressed in purple in the Eleventh Dimension during her Atsalat meditations. Along with Seth, she had already been pre-assigned to the ranks of the templar knights under the leadership of Buluc and Isaiah.

Yoro's counterpart on Shrah was Obasi. Isaiah had given the order to have all Mine War veterans reinstated to their ranks from the war as soon as they completed their training. Most of the veterans were sergeants.

The training facility was adjacent to Temple Alom and had been built several years before to train Shrah's combatants for service to the emperor during the Mine War against Lyndon. It had been used consistently since then to train templar knights and special forces and for general military training.

One cold desert night, just before the eleventh hour, Michael and Maya walked the training grounds after the nightly temple-wide Ch'o'Jonik class and Atsalat meditation. The stars were prominent in the dark firmament. Nights in the Shrah desert allowed for a spectacular view of the cosmos high above.

A few moments into their walk, Maya stopped walking and held her husband's hand, turning so she could look into his eyes. Michael stopped as well, knowing instinctively that she wanted to hold him close. He peered back into his wife's eyes and said nothing, but he silently attempted to convey to her that everything was all right. Maya knew better. She knew every square inch of his body and soul. She could see the weariness and concern in her partner's eyes and felt the overwhelming empathy only a lover could feel. She held him and said nothing.

After some time in her husband's arms, Maya spoke. "Seth is thriving in his training. What do you think, Michael?" she asked.

"I think he needs to finish with the class. Someday, he will be ajaw of our temple. He needs to spend as much time as possible with the military forces he will lead. What do you think, my love?" asked Michael in return.

"I agree with you. My biggest concern was his health since the attack on him was so recent, but he seems to be fine."

"His health has not been a concern for me. Noah cleared him for the physical toll of such training. Besides, he is your son." Michael smiled.

Maya smiled back at him. "I'm glad you realize that it's my genes that make him so strong."

"My genes make me just smart enough to know when not to argue with you," Michael countered playfully. "I've also heard Seth is becoming quite fond of Janina, so I doubt he would want to finish his training sooner."

Maya's smile disappeared. "Yes, I heard the same."

"It's to be expected at his age. Besides, how could she resist? He does also have my genes, you know," teased Michael.

Maya's smile returned long enough for her to change the topic of their conversation. "Can we discuss tonight's Atsalat meditation?"

Michael looked around to make sure there was no one nearby to hear their discussion. Once sure they were alone, Michael looked into Maya's eyes with an intensity communicating that he was ready to listen.

Before they could continue their discussion, a thunderous boom roared over the western sky, and a bright diamond light appeared there. Michael immediately grabbed Maya and pushed her behind him, standing between her and the diamond light. Michael knew his body wasn't enough to stop the power and intensity of the sound and light in the sky, but it didn't matter. He would be damned if his wife was killed while he was still alive. Even if only for a fraction of a second, he would have to be dead for any harm to come to Maya.

Standing behind her husband, Maya had already unsheathed her obsidian knife, which she held in a ready grip. Maya was a veteran of war herself, and warrior blood ran through her veins.

Michael quickly assessed that the entire City of Nacaome was in complete darkness. Then came the sound of all the windows shattering in an instant.

The shit hit the fan.

# CHAPTER 27: ACTION VERSUS INACTION

The people of Shrah were not the type to sit around when they felt threatened. Michael and Maya double-timed to the city center emergency meeting place they had designated for leaders. Since the threat remained active, all leaders headed to the outdoor staging area, where they were to gather in the event of an attack. Within a few minutes of each other, Shrah's leaders assembled, ready for orders.

Assembled were Maya, Michael, Seth, Isaiah, Kabel, Noah, Buluc, Danli, Obasi, and Janina. Janina had followed Seth to the city center. Buluc had brought two extra CO2 rifles and night vision equipment for Michael and Maya. All others had arrived armed and ready for any battle that might ensue.

Michael wasted no time handing out orders

to his team. "Isaiah, take charge of the templar knights and secure the perimeter of the temple while your forces take position to protect the city's perimeter. Noah, determine any injuries sustained with the breaking of the city's windows, especially by children and the elderly. Also, prepare the infirmary and temple for treatment of any injuries our citizens might sustain in the future. Buluc, find out what's going on with our electric power, and work on having it restored as soon as possible. Danli, work with Obasi to take charge of the special forces. Know you have my full authorization to use lethal force if you feel it is necessary. Maya, Seth, Kabel, and Janina, do not leave my side."

The ajaw had taken charge of the situation, but they still had more questions than answers. The bright light bathed all of Temple Alom and most of Nacaome City in its intensity. The source of the light approached the spot in the city center where Michael stood. Many attempts were made to shoot pulses at the object, all to no avail. Shrah weapons failed to shoot. It was the most helpless and vulnerable Shrah's fighting forces had ever been.

Michael felt vulnerable but, for some odd reason, not threatened by the light. Nevertheless, he had a firm grip on his obsidian knife and stood in a ready stance. His gun might not work, but his knife would never fail him. Hidden in the recesses of Nacaome City were several deadly operatives ready to defend their homeland.

After a few moments, Isaiah came out of the darkness, approached Michael, and whispered in his ear, "Sire, none of our weapons work. They're failing to charge, and our missiles won't power on."

Michael suppressed an expression of alarm. "Order our forces to switch to ballistics, and be ready to strike with blades. Our ancestors killed without technology, and so can we," he stated with remarkable calmness.

"Yes, sire. I have already given the order."

Michael had figured the order had already been given, but he'd wanted his cool, strong, normal tone to be heard by those standing around him.

The diamond-shaped light came closer and closer, but the ajaws were not going to hide. Michael stood his ground and prepared for what was to come, and so did everyone standing with him. The light came to a stop directly in front of the ajaw as if driven by an intelligent power that knew who was in command on the planet.

As the light halted, something came over the citizens of Shrah. Seth, who stood next to his father, said, "Father, I can't move a muscle! No matter how hard I try, I can't move!"

In fact, no one on Shrah could move. The entire population of the planet stood frozen in terror. Some feared for their own safety, but most were petrified of not being able to protect their ajaws from impending harm.

Escaping explanation was that the greatest fighter and most dangerous warrior on Shrah, Ajaw Michael Alom, was not immobilized by the diamond-shaped light. Michael, however, was far more concerned about the safety of his people than he was about his own.

Michael made a decision there and then. He decided he would most likely lose his physical life and enter the Eleventh Dimension, but he would take some of the attackers with him. It had been a while since he had spilled blood, but he was ready to do so again. He was the only one on the planet who could still move, so it was solely his responsibility to defend his people, and he was ready.

The light lowered itself directly in front of Michael to hover less than a foot from the sand. It became obvious to Michael that a group of beings was standing in front of the light, which he assumed was a spaceship of some sort. It was hard to tell because of the intensity of the light. Michael thought he could see two regular-sized beings in front and four larger beings behind them. The sheer size of the four beings behind concerned him greatly. He could tell by the movements of the beings that they were likely males. Michael had already run through the scenario in his head, deciding how he would attack, whom he would kill first, and how he would end their lives.

He judged that large creatures were at least nine feet tall. *They will have to be eviscerated or chopped in half quickly due to their size*, he thought.

All six beings were visible when he finished his mental preparation, but they weren't recognizable yet with the extreme brightness behind them. Michael noticed that one of the two normal-sized beings seemed to be leading the way. This being appeared to be a strong man of muscular build who carried himself with authority and self-assurance. This person exuded the aura and energy of a trained and vicious fighter who was a danger to any challenger. Michael could read that energy from a distance. Warriors gave off energy that other warriors could detect. The other normal-sized being seemed less intimidating in build and fell in step behind the stronger normal-sized leader. Michael could not see the details of their faces.

Michael focused his attention on the stronger being walking in front of the rest and prepared for a showdown. He tried to figure out whether or not these beings were of his species, and he settled on the assumption that the two normal-sized beings were but that the four large beings were simply too big to be. Michael had fought in a war that had involved aliens from the planet Tai-Anh on Magna Hermopolis, and he had not encountered beings as large and muscular as those that had just arrived. This would be new blood to spill.

The apparent leader of the alien group turned around as if to address the four large beings behind him. Michael could not hear what he said. It appeared he was giving instructions or requesting something. As the apparent leader turned to face forward once again, Maya, Seth, and Janina regained their ability to move freely. All four of them resumed their fighting stances and positioned themselves two abreast of their ajaw with weapons at the ready.

Michael spoke to his team. "The normal-sized being in the front seemed to give the order for the four of you to be released from their grip. If they wanted us destroyed, they would have done it by now." As soon as Michael finished his statement, the assumed leader of the group began to walk slowly closer to Michael and his protectors. All five Shrah natives prepared to attack.

Then Seth exclaimed, "Stand down! It's Andy Sauer!"

# CHAPTER 28: TWO SHIPS PASSING IN THE NIGHT

It was a cold night on Choluteca Island. The rain had subsided for a brief moment. Yoro and Hope were running on the sandy beach, getting in some additional physical training in preparation for what they felt was impending battle. The night air was damp on Choluteca Island's western seaboard. Tai-Anh's double moons lit the fine sand of the beach and made the Panthalassan Ocean seem as smooth and calm as a mirror reflecting the light of the celestial bodies overhead.

The moons were so bright that evening one would have thought they could touch them by simply reaching for the skies above. Their light danced upon the clouds over the ocean. Yoro wondered about the gravitational forces at play between the two moons and how they affected the tides of the planet.

Hope found Magna Hermopolis a bitter sweet sight. On the sweet side was the splendor that lit the night sky with majestic beauty. On the bitter side was the knowledge that it had been home to so much death and destruction during the war. She'd been there for most of the fighting. She was one of the lucky ones who'd returned home.

Hope was beginning to develop feelings for her lieutenant, and she knew that he had a fondness for her. It was the kindness behind the masculine smile and chiseled physique, the depth of his spiritual being that most attracted her to him. When she spoke to him, she felt that she had opened the door to her inner being and that he had stepped inside. She was just fine with that because she understood that he would treat her inner being with tenderness and care. He had the incredible strength of gentleness. Hope was afraid she had fallen in love with him. Before this, she had shut her heart. She was afraid of the vulnerability of loving and being loved. She didn't care much for being so very exposed.

After running for what seemed like miles on end, they stopped to enjoy the beauty of the moonlight on the ocean. They were both panting and sweating on the cold sand of the lonely island. After they caught their breath, Hope sat on the sand with her legs crossed, overlooking the moon's reflection as it shimmered on the ocean's surface. The calm before the storm. For a brief moment, there was no rain.

Yoro sat on the sand next to her and lay back on his elbows, also taking in the gray moonlight on the water and the wonderful smell of the sea breeze that caressed his face like nothing on Shrah could. He breathed deeply as his mind began to travel through space and time to a sad place. "You know, Sergeant, the night brings great melancholy to my heart," began Yoro.

Hope immediately noticed that he addressed her by her military rank. This lifted an invisible wall between them. At that moment, she saw him free of the restraints imposed by their disproportionate ranks. Sometimes, reality had a way of attacking tender moments and changing them. She knew that he was opening up his heart and allowing her to step inside it by discussing his melancholy. She was ready to listen . . . with caution.

He continued, "It was night when my father died. It was a dreadful night, Hope. He finally lost his battle. My father was the best friend a man could have."

Hope listened intently. Her mirror neurons of empathy began to align with Yoro's, and she was entrenched in his melancholy, now their melancholy.

Yoro wondered why he was pouring his feelings out to Hope, but it felt so right, so welcoming, so therapeutic. "He was strong, but he was also loving and caring. I was his only son, and his eyes screamed that he loved me, even on that awful night. We know our loved ones who have transcended into the Eleventh Dimension still love us. I just wish I could feel his strong physical presence sometimes. I should have told him just how much I loved him during his living years. His arms were the safest place in the universe for me. To this day, I can feel him hugging me. I can see him in his all-white clothes. My father always wore all-white clothes. He believed it was an expression of his spiritual and physical purity."

Hope listened, connecting at an even deeper level with the man who had once been given the task to sharpen her killing skills. "It makes me sad to know you hurt like that at such a tender age," she said. "Who was your male role model when your father returned home to the Eleventh Dimension?"

"Our ajaw, Michael Alom. He came to the hospital the night my father died. He held my hand as my father's spirit transitioned and personally took me to Temple Alom, assuring me that my father was safe in the Eleventh Dimension and that he would teach me how to communicate with him," answered Yoro.

"Did the ajaw teach you Atsalat meditation

to reconnect you with your father at that young age?" asked Hope.

"Yes, I visit with my father often in the Eleventh Dimension. Still wearing all white. Our ajaw seems to make you feel like you are the only person in the universe that matters to him, no matter your age, gender, or job. Every citizen of Shrah is welcome at Temple Alom."

Hope noticed that Yoro had referred to Michael as "our ajaw," and it made her feel warm inside. "Doesn't the ajaw worry about his safety with such open access?" she asked.

Yoro let out an amused snort at the question.

Hope turned red with embarrassment.

"I'm sorry to react like that," said Yoro. "I will explain. If the Great Creator allows for you to meet our ajaw, you will see for yourself why that question made me laugh. Attempting to harm him would be the biggest mistake of your life. First of all, you would most likely lose your life very quickly for attempting it. If you succeeded, guilt would drive you to take your own life before the planet hunted you down and resolved the matter for you. The ajaw is the living, breathing representation of light energy and love itself. I'm sure you heard that four assassins tried to kill his son, Seth."

"Yes. I did. How could someone try to kill someone so young? Who would have the heart?"

asked Hope.

"The same someone who tried to kill Janina after killing Hamilton. That's who. Exelcior is the personification of dark energy and hate. Only the Great Creator knows what he'll do next. Whatever it is, we will be ready for him. We have to be. We all await our ajaw letting us know when it's time," continued Yoro, noticing sadness and worry coming over Hope's face. "I'm sorry, Hope. Did I say something to upset you?"

"Don't be sorry," responded Hope. "I was thinking about Janina and wondering how she's doing. She's such a young and strong woman, yet she's so alone."

"Don't worry about Janina," said Yoro. "She is in Temple Alom now with the likes of Maya and Kabel. She is being trained by our ajaw, Isaiah, Obasi, and Buluc." Yoro could see that, regardless of what he was saying, tears were welling up in Hope's eyes. It struck him that it was Hope who felt alone in the universe at that very moment.

Then he did it. He hugged her and held her in a tight and loving embrace. He could feel the firmness of her breasts pressed against his body. This was dangerous territory for a commissioned officer. It didn't matter how romantic the moon was that evening. It didn't matter that they were all alone. It didn't matter that Hope was gorgeous. She was his subordinate, and the Shrah Code of Military Justice strictly prohibited fraternization between officers and enlisted personnel serving in the same unit.

Regardless of protocol, Yoro and Hope could feel the sexual energy and attraction between them. Love was a far stronger set of rules than a military code. They looked into each other's eyes and slowly leaned into each other's lips. As they moved closer, they could feel the electricity of anticipation shooting through their bodies. He could feel her soft skin. She could smell the sweet sweat on his body.

At that moment, it began to rain. The raindrops quickly fizzled out the burning fire, and Yoro returned to his role as lieutenant and commanding officer. He pulled away and looked at Hope with embarrassment. His heart pounded in his chest. Hope looked away too.

Yoro, who was not usually one to be caught speechless, was at a loss for words. He finally got out, "When this is all over and you are no longer in my unit, I will come looking for you."

"And you will find me when you do, Lieutenant Copan," Hope said with an understanding smile and obvious sarcasm as the rain began to fall harder.

To break the awkwardness of the moment, Yoro rose and began to run into the cold Panthalassan Ocean, feeling like a carefree child. Hope followed him into the cold water, removing her top on the way.

# CHAPTER 29: THE ARRIVAL

While in bed at Temple Alom in a battle with insomnia, I recalled my final day in the vessel that had taken me and the four travelers from Earth to the gold planet in Andromeda. I remembered sitting in the classroom with my four oversized instructors as we'd advanced through some sort of wormhole for months on end. My fellow travelers had been about to reveal their true identities. I didn't understand all the science.

During our travel time, the travelers had taught me about accessing the universe's energy superhighway in the Eleventh Dimension, unlocked my K'iché language abilities, and re-familiarized me with the Sacred Codices and Ch'o'Jonik lethal fighting arts of an ancient past, an ancient life. My past lives had been unlocked, and they were all with me on Shrah.

I had reincarnated as Andy Sauer with the ethnic and spiritual past of Earth's ancient Maya civilization. In a past incarnation, I had been an ancient Mayan ruler before my people had been uprooted from Earth and relocated to the dry yet inhabitable planet I now found myself on.

On our way to the dry land, my mission had been revealed to me. There was nothing left for me on Earth. My wife had left me for another man, and I did not have children, parents, or siblings still living in San Antonio, New York, or anywhere else. I visited my adoptive parents and grandparents in the Eleventh Dimension regularly, thanks to the Atsalat meditative trances the four travelers had taught me. I'd been able to tell my parents things I hadn't had a chance to tell them while they'd been alive. It was a second chance.

By then, I had no longer been plotting my attack on my captors. They were not my captors after all, and what they had unlocked in the deep recesses of my brain was fantastic. I was returning home, and I had them to thank for it. Besides, where exactly would I have gone in deep space by myself with no spacesuit? I had no clue how to fly the spacecraft, and even if I had known, where exactly were we going? The travelers had my undivided attention.

This was my conclusion: these beings had been sent by the Great Creator to transport me from Earth to Shrah so that I might fulfill an ancient prophecy for my relocated people. Shrah was where my ancestors had already been for centuries. I was to join them for a good cause. I had skills and experience they could use.

I knew that I was no longer just Andy Sauer. My Andy Sauer identity was just one element of a complex consciousness. I was much more than one person. I was the combination of many past lives, experiences, and civilizations, all bathed in bloodshed.

I was a legendary and fierce warrior who'd been revered by an intelligent yet violent civilization on ancient Earth. That part was almost too spectacular for me to process, but I needed to become accustomed to it. My people had been spared the extinction of a mass invasion from Europe that had come to be known as the conquest.

In my most recent reincarnation, I had been a Mestizo. I was the descendant of a combination of Spaniards and Mayans. That much, I knew about my most recent ancestry.

Though far from Earth, my journey had been a return home. I would be reunited with my people, and my role in the historical events that were about to unfold would be grand. My people on Shrah would recognize me by my former Mayan identity. At least, those who had transcendental knowledge of their past lives would.

I remembered that as we had begun our descent through the atmosphere of Shrah from space, fire had begun to build around the craft.

This golden planet had an atmosphere. The four beings I had once named the travelers had now been identified to me, and they terrified me to my core.

From high above the planet, I could see the beautiful gold land below before we flew into the darkness of night. The color reminded me of the look of Saturn back in Earth's local solar system. There didn't appear to be a cloud in the sky, just a slight haze of water vapor below. Dispersed blue light particles in the atmosphere added to the intensity and complexity of the yellow glow.

Out in space, I'd seen the two suns co-orbiting one another, one far brighter than the other. These were the Kinich Ahau binary stars that Shrah orbited. We continued to travel from light into darkness, where the light from Kinich Ahau could not reach.

The travelers had prepared me for the arrival, and in preparation for the landing, we were soon accompanied by another humanoid, who appeared to me as a complete blur. I had already learned that things would be revealed to me in due time, so I submitted myself to that reality. I didn't feel the slightest contact on the ground on Shrah. It worried me that the ground wouldn't be solid.

The hatch opened. The feeling of being on solid ground for the first time in months was euphoric. The brightness of the outer skin of the vessel was almost painful, the same as it had been when I had been recovered from Earth. My eyes had to adjust quickly, and I noticed other human figures standing outside the vessel. I prepared for a possible battle. I was sure the inhabitants of Shrah wouldn't appreciate our rude intrusion into their night sky. Although I was unarmed, I always packed my hands and feet.

The travelers showed us the way out of the craft. They stood behind us as we faced Ajaw Michael Alom, who seemed to be standing with other leaders from the planet. He was quite an intimidating man. I prepared myself should he choose to attack.

I was still processing that the leaders of Temple Alom were my brothers and sisters from ancient Earth. We were all sons and daughters of the Great Creator, and we shared the same ancestral blood.

The ajaw's people assembled, most of them unable to move, immobilized as I had been when the travelers had arrived on Earth. The first person I recognized other than the ajaw was his son, Seth Alom. He also recognized me.

He commanded, "Stand down! It's Andy Sauer!"

The ajaw looked at him curiously, seemingly wondering how he knew my name. The situation was not conducive to a long explanation about our training together in the Eleventh Dimension with the four travelers.

As Seth finished his statement, the four travelers rode past me on horses, of all things. Where these horses had been during the space flight remained a mystery to me. I noticed once again that the desert floor did not sag underneath the beasts' feet, and no sand or dirt was displaced. The traveler I knew best had skin that gave off a white glow like a white aura radiating from beneath his tunic.

The other three travelers, who rode behind him, gave off three different-colored glows: one reddish, one almost black, and the third a pale grayish color. They rode up to the ajaw, faced him, and stood two abreast of me.

I was impressed that the ajaw didn't flinch, keeping a strong and steady stare on all four travelers. He examined every detail of the beings. When done gathering the information he desired from his visual inspection, he turned his eyes to me and said, "I know who you are. The Sacred Codices speak of you. For your return, we are eternally grateful. Welcome home." Then he demanded, "Release the hold on the rest of my people."

The radiant white traveler responded, "Ajaw Michael Alom, we come once again to your land in peace. Order your people to stand down, and we will release the hold."

With that, the ruler of the land turned to

his people. "Stand down. You are witnessing the arrival of the four beings written about in the Sacred Codices. They come in peace, and we need to understand the reasons for their visit."

The people of Shrah were released from their immobility. They politely followed the strict orders of their leader. No one advanced a single step, but they remained ready to defend or attack on command. Their mouths hung open in awe as they realized the implications. Were we the ones they had read about in the Sacred Codices their entire lives? This could only mean that war was impending.

I spoke to the ajaw through a veil of nostalgia. "It's wonderful to see you again, my brother, after all these centuries and millions of miles between us." I walked up to the ajaw and hugged him the way one would a loved one who had risen from the dead. No words were needed between us. I had once known Ajaw Michael Alom as Votan. Michael knew me as Kinich Ahau.

I heard the collective gasp of awe as the people of Temple Alom realized which spirit lived inside my body.

Michael turned to a woman standing beside him. "Kinich Ahau, this is my wife, Maya Alom, who you once knew as—"

"—Ixchel," I interrupted. Ixchel, now Maya, approached and embraced me with the same love we all shared.

It was going to take some time to learn to address them by their Shrah names. We'd known each other in such an intimate and powerful way for so many centuries and past lives that it wouldn't be easy to change the way I thought about them.

I found it ironic that I was on an alien planet where the aliens looked just like Earthlings and where the hot, dry weather was similar to that of Arizona, New Mexico, or Utah a galaxy away. It did a great deal to make me feel somewhat at home.

Back on Earth, sailing the planet's oceans and solar system, taking lives in the name of freedom, or simply sitting on my back porch, looking at the moon and the stars, I'd always felt that humanity had not originated there. Earthlings were, in fact, aliens. There seemed to be one universal species of what Earthlings called the human being. This species was spread throughout the cosmos. I may have stood on Earth next to an alien from a distant galaxy, and I would have never known it. The first humans had been brought to Earth. In order to save the species, humans had to escape. It was either leave or die.

# CHAPTER 30: OLD FRIENDS

Back on Earth, the ancient Mayans and Romans had never fought one another. They'd never known of each other's civilizations. However, in the Kinich Ahau system of the Andromeda galaxy, they were on a collision course.

The four creatures had uprooted people and even entire civilizations from planets, transporting them to other galaxies in the universe. I was on a mission to assist my people in surviving the collision or to perish with them in what would be an all-out apocalypse.

As I stood on the alien planet, I noticed her for the first time. She had gorgeous brown eyes, brown hair, and golden skin. She was the most beautiful woman I had ever seen.

Michael noticed that I was mesmerized by the sheer beauty of this woman. "This is High Priestess Kabel Luu," he told me.

She took a step toward me, into the light, so I could see her features more clearly. She was even more striking than I'd realized. "Hello, Kinich Ahau. You once knew me as—"

"—Akna," I finished for her.

Her voice and her face were even sweeter in this incarnation than on Earth. I was smitten and hoped it wasn't too obvious.

It hit me at that moment that Michael, Maya, and Kabel had all their memories of past incarnations unlocked in their present dimension. They must have been elevated spirits. The path to elevation was a long one, but it was possible during a physical lifetime. Every so often, we experienced déjà vu. In these instances, our minds encountered information in our source memory banks. We usually dismissed these feelings, not realizing their true origin. Elevated beings were able to connect with past incarnations at a whole other level.

Kabel and I smiled at each other. I liked to think that we communicated a great deal to each other by the genuineness of our smiles and the betrayal of hidden feelings in my eyes. Thoughts raced through my mind. I would have to work harder at masking my affection.

The only person standing with the group who had not been introduced to me was a young lady who seemed to be about the same age as Seth. Kabel noticed me looking in the young woman's direction as I attempted to figure out why she seemed so familiar to me.

Kabel looked toward the woman. "Kinich Ahau, that young lady with Seth is Janina Preston. In another life, she was the daughter of Ix Chebel Yax and Itza."

"That means she was Ixtab," I stated, which brought a smile to Kabel's angelic face.

Michael, Maya, and Seth looked at Janina and smiled. Janina turned her gaze to Seth and stared at him, saying much with her eyes.

I turned to Michael. "Ajaw, with your permission, I would like to return to you the man standing behind me. He has requested to be allowed citizenship in your temple."

"All living beings who wish to be citizens of Temple Alom are welcome here. We are an open civilization. Who is this person you speak of, Kinich Ahau?" Michael asked.

As he asked this question, the man behind me stepped out to be seen, looked forward, and walked toward us. When he arrived at a spot where the temple leaders could see his face clearly, they recognized him.

Hamilton Nile grinned.

I'd once known Hamilton as Ahau Chamahez in a distant life and on a distant planet. The people of Shrah had heard he'd been killed on his home planet of Tai-Anh. But the travelers had gotten to him before the building had exploded. This appearance was like someone walking out of their grave.

"Hamilton! Is it really you?" Janina exclaimed. Tears sprung in her eyes, and she ran to embrace Hamilton.

Maya, Kabel, Seth, and three others I hadn't met yet joined in a group hug. I watched, giving them time to absorb all that was happening. Michael smiled lovingly at Hamilton but didn't move from in front of me. He was everything I had expected from the ajaw of our people on Shrah.

"Ajaw, who are the other three standing at your side?" I asked.

"They are General Isaiah Gabriel, Dr. Noah Mandel, and Sir Buluc Hix. Isaiah is our supreme military commander. Noah is the temple's physician and my childhood friend. And Buluc is the grand knight of the temple," Michael said with clear pride in his people.

"All three were part of the history lessons taught to me by the four travelers, and Seth has spoken to me about them in the Eleventh Dimension. They are born warriors," I replied.

"You will have to tell me about the world from which you come, our people's original home," Michael said with genuine interest.

"Yes, Ajaw. Much has changed on Earth, although spiritual apathy remains a major issue," I explained.

"The large muscular beings that brought you to us, the ones you call travelers, are the ones written about in the Sacred Codices," Michael told me.

At that statement, I turned around and signaled for the four beings to approach on horseback. Immediately and seemingly out of nowhere, a path of golden light formed on the ground in front of them, and they began to approach us. I saw the expressions of awe from the people of Shrah as they set their gazes upon the four large, powerful beings, each one bathed in a glow of color.

I explained to Michael that this moment represented the final act of intervention from the travelers. From this point forward, they would no longer interfere in the events of the Kinich Ahau star system conflict. They had rescued Hamilton from physical death and had brought me to be with my people, but that would be the last act from the travelers as had been ordered by the Great Creator. From now on, we were alone.

"Ajaw, these are the four beings that bring a message from the Great Creator of our impending doom. Their names in order are Conquest, War, Famine, and Death."

# CHAPTER 31: BECOMING ACQUAINTED

It had been an exciting night on my new home planet. Part of me was afraid to fall asleep for fear that I would wake up to the realization that what I was having was just a vivid and protracted dream. But what I had experienced was simply too real to have been a dream, and I wanted to see it to its conclusion.

The situation in Shrah was one of pre-war. There was a palpable energy in the air as the society prepared for war amidst escalating tensions. It was the first time I'd felt truly alive since the Great War. It was sobering for me to realize that war was what I lived for, but I felt right at home in armed conflict. I didn't have the luxury of time to ponder the philosophical implications of what I was.

When the stars shone their light into my

sleeping quarters, I had slept three hours. I awoke, knowing it was time to get to work with Michael. Shrah was his domain, and as long as I lived on Shrah, I would serve him and our people. I had no clue what type of training the military on Shrah had, nor the weapons and tactics employed. My time with the four horsemen, hurtling through space and time, seemed like centuries ago. I wondered just how out of shape I had become after seven months of not exercising regularly.

I couldn't say I was homesick yet, but I sure missed the oceans of Earth. They had been an integral part of my life as a USNSC officer. I had operated in the Atlantic, Pacific, Arctic, Antarctic, and Indian oceans. I had also rendered services in the Caribbean Sea, the Sea of Japan, the Philippine Sea, the Sea of Okhotsk, the Mediterranean Sea, the South China Sea, and the Persian Gulf. Furthermore, I'd served in many rivers, lakes, and other bodies of water. Earth's Third World War had made me a seasoned expert in amphibious low-intensity special warfare.

The ajaw and I had had a long conversation my first night on Shrah. One of my tasks on Shrah was to train our special forces in parachuting and amphibious warfare and to do so quickly. I would be working closely with General Isaiah Gabriel.

I'd noticed the night before that people on Shrah carried obsidian knives with jade handles. The blades were triangular and would get the job done. On Earth, we called knives pig stickers. I was sure they'd work in combat anywhere in the universe. The locals also carried more advanced close combat weaponry in the form of CO2 laser pulse technology. The lasers their weapons shot were engineered to become hot when they struck flesh, so hot that they would punch a baseball-sized hole through their victim. I worried that the Shrah citizens would make fun of me for using their backup method of shooting, but Earthly technology had not achieved laser weapons like these. Lasers were popular but not in weaponry.

The ajaw gifted me his own obsidian knife and explained to me how my amphibious warfare experience would come in handy for our people. Apparently, our hostile neighbor had geography that would accommodate war from the sea to the land. I had already asked the ajaw for night vision goggles, handheld explosives, and a Shrah combat uniform, which he provided. My dive gear was to arrive that morning. I had learned that Shrah had underwater aquifers inhabited by a friendly species that had once lived on Earth and had been relocated to Shrah like me.

There must have been sensors in my room to detect when I was awake because a minute after I rose from bed, there was a knock at the door. One of the templar knights had my dive gear in hand. The knight showed me how to operate the closed-circuit rebreather system, which allowed no air bubbles to escape while a diver was submerged. It absorbed exhaled carbon dioxide, and I would soon have a hands-on lesson in its operation. I was struck by how similar this equipment was to the kind we used back on Earth. I couldn't wait to try it. The air quality on Shrah seemed perfect for an Earthling, although the oxygen seemed thinner, like that at high altitudes on Earth. It was as if the cities of Denver and Tucson had had a child named Shrah.

I showered, enjoying the warm water, which seemed to have some heavier minerals in it. These folks needed water-softening systems. I then dressed in the standard temple uniform I had been issued. When dressed, I looked out the window at the beautiful golden mountains of the desert a galaxy away from Earth. I stepped out of the bedroom and into the majestic halls of Temple Alom.

Temple Alom sure was a magnificent place. The people who lived in the temple were busy fixing the windows the spacecraft had shattered as it had approached Nacaome City. It was interesting to me that my people on Shrah seemed to live in a sort of stone-age by their own choice. They had the technology to travel through space to other planets using nuclear propulsion and very advanced weaponry. Granted, many of these advances were due, in large part, to their involvement in the Mine War on Magna Hermopolis, in which they'd assisted Tai-Anh in fighting Lyndon. Tai-Anh's technology had made its way to Shrah. In a strange way, that war had helped the people of Shrah learn much about the advanced weaponry and tactics of Tai-Anh. However, Emperor Exelcior commanded forces that outnumbered Shrah's many times over. The only real option was to fight a low-intensity special operations war from the sea. In other words, my kind of war. A kind of war that was not easy to win.

There were people everywhere inside the temple, hustling and bustling. I passed an area where it seemed a stone statue might once have stood. Everyone had a job to do and obvious enthusiasm for doing it.

I was greeted with respect, admiration, and great curiosity. I could hear them whisper, "That's Kinich Ahau, returned to us by the Great Creator."

Quite honestly, I didn't care much for all the attention and awe. It didn't help my humility that the entire planetary system was named after my previous incarnation.

The views out of the large openings where windows had been were spectacular. The desert reminded me of those in Arizona, the Middle East, and the Hindu Kush. These views were made more stunning by the high altitude of Nacaome City on the mountain plateau. I figured it was at least 8,000 feet from ground level; there was no sea to create a level measurement like on Earth. I took it all in.

While walking the hallowed halls of Temple Alom, I felt someone approaching me from behind. I could feel their energy. I turned to lock eyes with the beautiful Kabel. It was way too early to deal with a Kabel sighting. I tried to pretend not to be shocked by her radiance. As many times as I had been in mortal combat, I had never felt the nervousness this alien made me feel. This was different. The attraction, at least for me, was centuries deep, and I was sure it was obvious.

"Good morning, Kinich Ahau. Did you sleep well?"

It took me a second to realize she was addressing me. My stupor must have been imprinted on my face, I realized, judging by the satisfied smile I saw on hers. "I slept well, Reverend. How did you sleep?"

"I slept very well," she stated. Then she walked past me and left me walking by myself, wishing for a longer interaction. When she got to the end of the hallway, she glanced back just in time to catch me looking at her ass. She most likely hadn't needed visual confirmation of it. No use looking away. I had no choice but to own that I had been busted.

A moment later, Isaiah rounded a corner from one of the temple's many passageways.

"Good morning, General."

"Good morning, Kinich Ahau. I was looking

for you. Our ajaw has received a message from one of our special forces operatives training on Tai-Anh, and the ajaw sent me to bring you to our Security Council meeting for debrief."

I nodded my understanding, and we began to walk toward what I understood to be Michael's favorite conference room.

On our way to the conference room, Isaiah stopped in a passageway and handed me a belt, holster, and pistol. "These belong to you. I see you already have an obsidian knife on you. It's a fine weapon, all right."

"Thank you, General," I said. "I'm no longer naked!"

We both laughed. The general and I understood one another.

# CHAPTER 32: UNFORGIVABLE ACTIONS

It was amazing how the general understood the importance of my being armed. I was thankful for it. We entered the conference room together. Michael gestured to where my seat was. Isaiah already had a place directly beside the ajaw. All present at the meeting could see the intensity on their ajaw's face as they quietly assembled in the conference room. Michael clenched his jaw muscles, making the scar across the left side of his face more pronounced. I knew that look anywhere in the universe. It came with the weight of responsibility for the well-being of others.

There were no side conversations before the head of the meeting began speaking. Michael made eye contact with every member present at the meeting for just long enough that they knew he appreciated their presence. He began the meeting. "I'm afraid I have bad news."

Maya, Seth, Isaiah, and Hamilton were already aware of the bad news. They'd discussed the matter with their ajaw. Janina knew something was awry in the universal energy that surrounded her, but she didn't know the details. Hamilton appeared especially distraught.

The ajaw continued, "There has been a mass murder on Tai-Anh."

The entire room took a collective gasp.

The ajaw allowed time for everyone to absorb the statement before pressing on. "There has been an explosion that has completely destroyed an apartment building in Gandolim. It was the building where Hamilton was living when the school was destroyed. It is my guess that they didn't find evidence that Hamilton's remains were present at the School of the Eleventh Dimension so moved on to destroy their next target. Perhaps Exelcior wanted to send a strong message to believers. Hundreds of lives were lost. My heart is broken for all the innocent victims."

Horror took control of the conference room. This explained Hamilton's appearance. The emotional assault on Janina was instant. She remembered the beautiful smile of the little boy named Max who had befriended her in the elevator of that very same building. A beautiful life extinguished in violence. The heat and horror the innocent child must have felt . . . and his mother . . . all of the innocent people.

Hundreds of thousands of miles away, Hope heard of the attack from Yoro and immediately sent light energy to her young friend on the neighboring planet. She felt a pressing need to return to Tai-Anh and stop Exelcior at all costs, including her own physical life if necessary. But that was much easier desired than accomplished.

Michael continued, "I have approved Lieutenant Yoro Copan's request to dispatch our special forces operatives on Tai-Anh to infiltrate the empire in a clandestine operation to retrieve recordings that would show the true intentions and actions of Emperor Exelcior. Lieutenant Copan is in command of the operation."

The leaders in the room smiled with the satisfaction of knowing one of their very best was in charge of the ajaw's order. Hopefully, the lieutenant knew what he was doing. The mission must have been in good hands from what I could tell, but it sure sounded risky to be training forces clandestinely. Ironically, this was one of the functions of special forces on Earth as well.

Michael felt pain uplift into the universal energy superhighway. He tapped into it. "You will soon get the opportunity to return home to deliver justice," said the ajaw, focusing on Janina and Hamilton.

Maya and Kabel felt Janina's pain as well. They had already embraced her from either side.

"There is more bad news," continued the ajaw. "Several believers have been arrested, and there is speculation that many have been killed. They were not the ones training on Choluteca Island. The exact number under arrest is unknown, although I sense it's in the thousands by now."

There was a collective gasp of surprise in the conference room as Shrah's leaders were struck by this statement. They already felt a kinship with those learning the Shrah Philosophy on the neighboring planet.

"Our philosophy is gaining momentum, and there is no way to know the exact number of believers living on Tai-Anh. That number is growing greater each day. Their light energy is uplifting into the energy superhighway exponentially. Emperor Exelcior's oppression is only making his people's faith in our philosophy stronger. His people are being pushed to us by their suffering and oppression.

"Our special forces have their orders. The killing of innocent people is universally punishable. I once hoped Exelcior would be a good leader for his people. It has become apparent that he is their greatest oppressor. Our planet, the Shrah Philosophy, and all who believe in it are in grave danger. The people of Lyndon live in misery, plagued by oppression and injustice. Their plight has become ours because we have an obligation to care for even the smallest of the Great Creator's creatures. We all have a calling to protect their dignity. As your ajaw, I have a responsibility to protect you as well. This time, the threat is on a neighboring planet, but it is only a matter of time before it spreads to our home again. I gave Copan authorization to choose his group. He is leading a team of four."

A loud bark was heard in the meeting room, coming from Obasi. The special forces had a way of expressing themselves that resembled a sort of barking sound. At least, that was what it sounded like to me as I remembered Earth and the American forces there. I smiled from ear to ear as I recalled the practice a galaxy away.

The somber mood didn't stop the leaders from asking questions. Buluc asked, "Is it time, Ajaw?"

"No, Buluc. Not yet," answered Michael. "I need proof for the masses before we take action, hence the orders to the special forces on Choluteca. One more item before we conclude. I have appointed Kinich Ahau to a rank commensurate with the responsibility he will have here on Shrah and wherever he serves. As you well know, Kinich Ahau is a distinguished war veteran from our home planet. He fought in a great war, the third of its kind, brought on by the existence of what Earthlings call nations. Different geographic areas on the planet have their own rulers, and they keep others out of their territories by building walls and fences called borders."

I could see baffled looks around the room as Shrah's leaders tried to grasp the idea of a world where people of one planet fought each other and forbade others from trespassing on their territories. Hearing this spoken by the ruler of an alien planet made me realize, for the first time in my life, the absurdity of the way Earthlings treated each other.

Michael continued, "He brings experiences we do not have. One of his special talents is amphibious warfare in oceans similar to the Panthalassan on Tai-Anh. This is the launch of combat strikes from water to land. Kinich Ahau has come here to join us and has asked me to employ his services. I have accepted, humbled by his offer and sacrifice. The Great Creator has sent him to us, his people, to help us preserve our existence. The four travelers who brought him home are those written about in the Sacred Codices. They signal the apocalypse that is headed our way.

"Effective immediately, Kinich Ahau will be leading the activities of our fighting forces as they pertain to sea, air, and land combat operations. This is new to us, and I have asked him to work with Isaiah in preparing our forces for combat on a planet that contains large bodies of water." The ajaw paused to allow his leaders to comment or ask questions.

Kabel looked over at me, and I pretended

not to notice her.

With that, the ajaw turned his eyes to me. "Welcome home, Admiral."

# CHAPTER 33: NECESSARY STEPS

As officer in charge of the special forces training detachment on Choluteca Island, Yoro assembled his team for the high-stakes operation to retrieve incriminating evidence of the actions of the emperor of Tai-Anh.

He chose himself to lead the mission because he was most qualified for it. He was senior, and this operation would be an extremely dangerous endeavor. They would enter mainland Lyndon and travel by foot into Gandolim under the cover of darkness to recover recordings that would once and for all show the citizens of Tai-Anh that Emperor Exelcior dealt in deceit, murder, and oppression. Yoro, who was not particularly known for being patient, was tired of waiting to expose the truth. Michael had given him full authority to command the forces on the island. His order was to proceed as he deemed fit, and he was ready.

The morning after receiving the order from his ajaw, Yoro stood in front of his troops, who were in formation, and explained the dangerous nature of the operation to enter Gandolim to recover the incriminating recordings of the emperor's activities. Every single trainee volunteered for the mission. Yoro made the command decision and selected his team as he deemed best. He chose a small group of operatives so that the chances of being discovered while operating behind enemy lines were reduced. This was to be a clandestine spy operation carried out by experienced special forces troops.

Yoro chose three veterans of the Mine War for the operation: Sergeants Anayansi Sula, Candice Lucia, and Quintus Salvius. Anayansi was the best choice in regards to experience and ability. The two new Lyndonite additions would be the key to navigating in and around Tai-Anh and Lyndon, as they were very knowledgeable about the layout of the landscape on both sides of the conflict. They would leave as soon as Kinich Ahau set in the western sky and disappeared behind the Panthalassan horizon.

Morazan, Areni, and Hope were to stay behind and continue training the special forces troops. Hope was not happy. She wanted to accompany her lieutenant into the dragon's teeth.

But she was outranked and had been ordered to stay behind. Such was the way of the military.

They would travel to the mainland in a team of four that would be transported by a small underwater transport vehicle that Lyndon had built and offered for their use. Lyndon's attempt to build a naval force using metals mined on Magna Hermopolis had been one of the reasons for the outbreak of the Mine War. The climax of tensions had spilled over after the Dark Dance Massacre. The massacre had been ordered by Tai-Anh's leaders. Then Colonel Joram Antipas had led the empire's troops, who'd carried it out. Lyndonite adults and children had swayed, suspended in mid-air as they'd hung from their necks long after their deaths. Tai-Anh's leaders had wanted to send the separatists in Lyndon a clear message as to the fate that awaited those who opposed the empire's iron-fisted rule. Their plan had backfired.

The people in the process of creating the Independent State of Lyndon had already armed themselves and prepared for war. They'd mined metals on Magna Hermopolis to construct a star fleet. The worst part was that Tai-Anh had been able to manipulate the people of Shrah into believing the Lyndonites were enemies of the entire Kinich Ahau planetary system, a ruse of the highest standards. It had made blood from Tai-Anh, Lyndon, and Shrah spill on the cold moon's soil.

Yoro was well aware of the dangers posed by a clandestine operation on Emperor Exelcior's turf and accepted the risk. He made absolutely certain that the three volunteers he selected to join him understood the risks as well and fully accepted them. This was a mission that could save many lives in the long run if they were able to recover recordings that could expose Tai-Anh's evil regime and perhaps bring a diplomatic end to the impending conflict. The four operatives met in private and prepared every detail they could think of. They picked up their camouflage uniforms, CO2 pistols and rifles, obsidian fighting knives, and night vision equipment. They would engage in Atsalat meditation that evening and would soon be underwater and under the cover of darkness.

That night, Yoro visited the Eleventh Dimension and received individual private communications. Morning came quickly, and no one had been able to sleep. All assembled to bid the departing operatives good luck.

Hope wanted to give her lieutenant a kiss goodbye but knew this was inappropriate and not an option. She had to wait until they were assigned to different departments so she could get to know him properly. She made eye contact with Yoro, and excitement and love flowed between them. No words were necessary.

The team set off into the Panthalassan

Ocean. A submarine was the best way to travel under the thermocline in depth. The transit to the main coast was done very slowly in the deep of the ocean. They rigged the small submarine vessel for ultra-quiet mode so as to maintain stealth operations on their approach, using global positioning coordinates.

The four arrived on the Lyndon coast the following night. The Panthalassan Ocean was choppy under a light rain as they surfaced their vessel. The wind wielded its invisible force on the surface of the water. The special forces prepared for the amphibian portion of their mission. They donned their swim gear and took up their night vision equipment, laser pulse rifles, guns, and obsidian knives. The Lyndon coast patiently awaited their arrival from the ocean.

Yoro led his team, having already plotted the course of travel he thought safest. He'd carefully considered the input of trainees from Lyndon and Gandolim. He felt a sense of protective responsibility for his followers. It was a price of authority. Yoro felt just how heavy that price was.

The team moved quietly, unseen by anyone in the city. Moving undetected was the way to avoid trouble. It helped that Quintus and Candice were natives of Lyndon and knew the city well. It made the task of navigating through the city much easier and safer.

This team was composed of two of Shrah's

top special forces operatives and two Mine War veterans well suited and trained for special operations. The only concern Yoro had was the physical fitness of the two recent arrivals, as they had not been in training nor combat in quite some time. They seemed to be operating just fine, though.

Roughly halfway through their journey, they came upon a more inhabited part of the city. For their safety and to remain undetected, Yoro split the team in two. He took Quintus with him, and Anayansi took Candice so that each of the two Lyndonites was accompanied by a Shrah special forces counterpart. The two teams advanced silently, hidden from sight, through the empty streets of Lyndon. No one dared to be out at night under the strictly enforced martial law. Yoro had ordered a rendezvous point not far from the park, where the Lyndonite believers had assembled the night they'd met with the Shrah special forces.

Yoro and Quintus arrived at the rendezvous point right on time. In military operations, punctuality saved lives. The lieutenant worried about the safety of Anayansi and Candice. As they waited, Quintus leaned over to whisper something in Yoro's ear, and Yoro felt it: the sharp stick in the neck, followed by an immediate rush of heat and numbness in his extremities. He dropped to the ground. He could see Quintus standing over him with the empty syringe in his hand just before he lost consciousness.

# CHAPTER 34: SWEATING IN PEACETIME

I was up before my star system namesake rose over the eastern horizon of my new home. I began my mornings with a run no matter what planet I was on. I needed to stay in the best shape possible. The more you sweated in peace, the less you bled in war.

The air on Shrah was bone dry. Gravity felt lighter than on Earth. I could move faster and jump higher. Running in the hot air seemed to singe my nostrils when I inhaled. I had to be careful not to succumb to a coughing fit by drawing in too much hot air. There was very little cloud cover and no humidity to speak of.

Kinich Ahau was relentless in the sky. It was hot, and it was dry. I couldn't stop running, for to stop was to die. Earth was a wonderful and distant memory. Bodies of water sure had a way of calming the soul. Water on Shrah was hidden deep below the ground in massive aquifers. It was the beginning of living with leathery skin.

*How does she manage to have such supple and radiant skin?* I wondered about Kabel. It hurt to simply think of her.

I saw the Great Pyramid in the distance with its metallic golden cap. It was fascinating to me how much it resembled the pyramids of Earth. There had to be a connection. These builders had come before us, but where had they originated? What was the purpose of these massive structures? In how many worlds in the cosmos were they built? One thing was for sure: the people on Shrah were just as baffled by them as the people on Earth were. I guessed the Great Creator in this galaxy had mysteries also. Maybe it was the same creator. Maybe there was only one universal Great Creator that existed across multiple universes.

This thought made my head spin, and I began to miss Earth. I especially missed the sounds of waves rolling onto the beach and pine trees swaying in the wind on high mountaintops. I even missed sitting in a stadium, watching a professional baseball game. Major league baseball had been expanded to the cities of San Antonio, Vancouver, Mexico City, San Juan, Santo Domingo, Havana, London, and Tokyo. I longed for a little Earth. But at least I wasn't going to miss

Earth's deserts much. Shrah provided a very large dose of that.

I kept running. The way out of town was downhill and didn't challenge me much. I wondered if Shrah folks ran much. If not, I would have to influence them to do so. Every military combatant needed to run regularly.

As I thought about this, I saw three groups of two in front of me. Michael and Maya were in the lead. Behind them were Isaiah and Noah. The last two were Kabel and Buluc. They were returning from their daily morning run already. They waved at me as they ran by. I had my answer, and I was miffed. These aliens were training earlier than me. That had to change immediately.

Later that morning, I moved back up the mountain into Nacaome City after a long, thoughtful run through the rough, rocky terrain of the desert. The people of Shrah were fascinated by me. I would have to get used to that. I guessed it had something to do with my being an alien reincarnated and returned to them from among the stars. I slowed my pace to a walk as I hit the stone streets.

Girls and boys in the city were playing, practicing their Ch'o'Jonik hand-to-hand combat techniques. It fired me up to see this. The folks on Shrah understood that being ready for combat was an essential part of life. It was critical to fight to survive. They appreciated that they had been relocated as an entire people by beings who served the Great Creator. Sometimes, extinction or survival depended on your ability to stop aggressors. The people of Earth knew this well, from Carthaginian conflicts to WWIII. Shrah was now alone, and the people's warrior hearts seemed on the verge of being tested. It was time to sweat.

In my walk through the city, I saw something that reminded me of Earth: a large red scorpion crawling on one of the rock walls. This scorpion was three or four times the size of an adult emperor scorpion, about the size of a New York City subway rat. Needless to say, I kept my distance from it and was glad to have a pistol on me.

Later that day, I was to join Isaiah's special forces and those in training and begin taking them through a crash course in amphibious warfare. We would begin high-altitude, low-opening (HALO) parachuting techniques as well as working on the four combat swimming strokes necessary. We would work on freestyle, backstroke, breaststroke, and sidestroke. We would also work on swimming without using arms and legs, drown-proofing, and dolphin-kicking. I would have to keep in mind that they had never seen a dolphin. The thought made me miss dolphins. The swimming training would happen in the Tela Mountain Range aquifer's Blue Hole.

I was looking forward to the cold water. I

missed swimming in the ocean, but the aquifer would have to do for the time being. According to intelligence reports, Tai-Anh's coasts were mostly rocky shore with very few sandy beaches. Therefore, my focus would be on swimming in the cold, dark waters of the aquifers. We might have to take the war from the ocean to their shores.

As I was walking into the city, the Shrah forces-in-training were running into the desert for their second run of the day, led by Obasi and Seth. I was so very impressed by Seth. He was the age at which most teenagers on Earth were just learning how to drive and figuring out how to court the opposite sex. This young man was already leading trainee officers, was capable of lethality, and had fought to the death, killing several attackers.

As Obasi saw me approaching, she brought the entire platoon of trainees to a halt, and they all stood at attention as I walked by them. Obasi called out, "Good morning, Admiral!"

I returned the salute as my responsibility hit me. I was becoming less and less a stranger in a strange land and more and more involved in a sort of forever war.

Who were Emperor Exelcior and General Antipas? What was up their sleeves next? How could we take on a planet so much more advanced and with such a strong numbers advantage over us? The odds were stacked so high in their favor.

I returned to Temple Alom, home of the foundation. I showered, then had lunch with Kabel. I found myself bumbling like an idiot whenever I was around her. I think it amused her somewhat to see me, and everyone else for that matter, so out of my element in her presence. I invited her to our HALO and amphibious training at the Tela aquifer, and much to my surprise and delight, she accepted.

Michael, Maya, Isaiah, Kabel, Noah, Buluc, Danli, Obasi, Seth, Janina, the templar knights, and the entire regimen of active and training personnel joined the training evolution in the Tela Mountain aquifer. It was my moment to share the experience I had gained on Earth.

I was amazed at how everyone on Shrah felt a sense of duty to take up arms to defend their homeland and their very existence. It seemed to come naturally to them after being persecuted in two different galaxies. This time, however, they were going to have to survive on their own. They had no choice but to fight to the death. Every able body had to do their part and serve. Every Shrah citizen was a student and practitioner of Ch'o'Jonik, Atsalat, the Sacred Codices, and shooting.

Training happened every day without exception. I had trained so many special forces soldiers on Earth that I had the HALO and water training curriculum already fully mapped out.

There was, however, one very big difference to training in the aquifers: the assistance of one absolute badass of a swimmer and fighter named Ruby.

# CHAPTER 35: SILENT FATE

When Yoro awoke from his drug-induced slumber, he noticed he was strapped down on a table at a forty-five-degree angle in a bright room. He could hear rain on the small windows that sat high on the wall to his left. The first thought that entered his pounding head was the safety of his people. He tried to regain control of his situation and looked for his rifle, gun, and knife. He was unable to move, so his Ch'o'Jonik abilities were of no use to him. He called the names of his sergeant and recruits in a worried frenzy. "Anayansi! Quintus! Candice!"

There was no answer. He focused his eyes on the corner of the room, where there was a silhouette of someone looking at him.

"You are wasting your time. Your sergeant and recruits are not here," said the voice coldly.

"Where are they? What have you done with them?" spat Yoro.

"Well, technically, Salvius is not a recruit.

He is one of our lieutenants in the Third Realm and a Noumeroi special operative who switched sides to the correct one. The good news is that Salvius is fine and has received a commendation for his service. You have to be more careful about who you trust, Lieutenant."

Yoro fought back the anger of Quintus's betrayal and his own failure to recognize his intentions.

"We also caught the other invaders with you. We exterminated them. They were more concerned with your safety than with their own. They were of no use to us. Little did they know that your incompetence would cost them their lives."

Yoro entered a whirlwind of rage, sorrow, and helplessness. Nothing mattered more than the safety of his subordinates, who he cared for with the tenderness of an older sibling. Tears welled up in his eyes, but he subdued his anger. He closed his eyes for a quick moment of respect and to send a message of love into the cosmos as he controlled his breathing. *Please receive them with mercy and love, Great Creator*, he thought.

Yoro switched his mindset to return to his mission. "Who are you?" he asked, wondering the identity of the captor he was determined to send to the Eleventh Dimension as soon as he was able.

"I am Joram Antipas, General Joram Antipas to you, Lieutenant. My duty is to make certain you tell us everything we need to know about your ajaw and the rest of your treasonous religion that has brainwashed so many of our people into opposing us. Your ajaws and general have brought great pain to our people. We understand that you are just a soldier who isn't responsible for their crimes. Tell us what we want to know, and you will be set free."

Yoro knew the statement was a lie. He would have to escape and find his way to Choluteca Island. Everyone there was in danger. He thought about all who were there in training, especially Hope, for whom he had fallen hard. "Take me out of these straps, Antipas. I am only one, and I am unarmed. I am of no threat to you."

Antipas laughed. "You must think me a fool, Lieutenant. Do you think we are unaware of your exploits during the Mine War and your extensive training? We know you are all fanatics. Unstrapping you would be reckless. You may as well get used to those straps and start telling us what we ask. Where is the ajaw presently? Where is Janina Preston? We already know the rest of your forces are training on Choluteca Island. They won't know what hits them."

Antipas waited for the anger of the threat to fully sink in. Yoro couldn't help but feel the heartbreak of knowing harm was coming to his troops on Choluteca. He thought of how Hope would fight and lamented that he wasn't able to fight alongside her.

Antipas continued, "You can save yourself, and maybe them, by telling us what we need to know. Tell us, and you will be set free after you publicly accept responsibility and apologize for your act of war on the people of Tai-Anh. You are then welcome to live with us here on Tai-Anh for luxury and safety. After all, your people on Choluteca Island and on Shrah will cease to exist very soon. You may as well save yourself, son."

Antipas's words filled Yoro with dread and overwhelmed him with helplessness. He was not to be bought. He knew the outlook for his people was grim. He began studying the room for dimensions, searching for possible courses of action or escape.

"Don't waste your time and energy, Lieutenant. You are going nowhere until you start talking."

"Do what you need to do, Antipas. You know I won't betray my people or my oath to protect them," said Yoro, knowing these words would seal his fate. He began his prayers for what was to happen.

"Very well, Lieutenant," Antipas replied. "Your torture will begin immediately and will end when you start talking or die."

Antipas left the room at Imperial Headquarters and made his way to Emperor Exelcior's master chamber. He passed the two Noumeroi guards stationed outside the chamber and approached the emperor, who was standing with his back to the door, looking out into the driving rain.

The emperor spoke without turning from his window. "I heard your discussion with Yoro Copan over the communications system. He won't talk. They never talk. We will show the people of Gandolim the footage Salvius took, showing the military training on Choluteca Island and the clandestine team operating with weapons on the sovereignty of their land. We can begin torturing him and record it. We will send it to Alom so he can see how we handle enemy infiltrators on our lands. The moment he attempts to transmit the message outside Shrah, the recording will self-destruct."

Without a word, Antipas left the room to carry out his orders as given. Exelcior smiled from ear to ear. Soon, Yoro's screams of agony began to come over the communications speaker.

The emperor ordered that the footage taken by Salvius of the training operations on Choluteca Island and Yoro carrying his rifle on Tai-Anh was broadcast and shown to the people of Tai-Anh and Lyndon.

Yoro's torture was recorded privately to be given to Ajaw Michael Alom as a self-destructing gift and a warning about the seriousness and brutality of the empire.

Flaying was one of the most uncivilized methods of torture and punishment. It was brutal to the bone, literally. It involved removing the skin from the body. It was done to Shrah's beloved son, Lieutenant Yoro Copan, in a slow process, lasting two days. His skin was removed so that he would bleed to death slowly. The empire's Third Realm torturers added a chemical to increase the pain exponentially.

Yoro drifted in and out of consciousness with the extreme pain and exhaustion he was enduring. He entered the Eleventh Dimension frequently. On the evening of the second day of brutal torture and with large amounts of flesh cut from his body, Yoro asked to talk. He would only speak to Emperor Exelcior himself. The torturers laughed at the lieutenant from Shrah, who was in no shape to demand anything from them, but his request was honored. Even the torturers had developed reluctant respect for Yoro's ability to withstand the brutality with which he was treated. They placed bets on just how much longer he could live.

A few moments later, Exelcior proceeded into the torture chamber. He had been listening to the agonized screams of one of Michael Alom's finest and most loved warriors. He was ready to hear what the lieutenant had to say, hoping to use it for anti-Shrah propaganda. Without a word, Exelcior approached the bloodied and broken body. This was someone on the verge of death.

"Can you hear me, Exelcior?" Yoro managed to whisper, despite having lost his voice from screaming.

"Yes," answered Exelcior with no hint of empathy for the victim strapped down in front of him. He couldn't believe what was left was still alive and talking.

"I am a warrior from Shrah and only serve my ajaw, Michael Alom," said Yoro in trembling whispers of agony. After a pause, he continued, "I will die at your hands. Sergeant Anayansi Sula and recruit Candice Lucia have already. You killed them for no reason. The worst thing you did was attempt to kill our future ajaw, Seth. For that, I will make you pay. It might not be in this life, but I will hunt you down and bring you to justice in a way ten times worse than this."

Exelcior laughed coldly, unsheathed his knife, and drove it into Yoro's heart.

Hope Zenobia's heart broke to pieces at 11:11.

Lieutenant Yoro Copan entered the Eleventh Dimension permanently. He flew over windswept green fields and came upon Crystal City. At the city bathed in white light, he proceeded through a long tunnel with a light at the other end of it. He walked toward the warm light, and as he approached, he saw the figure of someone dressed in all white. The identity of the individual was hard to determine with the brightness of the light coming from behind, but Yoro knew who it was.

"Welcome home, son. I've been waiting for you."

# CHAPTER 36: BROKEN ENERGY

Hope felt something was awry with the universal energy that surrounded her. It was as if a source of light had turned off around her. She knew something had happened to her beloved Yoro. Somehow, she knew he wasn't going to return. She was devastated.

First, it had been the killing of her parents, who she hadn't been able to protect from the empire many years before. Now it was the man she had fallen for. The opportunity to love him physically was gone, and the pain was unbearable. She decided not to enter Atsalat so she wouldn't receive confirmation of what she already knew. Lieutenant Yoro Copan had returned home to the Eleventh Dimension and left her alone for the rest of her physical life.

Hope walked off alone into the misty night, feeling loneliness consume her. She soon arrived at the very spot on the beach where she had shared such a wonderful moment with Yoro. The moons were barely visible in the dark, rainy sky. She thought about how wonderful it would have been to make love to him, to lie in the safety and comfort of his arms. Now that would never happen.

Hope began a trip down memory lane. It was a practice in lament and heartbreak. She found herself climbing up to the island's highest point on the northeastern portion of Choluteca. Under the dim moonlight, overlooking the vast Panthalassan Ocean, she decided life wasn't worth living any longer. She felt there was nothing left for her in the physical dimension. Hope walked to the edge of the precipice and looked down at the jagged rocks below. No living being would survive the plunge. She stepped closer to the edge, tears streaming down her face. It was time. She felt a sweet lover's breath on her face as she began to step off the edge of the cliff.

The breath on her face became a strong wind, heavy with the scent of Yoro. It pushed her back, keeping her from falling forward. She fell onto her back, still on the cliff floor, and immediately looked up in front of her. She was certain she had felt hands press her shoulders back, but she saw nothing. She curled up on her side and sobbed so bitterly she could barely breathe.

As she was beginning to catch her breath, Hope felt the love being sent over many dimensions to her. Yoro might not have been with her physically, but he still existed, and he still loved her. He obviously wanted her to live. That was reason enough to keep living.

She came down the mountain, climbed into bed, and cried herself to sleep.

Back on Shrah, it had been a while since anyone had heard from Yoro, and the enlightened felt the extinguishment of his physical life. An encrypted message came through to Shrah from Morazan, now the senior special forces leader on Choluteca Island, informing Temple Alom that the team of four had not been heard from. Morazan asked for permission to assemble a team for a rescue mission into Lyndon to retrieve his fellow warriors. He felt powerless. The message was addressed to Obasi since Morazan was unaware of the lieutenant's promotion to captain.

A video message was delivered to Michael, showing the torture and execution of Yoro. The lieutenant's warning to Exelcior was omitted. Omitted also were the mass executions of hundreds of Shrah Philosophy believers. It was heartbreaking and gruesome. Exelcior wanted Shrah to know what was in store for them should they challenge the empire. He was done hiding his intentions with those who threatened his reign.

The Shrah Philosophy was one of love. Unfortunately for Exelcior, it was also one of war. The philosophy gave Exelcior the same value as all other living beings in the universe. That, of course, was not good enough. Any movement without his endorsement was unwelcome in his empire and was punishable by imprisonment or death.

Michael and his entire leadership team viewed the video file at the temple in Nacaome City. Yoro never broke, even as his muscles were systematically sliced off his body. Michael watched all the footage of his lieutenant's suffering, his anger growing. Then he had a realization.

When the video ended, Michael turned to his leadership team. He looked all of them in the eye just long enough for them to know that he loved them. The ajaw settled his final look on Isaiah. No words were necessary between them. Isaiah knew it. Buluc knew it too.

The planning and training had come to a climax for the leaders of Shrah. Michael called a meeting of their war cabinet in his favorite conference room, overlooking Nacaome City. The members of the war cabinet were Maya, Isaiah, Andy, Buluc, Kabel, Noah, Danli, Obasi, and the newly promoted Sergeant Seth.

The ajaw began, "We are dispatching a detachment from Shrah to the new location on Tai-Anh to assist in combat operations. I understand our forces on Choluteca Island have not been trained as long as we would have hoped, but we are out of time at this point. Our inaction would result in their extermination. The odds are greatly against us, and we are in full preparation for an inevitable war with the Empire of Tai-Anh that could very well end with our extinction. Take some time to visit with your loved ones, then return for war planning. Isaiah and Andy, please stay behind to meet with Maya, Seth, and I."

With that, the war cabinet members knew that the ajaw did not open the floor for questions. They would have to psychologically prepare for unavoidable action that would change their lives for good very soon.

Michael, Maya, Isaiah, Noah, Buluc, Andy, and Seth sat closer together as the rest of the cabinet members left the conference room.

Michael said, "From this point forward, Seth will be joining every meeting I have on matters of official business. It is time for Maya and me to begin handing down our legacy of rule for the people of Shrah. Should Seth survive what is inevitable for us all, I ask for your support in helping him rule our people. The time is upon us. I am counting on you to plan and execute the launch of a detachment to Tai-Anh to assist our forces training there to evacuate. You have full authority to plan and carry out this mission. You are the senior military leaders on this planet, and as such, you are in command. Together, we will design the strategy we will implement. As you are aware, our fighting forces are outnumbered greatly. We need a strategy to protect our people who will be left behind here on Shrah, and we need a strategy to attack the empire at their home on Tai-Anh. General, you know Shrah's forces better than anyone and are our supreme military leader. Admiral, you are one of us and have returned home to our people with extensive combat leadership experience. Your experience fighting in oceanic and amphibious wars on Earth is a blessing from the Great Creator. We need you. It has been the greatest of privileges to be your leader. Let's get to work."

The war room, filled with Shrah's greatest military minds, began to create a strategic plan of defense and attack that encompassed the experiences of two galaxies. It was time.

# CHAPTER 37: THE CHOICE

They made love that night. Sex was a physical act, but they didn't have sex. It simply wasn't a strong enough term to describe the powerful flow of emotion and passion between them. Every contact from his mouth and hands sent shockwaves through her entire being, and the favor was equally returned. Lovemaking happened four-dimensionally for them. There was the physical plane, the psychological plane, the emotional plane, and the spiritual plane. All four levels of their psyches were interwoven into a rhythmic crescendo. There was a powerful physicality. They were both warriors and did nothing halfway. It was all or nothing. They looked into each other's eyes and consumed one another until there wasn't a drop left to waste. It was raw, intense, and all-consuming. No words were spoken between Michael and Maya Alom.

Afterward, in the temple master dormitory, the ajaw lay awake, sleepless. He existed in the oppressive silence. He could feel the weight of the darkness in the room. That night's darkness was unbearably heavy. The ajaw rose from bed quietly without disturbing his wife. She pretended to be asleep. He pretended not to know she was awake.

Michael took in the coldness of the floor at his feet as he looked out over the valley and down into Nacaome City. The moonless sky gave the desert a unique kind of beauty. The stars of the Andromeda galaxy pierced the black canvas of the night sky. Michael sat in his comfortable lounge chair, looking out into the night. Thoughts assaulted his mind. Melancholy bombarded his heart and strife his soul. The ajaw knew the years of harmony were ending. Peace was ephemeral. The decision had been made for him. War and the metallic smell of the bloodshed that accompanied it were once again upon his people.

Michael was ready. He had no choice. His people were being hunted. He was angry that his legacy was threatened. They had almost killed his son. They had managed to kill many of his people. Any believer anywhere in the universe was part of his people. They were dying for love. The pain of seeing the brutality with which Yoro's physical life had ended was almost unbearable. It broke Michael's heart. He also felt the pain of the scars on his young son's face. The pain was transforming into anger. Anger would soon become rage. He feared the danger of rage, the dark energy, which would drown the light of a soul in wrath. Nevertheless, the survival of his people was predicated by his ability to decide and execute. Striking first might be his best option.

Michael drew in a deep breath as he shot his eyes up into the cosmos. He closed his eyes and brought down his head to face straight forward with a slow exhalation. His heart rate slowed. At-salat.

Michael's spirit left his body and flew out into the cosmic superhighway. He found himself soaring through the clouds and over the wind-swept fields to Crystal City in the distance. His spirit approached, and he took in the beauty of the crystal cathedral in the Eleventh Dimension.

When he arrived, Michael entered a flowing tunnel and headed up toward the warm light. At the top of the tunnel, he came upon a being. As he approached, its identity began to become clear. Michael had known him his entire life. As a young man, he had seen him in his dreams. As an older man, he had sought his counsel in the Eleventh Dimension.

He stood in his traditional ceremonial Mayan garb. Michael was one of his own, and they had been related in many different ways and incarnations. They embraced.

The greatest Mayan warrior of all time, Ek Chuah, was happy to see Michael, but he had a singular focus on his reason for awaiting Michael's arrival. He had an urgent message to communicate.

When they visited, an urgent message was delivered, and Ek Chuah walked away, returning to the pantheon.

Michael was well known on Tai-Anh. The people of Lyndon feared him. The people of Tai-Anh respected him. Exelcior had done his best to change the sentiment of his people toward Temple Alom, but Michael was unsure of whether it had worked. He felt certain the systematic huntings, attacks, arrests, and executions of Tai-Anh's citizens would have given the people doubt. Michael didn't know. What he knew was that his silence was no longer possible. Under the guidance of Ek Chuah, Michael recorded and sent a public message to Exelcior, informing him and the people of Tai-Anh and Lyndon that Temple Alom had officially declared the Tai-Anh Empire, but not its people, an enemy.

*Third Day of the Sixth Month of the 746th Orbit After Relocation*

*To Herod Exelcior,*

*This is a message of love written in anger. It is generally my philosophy not to address another being until anger has subsided. That would be impossible in this instance, as my anger will not subside.*

*Earlier in this year's orbit, you ordered the*

*murder of my son and of our brother, Dr. Hamilton Nile. You failed. Unfortunately, that is not the case for the thousands of innocent beings you have violently removed from the living dimension for believing in a philosophy that is of no threat to you. You are also responsible for the financial oppression of our brothers and sisters in Lyndon and your own people on Tai-Anh. For these crimes, you have attempted to convince the people of Tai-Anh and Lyndon that the people of Shrah were to blame.*

*Your most recent attack on our people was the unnecessary and brutal torture of one of our sons, Yoro Copan. I know it is simply a matter of time before you attempt the complete extermination of the Shrah people, who have survived in multiple galaxies by the grace of the Great Creator.*

*I have a duty not to allow you to continue to exist in the living dimension for one second longer than I can control. There is no place in this universe where you will find refuge from me. Evil must be extinguished. Letting you live while there is a single citizen of Shrah with physical life is no longer an option.*

*Taking your life for attempting to murder my son would be my pleasure, even if it comes at the cost of my own.*

*There is not enough room for both of us in this dimension. Your time has come.*

*End*

The message from Shrah's ajaw was broadcast all over Tai-Anh and Lyndon, but not before the training detachment on Choluteca Island was relocated to a secret location in the Panthalassan Ocean. The news media outlets on Tai-Anh betrayed their emperor by broadcasting the message. This betrayal resulted in the immediate imprisonment and execution of many innocents. Regardless, the people of Tai-Anh and Lyndon heard the message from Shrah loud and clear.

At the time of transmission, the detachment from Shrah departed on a stealth mission to join the relocated forces-in-training to execute parts one of two in the overall strategic plan put together by the military leaders of Shrah.

# CHAPTER 38: LIGHTS FOR DARKNESS

Exelcior paced his dormitory room after waking up from a nightmare. In his dream, a faceless warrior had been jumping up and down in a pool of blood. Exelcior was unsure whose blood it had been in the pool, but he was convinced it was his. The realization of it sent chills through many dimensions of his existence, and he'd awoken bathed in sweat with a racing heart. He'd stood from his bed and began to pace the room with a throbbing headache and a dry throat, upset that the dream had had such an effect on him. He was ready for a fight anytime and anywhere.

But how real that dream had been. He knew well that the uncivilized savages from Shrah were capable of killing easily and without reason. It was why he bore the responsibility of exterminating them as soon as he was able. The universe

needed to be rid of these pests.
Exelcior rolled that thought around in his head as he paced his dark sleeping quarters inside the all-metal building. As usual, rain hit the dormitory window. Exelcior thought about the maniac lieutenant they'd had to torture to death and how brainwashed the fanatical animals from Shrah were. Exterminating them was the only solution.

Exelcior made the decision at that very moment that he would take action. He became far less concerned about the small and insignificant group training on Choluteca. His target would be the root of the problem: Shrah itself. An attack on Choluteca would tip off the Ajaw of Shrah that the empire intended to take military action by force against all believers. Time was of the essence. He had Antipas woken and sent to meet with him in the middle of the night and gave him the order, the final solution, as he called it. He would never again have to deal with Michael Alom or his followers.

A few nights later, it was especially dark. Then, without warning, night became day. In the distance were two streaks of firelight, which were to blame for the interruption of the stark darkness that normally blanketed the desert when Kinich Ahau lay to rest beyond the horizon.

The interruption that turned night into day had originated from far beyond the planet's atmosphere, on another world. It was carried through space in the belly of a beast, a beast piloted by technology.

The sound that accompanied the fireballs hadn't reached Nacaome City's Temple Alom, but the gas from the light that was closest was already there. It was a cloud of monopropellant fuel that completely blanketed the city. Then the second source of light came into the fray. The aerosol was detonated and engendered a shockwave of extended duration in an overpressure blast. All of Shrah was ignited with dispersed fuel as it caught fire and invaded every living space in the city all at once. The force of the blast sent shockwaves through Nacaome City. Not a single living creature on the planet's surface survived the blast. All exterminated. The final solution. Shrah's day had arrived at night.

Nacaome City had become the site of destructive horror. All life in the desert city was extinguished. The fires from the sky created an apocalypse. One dowsed the air with the mist of fuel; the other brought the fiery monster of death. They arrived with surgical precision and covered every square inch of the planet's surface. No living creature had time to find cover between first sight of fire and their death. All breathable air was consumed in seconds with a deadly pressure and wave of destruction. No dwelling, bunker, or tunnel was safe. Life at all altitudes above ground level on the planet ceased to exist.

Back on Tai-Anh, a world away, the empire was hunting the other believers down. The Third Realm was hunting them. The Noumeroi were hunting them. They were unaware that their fellow believers still on Shrah had been attacked and that Temple Alom was completely erased, gone without a stone left standing.

Choluteca Island was abandoned when the explosion took place. The entire island was charred and reduced to a level ground. The crater left behind made most of the island disappear into the Panthalassan Ocean, triggering a tsunami that assaulted mainland Tai-Anh's eastern coast. The believers on Choluteca had evacuated just in time.

And high above the rain-soaked clouds of Tai-Anh, although transports from Shrah approached the planet every week, Danli was taking no chances. He flew in complete silence to remain undetected. He wasn't even communicating with the spaceport in Lyndon. Danli was carrying plenty of cargo to justify his approach into Lyndon, but he would have a hard time explaining why he'd brought special forces operatives, templar knights, CO2 laser rifles, pistols, dive gear, parachutes, and night vision goggles along for the ride. These were the warriors who had escaped fiery death on Shrah. The ajaws were not among them. They, along with thousands of others, had been on Shrah during the horrific attack that had turned night into day.

They flew in HALO fashion. Not only were they going to jump out of the transport at 35,000 feet of altitude, they would do so over the ocean . . . at night. As they entered Tai-Anh's gravitational pull, they penetrated the skies slowly to reduce the friction of the atmosphere, the vibration that came with atmospheric re-entry. Danli reduced the weight of gravity return as they fell through the Tai-Anh skies.

The warriors from Shrah were suited up and ready for their free-fall HALO. Oxygen rebreathing apparatuses, dive gear, fins, altimeters, compasses, global positioning systems, underwater propulsion systems, night vision goggles, CO2 laser rifles, pistols, and obsidian knives were ready to go. They were warriors dressed in black and waiting for the rear hatch of the craft to open for their plunge into the Panthalassan Ocean.

They reached 35,000 of altitude, and Danli opened the rear hatch and gave the order for them to jump. Alien bodies hurled themselves into the darkness of night and began to plunge at terminal velocity toward the ocean. They checked their communications systems inside their headgear, and all systems were go. At 3,000 feet of altitude, after piercing through the water within the clouds, they deployed their parachutes, feeling the pull of the wind resistance slowing their free fall. As they splashed down into the ocean, they unhooked themselves from their parachutes quickly and swam away from them so as to not get caught in the drowning fabric. All jumpers reported no injuries and began their swim toward the shore. The alien admiral had trained them to swim as combatants. They all asked the Great Creator for protection.

They swam a quarter of a mile in cold ocean water and intermittent light rain. There was a special kind of terror that came with swimming in any ocean at night. These swimmers were not just any swimmers, though. They had trained in swimming long distances in the complete darkness of the underground aquifers of Shrah. But the largest fish in the Panthalassan Ocean was carnivorous and grew to just under forty feet in length, and they hadn't trained to survive an attack from an ocean beast.

These soldiers were war veterans who had trained incessantly for clandestine and highly dangerous situations. They swam under the light of Tai-Ahn's two moons. It was surreal to the swimmers that one of the moons in the night sky had been the location of so much death and destruction. It seemed like so long ago, but here they were, doing it all over again. Experience had taught this group not to expect routine. They weren't extremely experienced swimmers, but they were disciplined in their techniques and in top physical conditions.

The seven teams arrived on the uncharted island's shore and emerged from the Panthalassan Ocean. Their purpose was to kill the enemy by bringing the battle from the ocean to land and air. The ajaw and his wife had made the decision together. If their people were to die, then they would do so fighting for their lives, not hiding.

As the water combatants stepped onto the beach, the forces on land prepared for a firefight. All of their training on Choluteca Island came down to this moment. They were ready but unsure if the forces arriving from the sea were friends or foes. If they were foes, they were in for a fight, as over 100 heavily armed warriors were walking in from the ocean, heading straight for them.

The leader of the arriving group emitted the red semaphore light signals used in secret by Shrah's military forces to stop the troops on the island from engaging them in a firefight. It was a good thing because Morazan, Areni, and Hope were dug in with hundreds of warriors, preparing to do just that.

Once Morazan, Areni, and Hope knew their detachment on the island was safe, they stepped forward to receive the leader of the new arrivals from Shrah. Only the face of the leader of the newly arrived Shrah forces was visible as he removed his headgear and waterproof night vision goggles.

Morazan looked at the unknown facial features of the leader of the newly arrived amphibian warriors.

The leader challenged, "Bahlam Jol, burned for the second time."

"A conquest of the Queen of Naranjo," Morazan responded. He then noticed the rank on the leader's uniform and was confused, as he didn't recognize who was wearing it, but he knew he had passed the challenge. The stars on the uniform that detailed the rank were unmistakable.

Morazan rendered a hand salute to his senior and spoke for his detachment. "Sir, I am Sergeant Morazan Ceibo, and as senior, I have command of this special forces detachment."

The arriving senior returned his salute. "I am Admiral Andrew Sauer, the rank equivalent of general. I have permission to come ashore as granted to me by our ajaws. I am here to relieve you of command. You, Sergeant, are hereby also relieved of your rank. I am commissioning you as an officer in the Shrah Special Forces Group. You are hereby promoted to the rank of lieutenant. The work you have done here has been outstanding, and our time is upon us. You will debrief me as soon as we retreat inland undercover and get to know each other, Lieutenant."

# CHAPTER 39: NECESSARY PLANNING

"I stand relieved, Admiral," stated Morazan with great satisfaction. The two forces looked at each other with awe and a renewed sense of purpose.

Morazan led Andy to the dugout, and the senior leaders from Shrah followed. The dugout led into a vast underground cave accessible via long, narrow tunnels. The cave was large enough to house all of the warriors present and those newly arrived.

The arrivals from Shrah greeted each other. Kabel, Noah, Buluc, and Obasi all congratulated Morazan on his field promotion. Andy took the opportunity to also promote Areni and Hope to the rank of lieutenant.

The leaders from the Choluteca detachment and those from Shrah proceeded into a separate chamber to meet privately while the warriors from both planets became acquainted with each other.

Andy requested the presence of Seth. It was only then that it hit Morazan and Areni that their ajaw-to-be was a member of their special forces group. They met him with exuberance and awe. Seth had come all the way from a medical coma to militarized, promoted, and trained to fight in a war in such a short time. They had only known him as a strong young man who would someday rule the planet, but seeing him ready to fight for them was wonderful.

Andy allowed them to enjoy their moment uninterrupted, and the seniors simply observed, satisfaction in their eyes. This was a special moment indeed. Andy reflected on the thought that the people of Shrah were all warriors and that the ajaw's son was no exception.

"With me are Colonel Buluc Hix, Colonel Kabel Luu, Colonel Noah Mandel, Captain Obasi Sabina, and Sergeant Seth Alom, along with templar knights and Shrah special forces sent here by our ajaw," Andy said. "We have little time to act, Lieutenants. By now, the empire is likely aware of this location and may have been watching you, waiting for the rest of the Shrah forces to arrive before erasing this whole island from existence, all of us included. Let's get started."

Andy explained to the group that they

would be leading teams in a deadly and very risky strike against the leadership in Tai-Anh. He didn't mince any words that the operation was one with little chance of success and would result in overwhelming casualties. Their time had indeed arrived.

Seven teams of fighters were now operating clandestinely on Tai-Anh, working their way to their objective. The teams were led by Kabel, Buluc, Noah, Obasi, Morazan, Areni, and Hope.

Seth was to operate as Andy's right hand in combat and primary apprentice in strategy and leadership. Seth would have the privilege of learning from an intergalactic veteran of war who would be running the entire operation.

The leadership meeting and distribution of team, squad, and leader assignments and promotions of war veterans to the rank of sergeant ended just before Kinich Ahau rose over the eastern horizon, where it could be seen from the eastern entrances to the massive cave. For the remainder of this operation, sleep would come at daylight and action at night.

All team leaders were provided with hologram projectors that could fit in the palm of their hands. The devices contained detailed maps of the City of Gandolim and specific route information for the teams. The leaders were to become familiar with the routes and bring their team members up to speed on the operation. All equipment was to be prepared and fully operational for combat. They would be departing for the mainland as soon as Kinich Ahau dipped below the horizon on the following day.

That night inside the cave, Andy walked about. It was surreal to him to be in another galaxy, commanding forces he had not served for in battle before. He could see the warrior determination in these troops. These folks were born to fight. He could see it in their faces and their muscular builds. And he was one of them.

The cavern was dimly lit by red light sources brought in from Lyndon on an earlier delivery. Red light traveled shorter distances. They made sure to seal off all entrances and exits for the night and day to follow. As Andy walked around, all eyes were trained on him, watching his every move. All were awed by this alien from a distant galaxy, who had been battle-hardened after years of service and war. They noticed the way he stood with the confidence of someone born a warrior, and they submitted to allow him to lead them into the teeth of a mission that would most likely end their lives.

As Andy stood with his back to the troops in the cave, looking down at the ground with his thoughts a million miles away, one of the troops stood up and silently walked toward him. The warrior thought twice about approaching the admiral and stopped, turning around and walking away from him, regretting having approached him in the first place.

Andy spoke without turning to look. "I'm sorry about Yoro, Lieutenant. You will have a chance to avenge him soon. I will make certain that we do."

Hope attempted to thank him, but her voice failed her. She simply walked away. She knew her moment was coming, and she was more than ready to act.

Andy continued walking around the cave. In every chamber he entered, each occupied by a different team, he earned an immediate response of attention. It struck Andy that, just like on Earth, warriors here stood on their feet as a demonstration of respect to authority. Some behaviors cut through the entire universe. Other warriors practiced Ch'o'Jonik, and still others sat in quiet spaces in Atsalat meditative trances.

Andy stepped outside the cave to visit the forces standing watch in the exterior.

As he exited the cavern, Seth came up to him. "May I join you, sir?"

"Absolutely, Sergeant. I will be visiting our watch standers in the open night air," responded Andy.

Andy and Seth stepped out, making sure all light remained sealed tightly. They walked up to the location where they knew the sentries were positioned outside under the moonlight. Andy tapped on the communications device on the lapel of his uniform and informed the sentries of their approach. The sentries replied with their confirmation of transmission receipt.

Andy could feel barren sand beneath his boots. He could smell the sweet salty air of the Panthalassan Ocean and hear crashing waves on the shore. It reminded him of Earth, and he suddenly felt a tug of longing nostalgia at his heart.

As if on cue, Seth asked, "Does the smell of the ocean remind you of Earth, Admiral?"

"It does. There's nothing quite like the smell of the ocean. How about you, son? Do you miss Janina?"

Seth blushed and took note of the manner in which Andy addressed him. It struck Andy that Seth hadn't been on a planet with an ocean until now. It also struck him how young Seth was and the great danger he was heading into.

Seth looked into Andy's eyes. "What makes you think I miss her?"

"I was once your age. I remember how wonderful falling for someone can be. It devours you in a way you never forget."

"Are you saying Janina is devouring me?"

Andy laughed. "Not physically . . . yet. But emotionally. Did looking out into the ocean make you think of her?"

Seth smiled. "I guess so. Do I make it obvious that I'm attracted to her?"

"Not so obvious, but it's there to be seen."

Seth changed the subject. "Did the ocean make you think of anyone back on your Earth?"

His Earth. For a moment, Andy thought about how space travel could be a harsh mistress. Then he answered, "Just about every night. I'm haunted by thoughts of my ex-wife."

"Ex? Do you mean people stop loving each other on your planet?"

Andy pondered the deep meaning of Seth's question. "I don't know that people stop loving one another. It's just complicated."

"Complicated? I guess it must be to stop being with someone you love. Have you ever met someone you could love as much as you love your . . . uh . . . ex-wife?"

"You ask good questions for such a young man, Seth. I guess I could love again. I had history with her, and it took a long time to build that history together. That history strengthened our love. At least, it did for me."

"But not strong enough to keep you together."

Andy thought about it. "I guess you're right."

"Did you have children?" asked Seth.

"She was pregnant once, but the child's spirit returned home to the Eleventh Dimension before witnessing the light of birth," responded Andy.

"Do you visit with your child during Atsalat?"

"I do not. The Great Creator has her hidden for reasons that are mysteries to me. I see my parents and many warriors lost in Earth's wars routinely."

The two men stood silently for a while, looking out into the ocean. Then Seth broke the silence. "Did you think of Colonel Luu when you looked out into the ocean?"

Andy broke out into a startled laugh, then fell silent for another minute before he answered. "Is it that obvious?"

"I guess we're in the same situation, except you do make it obvious," Seth replied.

Both men laughed wholeheartedly.

Their moment was interrupted by the arrival of Kabel, who walked up from the cave behind them. She saluted the admiral, and he returned her salute.

Seth knew that he assumed the rank of the admiral when he accompanied a senior officer and returned Kabel's salute. "Good evening, Colonel," he said.

"Good evening, Sergeant," returned Kabel.

Then Seth stated, "I must return to continue preparations with my troops. Have you heard? We are going to war tomorrow. May I be excused, Admiral?" He instinctively felt he should leave them alone for a few moments.

"Absolutely, Sergeant," said Andy. "I'll be in shortly."

Kabel watched Seth walk away. "Did I interrupt an important conversation, Admiral?"

"It was a good conversation, and your arrival kept it good, Colonel."

Kabel smiled and looked out at the ocean.

A few seconds later, Andy spoke. "Do you think about anyone when you look out into the ocean, Colonel?"

Kabel blushed for the first time in a long while.

# CHAPTER 40: GRASS ROOTS ORIGIN

Kinich Ahau had broken over the eastern sky. Surprise was the Shrah soldiers' greatest weapon. The intelligence reports from Buluc were mixed between good and bad news.

"Admiral, we have received reports from our spies in Gandolim. They have communicated with us at great risk to their lives. By this point, everyone is aware of the ruthless torture and execution of Yoro Copan. Thousands have been imprisoned for suspicious behavior. Anyone suspected of empathizing with the Shrah Philosophy is being arrested on the spot. The empire is quickly constructing new penitentiaries, which we believe are akin to concentration camps."

"Somehow, we will honor them for the great risk they are taking and for the value of their information," assured Andy.

"It appears there is a leader emerging as a grassroots opposition to the Tai-Anh Empire. The leader is believed to be someone formerly associated with Hamilton Nile. We don't have confirmation of their identity, nor do we have a way to locate this leader, but our spies are working diligently to make contact. The fear is that they are presently imprisoned like so many others and unable to assist."

At Buluc's pause, Andy ordered, "Sergeant Alom, let Lieutenant Zenobia know her presence is requested outside my chamber and that I will see her as soon as I'm ready." Then he turned back to Buluc. "Continue."

"The bad news is that Choluteca has been leveled by the empire."

"It is bad news, Colonel. My assumption is that the Noumeroi are trained enough to know to use just enough explosives to destabilize any inhabitants on the island but not enough to destroy all evidence. It was just a matter of time before they arrived there after Quintus Salvius's betrayal. We must assume that the empire is aware that we are somewhere on their planet and that they are most likely hunting us aggressively. Thanks to the Great Creator, we evacuated our forces before they arrived with a superior number of troops, leaving us nowhere to run."

Buluc nodded his head, thinking how astute the admiral was, his respect for the experience of the hardened veteran of war deepening.

Andy opened his communication link and ordered Kabel and Noah to join Buluc in the meeting with Hope. Through Hope and her selection of seven of the most fervent believers, he put a plan in place that pulled knowledge from an event that had transpired on Earth; he hoped for a similar result today. Together, the team planned the entire action in excruciating detail.

As the Shrah forces made their way to the mainland, Danli arrived back on Shrah after delivering the warriors to the neighboring planet. He could see the golden hue of the small, beautiful planet he called home, suspended in the stark darkness of space. It was a glorious sight after being in the open vacuum with what he assumed to be broken communications equipment.

The planet was as beautiful as ever, lit on one side by the intense light of Kinich Ahau. Danli could enter the atmosphere of home at a faster rate since the glow of the ship's heat shields was of no concern, but he maintained radio silence as a precaution. This was not a secret mission to what was now an enemy planet but rather a return to the safety of home. Or so he thought.

Danli noticed that something was different about the color of the planet's surface as his bodyweight began to take shape with the force of Shrah's gravitational pull. Just off enough for his heart to begin pounding and for his stomach to begin tightening with sickening dread.

He attempted to contact Temple Alom when he was still several miles away. No response. No honing signal. Nothing. Somehow, the planet's surface seemed darker than usual. Perhaps it was an optical illusion created by the time he had spent in darkness in outer space, but he didn't think so. He had performed these flights many times before, and it looked different this time around. As an added precautionary measure, Danli decided to approach Nacaome City in ultra-silent mode from the outskirts of the desert far beyond the horizon.

The planet was indeed darker. The yellow ground surrounding Nacaome City had been replaced with the drab gray that came with the burning of things that had once lived and breathed. There was death everywhere. His heart began to pound louder as he took in the horrific scene of mass devastation.

Shrah as he knew it was no more. Sections of the Great Pyramid were gone and burned. As he approached Nacaome City, he noticed there were sections with a glassy look to some of the land. Heat had converted sand into glass. *The heat must have been tremendous*, Danli thought.

He landed in the city square and stepped out, armed with his rifle, pistol, and knife. He could smell the aftermath of the fiery death that had hit the city and its inhabitants. There were ashes and burned spots all over the city. Danli wondered if these were what remained of the beautiful people of Shrah. He searched for his family, the ajaws, Isaiah, and for anyone at all. The intensity of heat had surely consumed flesh and bone alike. He tried as much as possible not to step on the ashes out of respect.

Danli arrived at Temple Alom and regarded it with horror. He entered the temple and began to zigzag his way through it. The temple was devoid of windows and color. The windowless walls were the drab gray he had noticed in the desert. He began to call out his ajaw's name in shouts of love, pain, and desperation.

He entered the main living quarters of the temple through a missing outdoor window. He walked the hallowed halls of his people's temple. In a strange way, Danli was still a warrior, always ready. He looked down at his peridot ring and made sure he had his knife, rifle, and pistol at the ready, but there was nobody to fight. There was only the stench of burned matter.

He decided to leave the temple and city to gather his thoughts. As a warrior, Danli knew he should proceed to an elevated position where he could survive alone. He headed for the Tela Mountain Range. His spacecraft was able to hover and land, and he knew there was flat land high above the desert plains near the aquifer, where he would also have water at his disposal. It was the best place for him to go and have a chance of surviving alone on the desert planet.

Danli headed for high ground, allowing himself a moment for emotional catharsis. His home and all of his loved ones had been extinguished in a moment, and he was devastated. He would sleep his final night on Shrah, then head back to Tai-Anh and join the group of hundreds of Shrah fighters on a suicide mission against the emperor's Third Realm and the Noumeroi. Shrah warriors weren't hunted without a fight. They never had been and never would be, even after thousands had been murdered. Danli would mourn later.

Danli climbed to 8,000 feet and looked for any signs of life on the way to his destination. He had hoped he would at least find one living being in the mountains away from the city. He was disappointed. He found the entrance to the aquifer and the flat land he needed. He gently brought the craft down for landing with trembling hands.

Danli stepped out of the craft and felt the first coolness of the night. He donned warmer clothing for the chilly evening on the desert mountain. Then he began preparations for the evening. That night, he slept poorly, thinking about the suffering of his people and how his home was now a lifeless, barren place. Although he was fatigued beyond comprehension, he woke up and ate some of the provisions from the spacecraft's galley. He thought he had enough to make it back to Tai-Anh since the planets were close to one another.

Danli felt the terrible loneliness of being the only living being on a lifeless planet. He dropped to his knees, hung his head, and sobbed as anger ran through his veins. Overwhelmed with emotion and exhaustion, he lay on the ground and fell asleep in that very spot.

Hours later, Danli awoke and fetched the portable water tanks from his craft, taking them to the aquifer for refilling. He looked at the beautiful blue of the Blue Hole and stared down into the water at an image that became clearer as it came closer to his face. It was the eyeless face of a salamander named Ruby. He stood up, startled, and ran into someone standing behind him. He turned to engage the being in Ch'o'Jonik, and he couldn't believe his eyes.

The ajaw stood there with a smile. The men embraced.

Danli wasn't sure if he was dreaming, but the sight of his leader overwhelmed him with joy. "Ajaw! How could this be? I must be in the Eleventh Dimension!"

"You are not, Danli. This is me in physical form. Our people are safe, thanks to the Great Creator and Eurycea. Our brethren here in the massive aquifer system saved us from extinction. They gave us shelter and protection. We are deeply indebted to them. It's so good to see you. Did the troops make it to Tai-Anh safely?"

"Yes, sire!"

Eurycea and the descendants of the Mayan civilization had survived yet another attempt to erase them from existence and relegate them to historical tales. Food would be an issue, but they had planned as best as they could, and they would survive. Survival meant they would have the opportunity to fight, and fight they would.

Once Danli was convinced that he wasn't dreaming, he asked his ajaw, "Sire, our forces have been deployed and are already operating on Tai-Anh. Request permission to return and fight?"

"Permission granted, Captain. But you are not going alone," said the ajaw with a smile on his face.

# CHAPTER 41: ELEMENTS OF SURPRISE

After traveling to the Tai-Anh mainland on stealth vessels provided by the Lyndon Parliament, the Shrah forces hid in predetermined places on their advancing track during the day and advanced under the cover of darkness at night. It would be a long trek.

The teams had one of the most significant advantages combatants could have: the element of surprise. Exelcior was convinced he had annihilated all living beings on Shrah. He was not aware that Temple Alom had forged a most unlikely alliance with the salamanders living deep within the planet's aquifers. Unfortunately, Exelcior had extinguished the lives of uncountable animals on the planet's surface. This fact greatly saddened the ajaw and his people. The people of Shrah felt a spiritual connection to their animal brethren, and they mourned the senseless deaths of so many. It only added fuel to the fire of resolution for the ajaws and Isaiah.

Although the Shrah forces had the element of surprise in their favor, they were greatly outnumbered. Their fight was a sort of suicide proposition. It would be a low-intensity, highly clandestine operation that needed swiftness of violence and the intercession of the Great Creator. They understood they would most likely not leave the planet alive but hoped to begin the process of ridding the universe of Exelcior's evil. They simply could not stand by any longer. An even more certain suicide would have been not to fight.

The point of entry for the Shrah forces would be along the Bructeri River, which flowed from northwest to southeast, cutting across the City of Gandolim and through Lyndon. Moving silently and undetected was key. It was an exercise in patience. The teams' movements had to be slow and imperceptible. Anything that would tip off imperial forces would have deadly consequences. The teams moved at night and benefited from the guidance of Hope, Janina, and the believers who were natives and knew Gandolim well. All the planning for the mission was done on the stealth spacecraft flown by Danli from Shrah. The maps of the complex drainage systems below ground, with location details, were memorized by all team members. The team and squad leaders had navigation equipment, but the people of Shrah never depended on systems outside their bodies. They relied on their own senses, intelligence, and lethal Ch'o'Jonik training far more than advanced technology.

There was a part of Michael that felt the weight of his decision to send his people into combat. Another part felt the weight of risking the life of his son. Deep down inside, he knew the choice had been made for him the day his son had fought the four attackers in the Shrah desert.

Regardless, the teams moved in slowly and in a predatory procession in an attempt to kill before being killed. The rain kept driving down on the metal planet. The moisture soaked into the skin of the aliens from Shrah. Their laser pulse rifles were a safety switch away from firing. The defrosting function kept the holographic sites atop their rifles clear and ready to acquire targets. Their best weapon was their clandestine status.

Andy enjoyed the feeling of salty humidity that came with operations near an ocean. He reminisced about his home planet and all the miles that led to it.

As the Shrah special forces moved closer to Gandolim, they began to see the glow of the city's lights reflecting in the clouds high above. The combatants from Shrah were, for the first time, mesmerized. The time for bloodshed was drawing near. They would rest during daylight and advance to their first attack the following night. The teams arrived at their predetermined spots and settled in, out of sight, well ahead of Kinich Ahau's rise over the horizon.

It was imperative that the teams not arrive at their spots ahead of time or after so that they wouldn't compromise the mission. It was a great asset that Shrah engineers had dedicated many resources and a great deal of research to the development of stealth technology. They had learned of its importance during the Mine War.

Although it was daylight on Tai-Anh, the teams from Shrah saw no light of day in the underground drainage system, a complex structure built to deal with the constant rain on the planet.

Andy joined Hope's team for entry into the city. The teams were then to break up and proceed to their respective targets.

As the binary stars fell past the horizon, Andy stepped out and confirmed that the night was dark enough for a further advance to their destination. Hope was allowed to keep charge of her team. Andy was impressed with her leadership style and decision-making skills.

Hope announced to her team, "On this team, the intent is to go into harm's way and fight. I intend to do so, and I expect all of you to do the same. If you have any reservations about risking your life and taking those of many, this is the time to let me know so we can figure out how to keep you from battle."

All responded that they understood the requirement.

"Great," said Hope. "My commands are only overridden by Admiral Sauer, who commands the entire theater."

The advance continued but in separate groups. The teams were to arrive just in time to attack simultaneously. Andy explained that their forces would arrive in time-on-top fashion.

Seven soldiers, selected carefully, had gone ahead of the teams to the respective destination locations and were already beginning to relay back critical information on the status of the targets for attack via secure link.

Hope didn't quite know how to feel about having Andy pick her team for advance. She wondered if his selection stemmed from his lack of confidence in her leadership ability or if it was the strongest statement possible of confidence in her abilities.

Hope observed the way Andy carried himself. She noticed the strength of his posture and the self-assured strut only found in the most confident of warriors. She could only imagine the violence his eyes had seen millions of miles away. Hope couldn't help but wonder if Yoro would have carried himself the same way if he'd had the chance to grow older. Regardless, she was happy to have such a strong and experienced combatant with her.

Andy observed Hope's battle-hardened poise and how a life of combat had shaped her into a walking lethal weapon. She reminded him of some of Earth's greatest fighters. At the next rest stop, he had the opportunity to speak to her in private while Seth checked the readiness of the team's equipment and spirits. "This task would have been much more difficult if it were not for your in-depth knowledge of the underground tunnels of this city."

The statement filled Hope with great pride that was obvious in her facial expression.

"It's my understanding that you worked in public works and infrastructure projects for the empire after the Mine War," said Andy.

"Yes, Admiral, that is correct," Hope told him. "The honor is mine to serve the people of Shrah and fight the empire for as long as I have breath."

"Very well, Lieutenant. You know the demands of combat on the psyche, so I won't lecture you about it."

After a brief pause, Hope said, "Admiral, I will do everything in my power to protect our ajaw-to-be. I worry that I will fail to protect him when shooting common—"

"Don't you worry about Seth," Andy interrupted. “He is fully qualified to handle himself. Seth has been a warrior for centuries. He was born for this. Stay focused on all your sergeants equally, and they will take care of their assigned members.”

“Understood. Do entire families fight back on Earth, Admiral, or is that reserved for the young and able only?’

“That’s a great question. The answer depends on who you are fighting and whether or not you are being invaded,” Andy replied. “The folks who are invaded must fight, submit, or run to live. Earth has had three great wars. During the second, a tough group of Earthlings called Russians fought, and millions of their citizens died. The invaders miscalculated just how tough they were and the resolve of every single Russian citizen. The Russians won that war with the help of other groups that allied with them. The group I belonged to were called Americans. They were allies of the Russians for that war. For that specific war, the American Navy allowed five brothers to serve on the same surface ship in an ocean called the Pacific. Their last name was Sullivan. The ship was sunk by the enemy, and all five brothers onboard perished together. It was the last time the American Navy allowed family members to serve aboard the same ship during war.”

Hope mentally sent light into the energy superhighway to travel to the Sullivan brothers and their family, whatever dimension they might be in.

Seth approached. “Admiral, Lieutenant, it’s time to continue advancing.”

# CHAPTER 42: ANATOMICAL SIMILARITIES

It had been some time since I had shed blood, but making my enemy bleed was my specialty. This whole experience was so surreal. There were some important similarities between my home planet in the Milky Way and my brave new world in the Andromeda galaxy. We all looked the same. There was no doubt we had been created in the image of one creator. The little green man image built into our psyche as a collective pop-culture idea back on Earth was simply that, an image built into humanity, filling in imaginary details in the absence of concrete experience with alien life. There were good and bad, fear and courage, integrity and betrayal, life and death, passion, lust, love, and hate in each galaxy.

Anatomically, we appeared to be exact replicas of one another. I thanked the Great Creator that Kabel Luu was such a wonderful specimen. It was also a good thing that I knew the physical anatomy of my enemies. I had spent a lifetime exploiting the human body's fragility and vulnerability to end enemy lives decisively and swiftly. Unfortunately for me, they'd done the same. Arteries, spines, hearts, viscera, lungs, brains. They were all in the same location and functioned identically. That would come in handy very soon.

There were also key differences between us. We were two worlds apart. Earth had a longer and deeper history of violence than Tai-Anh. People on Earth were brutal with each other. In thinking through the customs and behaviors of the people of Tai-Anh, I could see a strong connection with the Ancient Roman Empire.

The differences resulted in disadvantage for the Tai-Anh Empire. They had not faced an attack in their own backyard before. There was a certain sharpness that came with either defending your homeland or attacking an enemy's to prevent an attack on yours. The City of Gandolim hadn't been attacked since the Mine War, and even then, the threat to the homeland had been minimal. I assumed they were prepared to defend themselves.

What I wasn't sure about was whether or not they believed the people of Shrah to have been wiped out by their attack, although I assumed they had already sent in reconnaissance missions to determine that there were no Shrah native remains to be found anywhere on the surface of the planet. Better safe than sorry. If any of Shrah's warrior citizens had survived the attack, what were the odds that any of them would be able to attack the empire at home? We would soon find out. When Kinich Ahau set next, we would move in for our final approach on Gandolim.

As night fell, Hope became our expedition leader. She was familiar with the geography of her homeland, especially the underground tunnel system of the city. There was an eerie and discomforting quiet about the city above. There were no sounds of machinery or animals. There were no sounds of vehicles on the ground or in the air. Nothing. Hope confirmed that the quietness was abnormal.

As we began to stealthily enter the city's outer perimeter, a smell I would never forget reached me: that of burned flesh. The overwhelming realization came over me that Exelcior had unleashed his brutality on the people of Lyndon for their support of the Shrah Philosophy. Vehicles, buildings, and structures were still smoldering in the city. I made a move to see with my own eyes the conditions on the streets above. It was an eerie sight. The power was shut off to the city, and the only light present in the dark night was the ember glow left behind by mass destruction. It was a sight I had seen before during

Earth's Third World War. What I also noticed was that Kinich Ahau wasn't far from rising in the east. We'd have to stop advancing soon and begin staging for attack when the binary stars set.

I could feel adrenaline pumping through my body, sharpening my senses as combat drew close. Everything was set up for the seven teams by seven advanced scouts. That evening, the seven teams would attack seven different buildings within the same complex. The plan was to attack simultaneously to increase confusion and optimize surprise in the darkness of night. We were greatly outnumbered but well equipped with the necessary night vision aids to move swiftly through the complex. We were to attack as many as possible and retreat quickly into the underground tunnels of the city before the empire could organize a retaliation.

The complex was adjacent to the Bructeri River, and the cold, damp air made for an uncomfortable attempt at resting before the offensive operation where we would fight for our lives. The river was shallow at the point of entry, no deeper than chest high. This allowed for good cover, especially in dark water. The complex would have little moonlight with the heavy cloud cover.

The riverine position would also provide excellent observation perspectives just prior to entering the complex. Footpaths from rivers were usually perpendicular to the water and provided seven separate entry trails from the river, heading toward the perimeter wall. That was the basis for our seven combat and scouting teams.

In the darkness underneath the city, we warriors entered Atsalat trances and prepared for the fact that it just might be our last day of physical life. The Great Creator held the fate of many in mystery. It was an act of mercy to keep certain fates secret.

I entered Atsalat and flew past the windswept green pastures on my way to Crystal City. I arrived at the crystal castle, bathed in white light. There, I saw my mom and dad waiting for me. They looked so wonderful. Dad was as strapping as he had been earlier in his life, with a strong-set jaw and powerful lines on his face. Mom was beautiful as usual, with those kind eyes full of the love that I missed so much. We embraced for a good while. It was a blessing to be able to visit them in any dimension, especially when I was about to enter a battle for my life. It reassured me that I was never alone anywhere in the universe.

Loving energy didn't adhere to the laws of physics. It transcended all space, time, and dimensions. Love didn't play by scientific formulas. The power of that fact filled me to a spiritual maximum. When it was time to return to the present dimension on Tai-Anh, my father handed me a small gift, which he called hope.

When I returned to the present dimension,

I noticed Seth sitting beside me, already returned from his own Atsalat meditation. In the darkness underground, I checked his biometric readings, displayed on the inside of my helmet, and it surprised me that his heart rate matched that of an athlete at rest. I was convinced this young warrior's heart pumped ice water. Nothing seemed to unsettle him, not even his possible death in a few hours.

I checked my own biometrics and found it ironic that my heart rate was the same. It was a nice feature to be able to see the biometrics of my entire team displayed on the inside of my face shield. It would have been nicer to see the biometrics of my enemies. I found myself feeling the irony that I was about to fight on another planet. It seemed that I simply had to fight, no matter where in the universe I found myself.

For the first time, however, I was going to use an obsidian knife as my weapon. The sharpness of its triangular edge was lethal, especially on exposed necks, arteries, and eyes. I was ready, and judging by the biometric readings of my team, so were the other fighters from Shrah and Lyndon.

# CHAPTER 43: FROM THE GROUND UP

A little before Kinich Ahau set, Andy checked in with his team leaders using short-range encrypted secure link transmission to establish confirmation of their readiness for battle. Teams one (Noah), two (Buluc), three (Kabel), four (Obasi), five (Morazan), six (Areni), and seven (Hope) were set and ready. Sufficient darkness had fallen to commence the attack. It was time.

The teams would advance out of the underground drainage tunnels at the point where rainwater drained into the Bructeri River. They would then approach the target facility in low-profile fashion. Each team would assault the part of the installation that corresponded to them. Andy would float to where he was needed to lead the expedition. Seth was to follow his every step.

Andy ordered the teams to proceed into the

Bructeri River. The teams exited the tunnels from seven separate drain exits. They entered the river, minimizing splash, visual profile, and sound. The tide was low, as was to be expected. They proceeded to tread into the river, upstream of where they would exit back onto land for the final approach to the complex. The river would effectively hide the hundreds of incoming warriors. The cold river water would mask their infrared heat signatures. They also had the element of surprise because they were not attacking a military institution.

The seven advanced scouts who had been sent ahead to provide intelligence information on the seven targets had proceeded to their second objective in Lyndon and were making contact with Broteas Ovidius. Intelligence reports provided information that Ovidius was no longer in prison. He had been released for fear that his continued imprisonment would incite rebellion among the people. The teams were to reconnect with him to arrange military support for the operation.

It began to rain harder. The hundreds of armed fighters stopped inside the Bructeri, awaiting the final order to proceed. Andy took all spotter reports provided and gave the order to proceed out of the water. When all team members were out of the water, within proper distance and ready, Andy gave the order for the explosives to be placed on the outside walls.

There were seven simultaneous blasts that created seven separate points of entry, through which Shrah's finest gained quick entry and spread out. They poured in and opened fire on all enemy combatants at the corrections facility. The prison held over 20,000 prisoners, many of whom were wrongfully imprisoned believers. They had been treated with brutality for suspicion of practicing or sympathizing with the philosophy. Imprisoning them had been a mistake. Imprisoning them together had been a bigger one. Not realizing that many were trained war veterans had been the biggest of all. Erecting the facility along the Bructeri River had also been a lapse of reason.

The seven targets were large cell blocks. There were approximately 3,000 prisoners in each building. Each contained a watchtower with laser pulse guns to control the prison population. All seven gun towers were commanded by one main tower located in the center of the complex. The team leaders were personally responsible for taking control of the towers. Andy, with Seth at his side, would take control of the main tower.

The shooting at the central penitentiary commenced almost immediately after the breaching. The first shot of Operation Freedom was taken by Buluc. The laser pulse removed the entire left side of the guard's head before he was able to level it for a clean return shot. The guard dropped on the spot. His weapon was quickly recovered by special forces.

As the firefight continued, the training of and surprise by the Shrah forces quickly overwhelmed the empire's prison guards. Within a few minutes of the invasion, Areni's team came under heavy fire. The roving guards had been responding to unrest in that particular building before the breach, and as a result, they were present there and heavily armed. Areni was moving forward to overtake the tower for the building when she was engaged from multiple directions with enemy fire. She knew some of her team members had been hit; injury and death reports were already coming through on her communications channel.

Then Areni felt the extreme pressure of a shot to the leg, and she knew loss of mobility would take her out of the fight. She looked down at the condition of her right leg and realized it was broken at the femur. Her leg was dangling, and she bled profusely. She could smell her own blood as it spilled onto the ground. She was lucky the shot had missed her femoral artery. She controlled her breathing and communicated with the admiral, reporting her condition and requesting support.

The call was heard on all leaders' circuits. Hope, who was closest to Andy, looked to him for guidance and orders, but all she saw was a glimpse of his back. He was already on his way to join team six in the fight. She saw the flash of Seth closely following behind him.

As Andy proceeded to join team six, Hope took command of the push to control the main tower.

Before the admiral arrived to join her team, Areni was struck on the same leg's hip. She knew she would lose consciousness soon. The final shot struck her neck, and she bled out on the spot. Her spirit entered the tunnel of light connected to the Eleventh Dimension.

Andy arrived and announced the passing of Areni via his communication device. Then he took command of the team left behind. Andy and Seth leveled their rifles and proceeded. They made their way to the head of the firefight, killing many armed guards.

The entire team was amazed at the precision and exactitude in the admiral's killing of the enemy. He was an efficient and experienced killer, and they thanked the Great Creator for having him to lead them into battle.

Andy was unfazed by deadly laser pulses passing just inches from his face. He didn't have time to be distracted from taking lives. This wasn't his first firefight; he was a war veteran in two galaxies. The Milky Way already knew his excellence in war. The Andromeda had no idea of the totality of what they were about to witness.

Andy and Seth took control of the tower and the secondary forces of each team and began breaking down the walls of the installation to allow the prisoners to escape. The prisoners had begun making noises like caged animals. They figured very quickly that this was the promise of action being delivered to the empire by Michael Alom from Shrah. Most of the prisoners were young able-bodied adults who were trained military veterans from the Mine War. They were a combination of citizens from Lyndon and Gandolim who had been robbed of their freedom by an empire that planned to exterminate them. Within the prison walls, their belief in the Shrah Philosophy had only strengthened. In the prison system, they'd found a leader. Practice of the Shrah Philosophy was punishable by the removal of the right hand. There was a large pit full of the right hands of believers.

As the walls came down, the prisoners were informed that they were not the target of the attacks. The prisoners were relieved greatly by that. They were unarmed and enemies of the empire. Many of them had not been believers to begin with, but they'd quickly converted while incarcerated. The empire had greatly accelerated the spread of the Shrah Philosophy, and the new believers were now being set free to join the fight. It was time to find their in-house leader.

The prisoners emerged with their hands in

the air and were greeted with orders to remain in their cells until the guards were neutralized. The Shrah combatants noticed in horror how many of them were missing their right hands. Thousands of freed prisoners heeded the order, while others simply escaped into the night. Many, male and female, began to shout a name. With the chaos of laser fire and dying screams, it was difficult to distinguish what the prisoners were saying.

Kabel was in charge of freeing the female prisoners from buildings three, four, and six, helped by Obasi and Andy. The empire had no qualms about jailing women who were believers in the Shrah Philosophy. As more and more prisoners left their cells, they were told to follow the Shrah team members underground.

One of the newly freed females from building three spoke to Kabel. She was a young woman with strong features and the appearance of a war veteran. "We will follow you! You need to find our leader. He will be killed by the imperial forces if you don't save him quickly!"

Kabel responded, "Who is your leader, and where do we locate him?"

"His name is Cedano Jole, and he is in building seven. You must hurry!" shouted the woman.

It struck Kabel that Cedano Jole was the believer who had not made it back to the departure point for training on Shrah. He must have been arrested before he could. It also occurred to Kabel just how much the prisoner cared for her leader within the prison. Kabel realized the importance of connecting with him immediately.

While Kabel spoke to the prisoner, Hope stopped herself just a trigger squeeze away from taking yet another life. It was her long-lost friend Cedano Jole. He wore a great smile on his face. They embraced. “It’s so good to see you alive, Cedano!” Hope said.

“You came just in time, Hope! How many fighters are with you? What’s the plan?”

“We’re evacuating immediately using the underground tunnels. We don’t have much time. We’ve connected with Ovidius, and he has confirmed that Lyndon will be assisting. Our commander is an alien. I’ll explain later.”

Cedano stood there for a second, wondering what Hope meant with her comment about the alien commander, but he accepted that it wasn’t the time or place to ask for clarification. Hope knew she had to connect Cedano with Andy. Kabel and Hope contacted the admiral simultaneously, telling him of Cedano’s importance in leading the prisoners.

The admiral promised to meet with Cedano after they retreated into the underground tunnels.

The killing was rampant inside the prison complex. The Shrah warriors were beginning to slip on the large amounts of enemy blood spilled on the floors. The element of surprise and their arms, training, and leadership planning created a great advantage for the Shrah special forces. The members of team seven were able to see how effectively the admiral cleared a room as he performed with the experience of an urban close-quarters combat veteran. He swept his rifle and killed one enemy after another. The enemy combatants had never stood a chance against him.

Team members reported the effective elimination of the enemy combatant threat. It was time to evacuate back into the drainage system and advance to their next targets. Andy requested status updates. The number of confirmed Shrah combatants killed in the action was nineteen. This number included one officer, Areni Dayami. They'd killed forty imperial combatants for every Shrah operative. There were thirty-one more injured to different degrees. Andy had made it clear that no Shrah combatants would be left behind in the field of battle. His soldiers were never to abandon the bodies of their fallen for the enemy to recover. They would take with them into the tunnels any remains belonging to their own. This they did.

# CHAPTER 44: A PUSH FROM BEHIND

Once underground, I requested further reports from the team leaders as we advanced to our second respective targets. It felt great for me to help my people in the Andromeda galaxy. I was starting to miss Earth more and more. However, the time to miss Earth was not in the middle of a fight to the death. I had noticed that many of the prisoners were emaciated. The empire had not spent too many resources on the believers. They had planned a mass execution. We had arrived just in time.

The prisoners had been starved by the empire and kept in roach-infested cells. The alien roaches were a sort of cross between a spider and a roach, with fangs to inject venom and spinnerets to weave silk or trichobothria. They were a dark red color and could grow larger than those on Earth, up to about the size of a rat. They had eight eyes and flew poorly. They were carriers of disease, just like those on Earth. Their only good attribute was that they were high in protein if there was no other source of food. Chewing through the eight eyes would be rough, I had to admit.

We had to move fast. We advanced through running rainwater as we got closer to our inner-city destination. I remained in command of team six after the loss of Areni. She'd seemed extremely sharp, and the team leaders seemed to miss her already. Unfortunately, she would most likely not be the only officer lost in the war. The previous war between Tai-Anh and Lyndon had made for many veterans. Many of these prisoners had fought for and against the empire on Magna Hermopolis. Their experience using weapons and combat tactics was useful, but the war on the moon had not been a close-quarters combat situation in an urban setting like this was. Magna Hermopolis was a mountainous moon, and the war had been similar to a war on a sierra or desert mountain range, with large caliber weapons firing from long distances. This war we were now fighting was my kind of war, a kind the special forces under my leadership would have to learn on the fly as they killed or were killed.

The freed prisoners from each building within the complex were to stay with their respective teams and follow the orders of the team leaders. Anyone challenging the team leaders was to be shot on the spot. There was no time for insubordination. In fact, there wasn't time for anything. The team members from Shrah all had night vision goggles, which made moving in the drainage tunnels possible despite the extreme darkness underground. The prisoners were to stay close behind. Everyone would have to move through the tunnels with approximately thirty prisoners between each team member. The distances to the next spots were much closer, so the travel time was shorter. Our movements would be more methodical. At a specific predetermined spot, the forces of Lyndon would meet with our forces and would provide much-needed food, weapons, and equipment for the former prisoners. Our force was now thousands strong.

Our next targets would be the seven largest weapons depots. The mission was to take small arms and portable explosive weapons for our use, to destroy the non-portable weapons, and to kill as many enemies as possible. Our scouts had confirmed that they'd made contact with Lyndon's leaders, who knew where to meet us and what was required. Only five of the scouts arrived in Lyndon to deliver our plans. Two others were either dead or arrested. The forces from Lyndon absolutely had to be at the right place at the right time with the right equipment.

At our next stop, I would have to locate Cedano Jole, as it seemed he had been instrumental in uniting the prisoners and propagating the Shrah Philosophy within the prison compound. I understood he'd been a believer with Hamilton Nile, who'd been jailed when the Shrah special forces had first arrived in Lyndon. Cedano had influenced many with his teachings of the Shrah Philosophy, Ch'o'Jonik, and Atsalat.

Killing empire guards was satisfying in a dysfunctional way. The metallic smell of spilled blood that permeated the air took me back to memories of war on Earth. I hated having flashbacks to memories I didn't want to remember. The warriors from Shrah were brave and capable. War was the same in both galaxies. The brutality of it did not diminish with the vast distance. It seemed to be the nature of those created in the image of the Great Creator.

The tunnels ahead had running water in them. This told me that it was raining steadily enough topside for the rainwater to flow into the tunnels below. We had to press on quickly. There were thousands of us, and there was no time to rest. Stopping meant dying, so we kept moving. I began to think to myself how ironic it would be if I was killed in a foreign galaxy after surviving so many battles on Earth. Unfortunately, that was how it went sometimes.

As I thought about the irony of war, we

advanced toward our next objective. Each team was taking a different route. By that point, I figured the imperial forces were aware that we had evacuated using their underground tunnels, and I assumed they would be mobilizing to rendezvous with us underground. That was why the dispersal of the forces along multiple routes was so important. The next battle would not be with their prison guards or city police force but with the battle-hardened Third Realm's Noumeroi. We were ready. We were not on the planet to talk about our differences.

Reinforcements from Lyndon were to join us before the attack. They would bring with them additional weaponry for the freed prisoners who were now with us. We had brought additional equipment with us, but it wasn't nearly enough to cover the needs of what we estimated to be 19,000 new fighters. The prisoners were given the choice to flee or to join us in the war. The vast majority chose to join us. Many were trained military personnel, but how many were trained versus untrained, we could only guess. Regardless, we would all fight to the death since death was certain without a fight.

What seemed strange to me was that the prisoners hadn't been executed and that the prison personnel seemed to have been completely surprised by our attack. But the element of surprise was no longer. I was convinced the empire had spread the news that Shrah and the believers had staged an attack on their sovereign land to free the "dangerous prisoners" they had tried to lock up to protect the people of Tai-Anh.

After attacking the weapons depots, our survivors were to advance on land toward Imperial Headquarters. For the time being, we were advancing in underground tunnels. It felt great to do what I did best. In a morbid way, it felt great to kill in combat again. It was as if that was what I'd been born to do. I may have been addicted to the rush of it. It wasn't the most opportune time to investigate the concept, but it did bother me. Soon, I would think more about it. Oh, the troubles of traveling to other galaxies to kill aggressive aliens.

As approached the weapons depots from underground, I received a ping on my secure communications link. It was an emergency message from Hope. It appeared that Cedano was with her, advancing with the rest of us. He had been provided communications equipment, and I needed to speak with him without losing time in our advance. The man named Cedano Jole could be our most powerful weapon yet.

# CHAPTER 45: ENEMIES TURNED FRIENDS

Andy was a stranger in yet another strange land, and he had taken the lives of many enemies. There was little time to waste as the soldiers advanced steadily toward their second targets. Unlike at the prison, they were not in the same compound, but they were relatively close to each other. They would have to divide and conquer.

They would meet separately at several large connecting underground atriums, where they would receive fighting equipment brought to them by Lyndon military forces. Andy was in command of team six, and he was waiting to see what the Lyndonite forces were all about. In the meantime, he would communicate with Cedano via two-way secure voice communications and learn as much as possible about the augmented forces advancing with them.

"Cedano Jole. Are you on the line?" Andy said.

"Yes, sir. I am," said Cedano.

"Cedano, it's my understanding that you are a Mine War veteran."

"Yes, sir. I am."

"Lieutenant Zenobia informs me that you killed two guards with your bare hands during your liberation. Impressive," noted Andy.

"That is true. The Ch'o'Jonik lessons with Lieutenant Zenobia came in handy, Admiral."

"I'm sure they did. I am certain Lieutenant Zenobia informed you that Hamilton survived the attack."

"She did!" Cedano exclaimed. "What a gift from the Great Creator!"

"Yes, it is," agreed Andy. "Tell me what information you feel I need to know most urgently. Time is short."

"Yes, sir. I was imprisoned the night Colonel Kabel Luu first arrived in Lyndon. I became aware that I was being followed, so I continued on a course far away from where the Shrah forces were until I allowed myself to be apprehended. I never talked. They amputated my right hand."

"I'm sorry. Please continue," stated Andy with great empathy.

"Thank you, Admiral. It's all right. I'm now

left-handed," replied Cedano with a mix of cynicism and optimism.

"What else do you think I should know?"

"Conditions in the prison camp were terrible. We slept on the cold, hard floors. Many died of starvation and disease. I'm convinced I was left alive because they felt I could be of use to them at some point. Many of us are weak and malnourished. We will fight anyway, but you should know our physical limitations."

Andy was impressed by the fact that Cedano had survived the amputation of his hand with no medicine, still refusing to provide information to the empire. *This man is a hero*, he thought.

Cedano continued, "Their biggest mistake was allowing us time to think and the opportunity to communicate among ourselves. They would have amputated our tongues had you not shown up when you did. It was just a matter of time. It's something the empire does to stress the importance of silence."

Andy remembered that Seth's assassins and the members of the detachment defeated on the Tela Mountain aquifer had had their tongues removed. He responded, "I'm sure they didn't execute all of you because of the repercussions this would have had on tens of thousands of families on Tai-Anh. They were attempting to convince the people that the true enemies were from

Shrah."

"I agree, Admiral," said Cedano. "We took advantage of the opportunity to communicate since we had one another's undivided attention. Thousands of us had our right hands amputated, and many died of infection. They offered no anesthesia or reparation of the tissue. They let us heal on our own. In prison, we made a commitment to destroy the empire or die trying to. We are ready to fight and die if need be. Prison and the brutality of the empire have made believers of us all. We are at your disposal and here to fight with you as you order, Admiral."

It was the first time Andy had had so many untrained fighters in his forces. It was a conundrum for sure. On one hand, he had the augmented numbers of veteran fighters. On the other, he had untrained and unarmed fighters who had not been incorporated into his well-oiled fighting machine. Regardless, these were the circumstances, and he needed to make them work. Soon, they would have more weapons provided to them by Lyndon. Andy said, "Thank you, Cedano. Soon, you will be armed. Follow the lead of Lieutenant Zenobia."

"Yes, sir."

Andy switched communications channels to check in on his team leads.

"Noah, what is your readiness status?"

"Team one is a go, Admiral."

"Buluc?"

"Team two is a go, Admiral."

"Kabel?"

"Team three is a go, Admiral."

"Obasi?"

"Team four is a go, Admiral"

"Morazan?"

"Team five is a go, Admiral."

"I will self-report for team six as a go," Andy said. "Hope?"

"Team seven is a go, Admiral."

"Very well. Advance to underground atriums for rendezvous with Lyndonite troops."

Each team advanced to large underground atriums for replenishment of weapons. Hope had been in constant communication with the Lyndonite troops and had confirmed exact global positioning coordinates, locations, and times.

Team six arrived at their location at the projected time and sent confirmation. The other teams did the same.

Andy could see Lyndonite forces approaching through the darkness. All armed forces were ready to fire should the approaching forces be enemies. Andy could see that there was one figure leading the troops as they moved closer, so he stepped out with his finger on the trigger of his rifle. His forces backed him up, preparing to fire at a split-second's notice. The tension in the air was palpable.

Andy couldn't believe his eyes. On the breast of the uniform of the leader he was facing was the symbol of the School of the Eleventh Dimension. It was the same one all his troops wore. It appeared that Lyndon had officially adopted the Shrah Philosophy as their own!

Andy allowed for a direct and secure communications link between himself and the leader standing before team six.

"Bahlam Jol burned for the second time," stated the leader.

"A conquest of the Queen of Naranjo," responded Andy.

These were the secret words spoken to confirm and cement the solidarity of two societies living on neighboring planets. Both of their anxieties eased some.

"I am Admiral Sauer," Andy declared. "I am here under direct orders from the Ajaws of Shrah to eradicate the empire threat."

"And these forces behind me are now your forces, Admiral. I am Broteas Ovidius, and it will be an honor to fight under you."

"The honor is mine. I'm afraid we don't have much time before we attack. I have received confirmation that our individual team leaders have connected with your forces. Job well done."

"Thank you, Admiral."

"Do you think you were tracked in any way by imperial forces?" Andy asked urgently.

"No, sir. I can tell you that the empire has scrambled their forces. I believe they were surprised by your attack but are looking for you now," said Ovidius. "You have moved very quickly. It's a matter of time before they find us here once they realize there are no living heat signatures above ground. We made sure they didn't follow us and discover our military forces, but we do not have much time."

"I agree. We must be out of the underground tunnel immediately. A fight down here would be catastrophic for us. We will bring the fight to them." Andy keyed up his secure communications link and transmitted. "Team leaders, this is Admiral Sauer. As you are aware, we have located ourselves under the appropriate weapons depots. Our movements are to be silent from this point until weapons discharge. Debrief team leaders from Lyndon so they may disseminate relevant regrouping information after engagement with their forces. These forces are now under your command. Take charge of your forces. We will move swiftly and smartly, minimizing noise in the rising water, upon my command."

"Team one copy," confirmed Noah.

"Team two copy," confirmed Buluc.

"Team three copy," confirmed Kabel.

"Team four copy," confirmed Obasi.

"Team five copy," confirmed Morazan.

"Team seven copy," confirmed Hope.

"Very well, I will do the same now for team six," reported Andy.

# CHAPTER 46: SHOCKING AUDACITY

Emperor Exelcior paced the room furiously. He had just received confirmation that it had been combatants from Shrah who had attacked the prison complex. His veins pulsated in his temples. *How dare they invade the sovereignty of the empire? I will have Antipas executed when this is done.*

He wondered how it was possible that there were no dead enemy bodies to be recovered at the prison. It had to be due to one of two reasons. Either his forces were incompetent or the enemies had taken their dead into the tunnels. Either scenario was unacceptable. This meant that few enemies had been killed. Exelcior ordered the immediate execution of the prison warden. Unfortunately, Buluc Hix had already delivered that very consequence for him with a laser shot to the head.

*At least the Aloms and their temple are destroyed now,* Exelcior told himself. *This attack had to be orchestrated by the misfits from Choluteca. As soon as we kill all of these attackers, I will order the destruction of Lyndon. I want everyone dead, just like the people on Shrah.*

Exelcior stood up, walked over to the large window, and looked out into the rain in a northwesterly direction. He could hear laser shots, screams, and explosions in the vicinity of the weapons depots. He called up Antipas to put their plan into action.

The operatives attacked from seven different directions simultaneously. The first to shoot and land a kill was Obasi. It was a center-mass shot placed from the street onto a terrace four floors high. The imperial forces were in a heightened state of readiness since the attack on the prison, but they didn't know where exactly the believers would attack next. There were many forces at their armories, picking up weapons in preparation for impending battle.

It was apparent to Andy and the Shrah leaders that the attack on the prison had been a surprise. Before the attack on the prison, the empire had believed that all the fighters on Shrah and Choluteca had been killed. They hadn't verified quickly enough whether or not that was the case, and their mistake would cost them dearly.

They had an advantage in the number of combatants who were fighting on their own soil, though. These fighters were not prison guards but infantry military forces.

The believers shot on target. The empire returned fire. Blood flowed.

Andy could hear the firefight in which team four was engaged. The team was engaged in heavy fighting by the time targets began to appear ahead of him and the rest of the teams. The brightness of the city lights assaulted his eyes for a few brief seconds as his pupils adjusted. Then he joined the shooting. The enemies in front of him were in elevated positions in windows and balconies of higher floors. As the bodies hit the ground, he was reminded of that disturbing sound. It sounded like watermelons striking the ground and exploding. Fortunately, or unfortunately, it was a sound he was accustomed to. He pressed on.

Andy swept the battlefield side to side and up and down the buildings, striking targets. Every few seconds, he heard laser bursts speeding past his head. This was a good thing. It was the shots never heard by the targeted victim, moving faster than the speed of sound, that were a problem. Most laser-shooting victims never heard the shot that killed them. Andy wondered what being struck by a high-energy burst of light so powerful it could irreparably obliterate flesh felt like. He couldn't focus on that danger. The admiral could hear that some of his troops were being struck by enemy fire. It was a battle to the death. After this attack, they would proceed to their final destination. Their element of surprise was officially gone. The empire would kill all of them if they re-entered the underground tunnels of the city. Their next target would be reached above ground.

Andy was in constant communication with his team leaders. They were beginning to report casualties. Many of those killed were the former prisoners, who were in poor physical condition, undernourished and untrained. The special forces were taking casualties as well.

Andy could hear the rotary craft in the distance approaching. The question was whether or not the craft carried friends or foes. He soon had his answer when one of the craft exploded. They were Lyndonite troops arriving to reinforce them. Several craft exploded in flight as they approached. Some landed and unloaded troops under heavy fire, with many Lyndonites killed as they exited. Souls began flowing into the Eleventh Dimension in a steady stream. The teams were able to access the weapons depots with their explosives. As soon as team six breached the main door of their depot, they heard a second set of aircraft approaching. These ones brought foes.

Explosions began to shake the ground as troops from Shrah were blown to pieces on the streets of Gandolim. The entire neighborhood was engulfed in flashes of laser pulses, explosions, smoke, the smell of burnt flesh, and the metallic smell of spilled blood.

Andy checked in with his teams for status updates, preparing to redirect support if needed. "Noah, report status."

"Team one is in the fight. Multiple casualties. No need for additional support."

"Buluc, report status."

"Team two is in the fight. Multiple casualties. No additional support needed."

"Kabel, report status."

"Team three is in the fight. Some casualties. No need for additional support."

"Obasi, report status."

"Team four is in the fight. Several casualties. Request permission to support team five. It's bad over there, Admiral."

"Morazan, report status," inquired Andy.

There was no response.

Andy repeated, "Morazan, report status."

No response.

"Obasi, permission granted. Provide support as necessary. Seth, are you on this net?"

"I am, Admiral."

"Seth, take a detachment and provide support as well. You assume command of team five as you deem necessary," Andy ordered. "Hope, report status."

"Team seven has two casualties. No need for additional support."

"Very well, team leaders. Team six does not require additional support. Advance to final assault on my command," said Andy.

All team leaders responded with their understanding and continued to take lives. There were thousands of combatants fighting to the death in seven different scenes of carnage. The surviving fighters from Shrah pressed on, well-armed after raiding the seven empire weapons depots. The depots chosen for the attack were strategically located near Imperial Headquarters.

The freed prisoners fought with a passion that greatly impressed the much better-trained forces from Shrah, Choluteca, and Lyndon. Cedano managed to kill dozens while shooting with his non-dominant left hand. The empire had forgotten to amputate his spirit. This was his most dangerous weapon of all.

Andy gave the order for the troops to fight their way to Imperial Headquarters for the final assault. The troops began to move through the large metal buildings of Gandolim in the driving rain. They were facing a hail of laser pulses from airborne aircraft and arriving troops.

Andy began to feel the pressure of his troops dying in droves. Doubt began to creep in, as he could see the dead bodies around him along the route to the tall Imperial Headquarters building in the distance. The empire must have sensed where the troops were headed, as more reinforcements began to arrive. Most of the Lyndon fighter craft had been destroyed. The tide had turned in favor of the empire.

Andy's fighters were being slaughtered on the metal street. He received confirmation that Morazan Ceibo had been decapitated at the weapons depot. Andy felt the loss of another great warrior fighting for the freedom of his people. Seth assumed command of team five as the teams advanced along the Panthalassan's edge, approaching their final destination.

This route on the water's edge had been chosen to enable the teams to see any incoming attack from the ocean. A major attack there would come from the air or water. The teams would be able to spot and defend against either.

As he progressed, carefully but swiftly, Andy thought about impending doom. The empire had most certainly reinforced defenses at Imperial Headquarters. They would be expecting them and would have plans to intercept them. They had to move fast.

They arrived just outside Imperial Headquarters, and Andy could immediately tell that they were looking at a fortress. His heart sank to his stomach. The troops had fought valiantly.

He sent a final message to the few thousand fighters who had survived to that point. "Believers, this is Admiral Andrew Sauer. Our final objective is to attack a fortified and heavily defended compound that is fully expecting our arrival. We did not come here to lose a war but to gain our freedom from an evil regime. That was the only choice we were given. Our choice now is not to retreat. This would ensure our deaths and leave a legacy of cowardice in the face of our enemy. We will fight until we can fight no more. This is what our ancestors did, and their legacy runs through all our veins. It has been my honor to fight with you. Let's finish what we started."

As Andy finished his broadcast, he could see a dim light approaching from the horizon over the ocean. The rain ceased. The light was barely visible as it skimmed the surface of the Panthalassan. The imperial forces stopped advancing and stood their ground, trapping Andy's troops between superior batteries and the ocean. The light grew brighter as it headed right for them. The craft launched a large missile at them. They scrambled to take cover.

# CHAPTER 47: INCOMING

They took cover behind anything they could find. They broke down doors and windows and braced for impact. Fortunately, the empire had disarmed their citizens. Breaking into living quarters did not lead to attack. They could see the flames of the propulsion system as the missile drew closer. It was silent; the deadly weapon was traveling faster than the speed of sound. They darkened the visors of their helmets to protect their eyes. They could hear the missile screeching overhead, and the loud explosion that followed made their chests rattle.

Miraculously, Andy was still alive. He didn't know yet who had been struck by the weapon and who remained alive. Judging by the thunderous sound of the explosion, he expected many casualties. "Team leaders," he said into his communications system. "What is the status of your teams?"

Noah was the first to answer. "Admiral, I could see the missile strike from my vantage point. The missile missed us and struck the imperial compound's outer wall, facing the Panthalassan."

The next voice belonged to none of the team leaders. "The missile did not miss, old friend. Captain Danli Itzamna doesn't make a habit of missing his targets." There was a cheer from all the team leaders as they recognized the voice of Ajaw Michael Alom. Michael continued, "We are on the ground with a fresh team from Shrah, Admiral. Isaiah will retain command of the newly arrived troops, and you retain command of yours. Carry out your plan of attack. We are here to fight with you."

The large space transport had delivered the troops from Shrah just north of Imperial Headquarters in full-stealth mode before heading out over the ocean to approach for the missile attack. On the ground in Gandolim, more highly trained troops headed in for the assault on the heart of the empire.

Two more explosions. One was a missile striking a metal building, the other a missile striking a spacecraft. Danli managed to get another direct hit on Imperial Headquarters. He fired both missiles low and at the perimeter walls so as to create an opportunity for the Shrah combatants to infiltrate the complex. But his craft did not have the maneuverability to escape the empire's surface-to-air anti-aircraft batteries. The explosion tore him to pieces, killing him instantly. Without a spacecraft, Danli flew over sweeping green plains. In the distance, he saw Crystal City, his new home.

Danli was physically dead, but he had accomplished his duty. There was a path of entry into Imperial Headquarters, and the surviving believers and newly arriving reinforcements from Shrah had a final assault.

Michael was in his element. He was fighting for his people's very existence. He could feel the pressure of an entire planet and the weight of all the years of his civilization's struggle to exist. They had survived attacks in other galaxies, and it was time for their final struggle for survival. All those eras had come to a head, and he was at the focal point of their destiny. He would either exterminate or be exterminated. The moment had come. The ajaw was ready.

Maya was in her element too. The Emperor of Tai-Anh had attempted to kill her son. It couldn't get more personal than that. The empire had drawn her wrath. Emperor Exelcior deserved to die. *That animal did his best to end my son's life*, she thought to herself. She was there for her people, employing the fury of a mother protecting her child, working to exterminate the threat to the ones she loved.

Isaiah was the supreme commander of the fighting forces from a planet of warriors. He was part of the Alom family and the person the ajaws trusted most in matters of life and death. The general had earned his title, and he epitomized it. Although he was the supreme leader, he was the first to fight. He was a man of few words. His strength was action, not discussion. It pleased him greatly to be in the thick of the fight. There was no better military leader anywhere in the star system.

Noah had to suppress his desire to act as a doctor and care for the injured on the battlefield. The believers understood they were fighting for their collective survival. Sacrifices needed to be made to accomplish that task. If they failed at toppling the empire, it meant death for them all. Noah was there to take lives, not save them.

Buluc was taking lives again, and now it was personal. He channeled his anger into fighting fury. He'd traveled to the neighboring planet to exact justice for numerous transgressions against his people. The sum of enemies who'd died by his hands was in the thousands. The best fighters from multiple eras had found their ends at his feet. He was Shrah's most decorated combat veteran, and he was exactly where he needed to be.

Kabel killed efficiently. She focused her attention on taking lives rather than sending light energy into the universe's energy superhighway. She was no longer acting as a priestess but as a special forces colonel fighting for her civilization's survival. She had done so in another incarnation in another galaxy. She was doing what she was born to do: fighting.

Obasi had been born to kill, and that was what she did best. The Mine War seemed so far in the past. In a way, she never felt quite at home during peacetime. Even as a young girl, she'd known the blood of a warrior coursed through her veins. She had learned how to fight from Isaiah. She had the intelligence and ferocity of a special forces leader, a born warrior.

Seth had replaced Morazan as leader of team five. It was his first military battle of this incarnation, but it was far from his first ever. Seth was a natural leader. The team members quickly fell into step behind him and were rewarded for it. Their leader made the right calls and gave effective orders to minimize loss of life. He was well aware that both his parents were in grave danger as they approached the teeth of the dragon in a fight to the death. Seth also knew that he was responsible for his own team of fighters and had to do his part to lead them in their mission. He could either worry about two lives or think of the survival of his entire civilization. He decided that he was there to fight.

It was the second war of Hope's present incarnation. The depth of her despisal for the empire ran deep. The persecution of her fellow believers and the killing of Yoro Copan had added up. This was as personal for her as it was for the Aloms. She was turning her hatred into action, and it was very satisfying.

Janina was officially militarized and trained for the battle at hand. She had finally found a place in the universe, a purpose, a home, a family. It struck her how wonderful it felt to be in Gandolim, running at, not from, her enemy. It hadn't been long since she had found herself feeling alone and powerless, fearing for her well-being. Now it was a different story. She was still in grave danger, but somehow, dying wasn't her concern. Her concern was killing the enemy.

Andy saw large vehicles coming toward them from every direction. Some hovered in the air, while others levitated along the metal streets. The admiral may have been an alien from another galaxy, but he knew military tactics and weapons systems anywhere in the universe. The vehicles looked like troop transports, lots of them. He spoke into his communications system. "Isaiah, this is Admiral Sauer. Do you see what I see?"

"I do."

"Noumeroi?'

"Yes, Admiral," said Isaiah. "Lots of them."

"Great. Let's kill them."

Isaiah smiled wildly.

# CHAPTER 48: MORE TIME TO KILL

They could see the Noumeroi arriving in the rain to end the nonsense outside the headquarters walls. Unlike their counterparts from Shrah, Emperor Exelcior and General Antipas were nowhere near the field of battle. They were running the operation remotely from a point where they had a view of the battlefield.

On the battlefield, Andy ordered, "Team leaders, take charge of your teams, spread out, take cover, and fight. These are Noumeroi. They bleed just like us."

Isaiah ordered his team to do the same.

The assembled forces from Shrah and Lyndon took cover inside and outside the buildings that surrounded the empire's complex. To their surprise, the people of Gandolim provided them no resistance. The anti-weapon laws were formidable on Tai-Anh. Exelcior's iron-fisted brutality didn't motivate his citizens to fight the heavily armed and trained combatants from Shrah either.

The Shrah fighters were effectively in a low-intensity, close-quarters combat situation with the Third Realm's Noumeroi. Andy could see more and more vehicles setting down and stopping all around them to unload troops. It was impossible for thousands of fighters to hide indoors, but they found the dark places and hid as best as they could in preparation.

Isaiah launched the stealth drone to investigate the battlefield. He could see inside his visor the five streets leading to and from Imperial Headquarters running east to west and four running north to south. The troops unloading for battle were heavily armed. There were no ships at any of the piers. Isaiah relayed all he saw to Andy. The two military supreme leaders communicated as if they had been doing so for several battles.

The main Imperial Command Building was in the center of the complex. The missiles launched by Danli had broken open the formerly impenetrable wall surrounding the complex. The first had struck the eastern wall closest to the ocean. There was a field between the eastern wall and the bay. The second missile had struck the western wall on the southern extreme, facing the Gandolim residential buildings.

Andy ordered his teams to break up and

attack specific locations while Noumeroi forces were still unloading. Two teams attacked the upper northern streets, two attacked the lower southern streets, and three attacked from the western side. The recent arrivals from Shrah, under Isaiah's leadership, attacked the western side, where there was an open field, along with an opening in the wall between Imperial Headquarters and the bay.

The element of relative surprise allowed them time to hide before the Noumeroi arrived. Another advantage was that the citizens of Gandolim were disloyal to the empire. Had the situation evolved on Shrah and the tables been turned, the enemy combatants would have been in a fight for their lives with every single citizen of Nacaome.

The first shot was fired by a squad leader on Buluc's team. It was a direct lethal hit on a Noumeroi. Then all hell broke loose.

The Shrah teams broke off to engage the Noumeroi. Staying in place was not an option. They advanced, relying on the urban close-quarters training they had received.

Andy could smell burned flesh, bone, and blood, and he could hear the sounds of killing and dying. Laser pulses fired in all directions. The use of holograms intensified the confusion. Two of the universe's greatest fighting forces were meeting in a struggle and would battle until one was exterminated.

The general and admiral planned on eliminating as many of the Noumeroi as possible outside Imperial Headquarters, then working inside the complex and continuing to clear the buildings one at a time. Before that, they had to win the battle to control the streets. The empire had all their warriors on deck, and it was a bloodbath.

Buluc's team was the first to engage in a firefight. They were the southernmost team attacking the western wall. As expected, the Noumeroi greatly outnumbered them. The templar knights and special forces held their own, killing Noumeroi at twice the rate of their own casualties.

The next teams to engage in firefights were Andy's and Hope's. They were both attacking from the south in the much narrower, darker alleys of the area. They were outnumbered and in an intense struggle. The Noumeroi got to see firsthand an alien who had been part of, arguably, the most elite special forces on Earth. Andy mostly used his laser pulse rifle but switched to his silenced laser pulse pistol and fighting knife when necessary. He had sliced the throats of seven combatants already.

After the southernmost teams came the other two teams on the western side of the complex, led by Seth and Noah. The streets running west to east were much broader and better lit. The light and fewer places to hide were disadvantages to both sides of the conflict. The death and casualty tolls climbed rapidly.

The next two teams to exchange fire were led by Kabel and Obasi. They fought along the northern wall among the tallest buildings in the area and had access to underground tunnels, which made their route especially deadly. They had to continually watch their backs because there was a northern pier, where more troops could arrive from the ocean. Kabel and Obasi were two of Shrah's finest, and they had their work cut out for them on the northern front.

The final team to engage in the fight was Isaiah's. His team encountered the most elite Noumeroi at the eastern gate. These troops were led by Antipas himself, and they outnumbered Isaiah's team. The small Shrah detachment was fresh, as they had not fought yet, and Danli had dropped them off secretly into the ocean very close to the shore so they didn't have to swim very far. The ajaws and Janina had full confidence in the general's tactics and in the abilities of their fellow templar knights. The killing was rampant at the eastern wall. Michael, Maya, Isaiah, and Janina were at the head of their team.

Buluc's team bore the brunt of the Noumeroi attack. Seth and Noah's teams provided support as needed while fighting themselves. A group of fighters from Lyndon joined Buluc in the fight, while the former prisoners fell back to reinforce and did as best as could be expected from prisoners with no training or physical conditioning. The prisoners began to die in droves in the battle, which greatly distressed Buluc. The surviving combatants began to slip in the spilled blood and flesh of the dead.

The intensity of the fight increased as the battle approached the opening to Imperial Headquarters. Exelcior ordered reinforcements to the area. A group of imperial combatants began to mow down the freed prisoners. Buluc responded by leaving the fight he was engaged in and placing his top sergeant, Tejad Jazon, in charge of the active fight. He entered the fight when the Noumeroi were already in complete control of the situation, firing down on them from elevated positions.

Buluc saw a young prisoner fall to the ground as his leg was blown off. The look of terror in the man's eyes called out to him. Buluc dashed toward the helpless prisoner. He felt the piercing pain of the laser pulse as it traveled from one side of his body to the other, sizzling through his abdominal cavity.

Mortally wounded, Buluc covered the young man with his body and dragged him to safety. He sent a secure message to Seth, informing him of the situation. Seth responded with fighters from his and Noah's teams.

In the rain of laser pulses, Seth found Buluc and informed Noah that there was no need to respond. He held his trainer, mentor, and most loyal friend.

Buluc choked out his final words. "I love you. I'm sorry."

Seth thanked him for being a pillar in his life. He sobbed with his friend in his arms until the end. Buluc Hix, one of the most feared and loved men ever to have lived, flew past grassy fields on his way to Crystal City. He left behind a legacy of honor, courage, and commitment.

The greatest of all Mayan war gods, Ek Chuah himself, waited to receive him. "Buluc Hix, you are restored to your permanent identity, Ah-Tabai. We have been waiting for you to join us. You have earned induction here."

Ah-Tabai walked into the Pantheon of Warrior Gods.

# CHAPTER 49: HEAVY TOLLS

Shrah fighters continued to die and kill.

Noah pressed forward. Team members dropped under enemy fire. He stayed focused on the task at hand and provided guidance to both Seth and Tejad Jazon. Tejad was one of the sharpest young fighters from Shrah. He hadn't been a war veteran before arriving on Tai-Anh with Andy. Seth and Tejad fought valiantly, counseled by Noah and Andy.

Obasi and Kabel fought hard in the rain on the northernmost wall of the complex. Shrah's forces had been augmented significantly by the freed prisoners and Lyndonite forces. The augmented forces were holding their own when Obasi and Kabel heard the call from their team members, notifying them that they were being attacked from the north extreme.

Obasi could see the detonations to the north. She could hear the agonizing screams of her team members being slain, one after the other. The two women decided to double-time north, away from the complex and into the thick of the northern attack. They had killed many enemies when the flash happened. They never heard the explosion.

A few seconds later, Kabel opened her eyes. She could tell she had been pulled to safety behind a short metal barrier by one of her subordinates. It was very difficult for her to perceive depth or see a full field of vision. She soon realized that she had lost sight in her right eye. She could only hear ringing. Her torso and arms appeared okay. Kabel tried to stand up to continue fighting, but she didn't have the strength or balance. She looked down to see that her right leg was no longer attached to her body. It was gone and destroyed.

Noah arrived at the scene after hearing the fiasco on the communications channel. Obasi had also been dragged away from the fighting. A window opened in the building adjacent to them. A man called out to them, letting them know they could bring Obasi indoors to care for her. They carried her into the building and into a humble apartment, where the man lived with his family. Noah laid Obasi on the floor, and she lost consciousness. Noah began cardio-pulmonary resuscitation compressions.

Obasi flitted in and out of consciousness. Her injuries were severe. Finally, she took her last breath on the warm floor of the small apartment.

Noah held her body tightly and sent his light energy into the energy superhighway to be part of the wind propelling her over the grassy fields of the Eleventh Dimension.

When Obasi arrived in Crystal City, all thirteen of the grandmothers surrounded her in a circle. "We have been waiting for you," they exclaimed harmoniously. She was in great hands.

The family who owned the apartment wept. The father, who had invited them in, pulled Noah aside before he left. "Thank you for fighting for all of us. This home is a home of believers."

Noah smiled and exited. He carried his patient's body out of the apartment, thanking them on his way out to resume fighting.

Andy engaged enemy combatants on the southern front, expertly picking off one after another with expert marksman shots of deadly laser pulses. He was feeling the great advantage of the extremely low recoil of the laser pulse rifle. The situation had turned into a free-for-all.

Andy and Hope's teams joined together to fight as one. They had advanced enough to engage the enemy on the same battlefield just outside the southern wall of the complex. There were over a dozen Noumeroi firing at Andy at the same time, as he was closest to them.

At the far end of the wall, there stood a single Noumeroi fighter with a large beam weapon. From that distance, he could see that Andy was wreaking havoc on his fellow combatants. He had a clear shot at the side of Andy's head. Andy was too preoccupied with killing other Noumeroi to see him. The Noumeroi fighter aimed his weapon at Andy's right side. He squeezed the trigger. The head exploded before the trigger traveled far enough to release the beam. The shot from Hope's rifle hit its target just in time.

Cedano was redirected by Hope on an important clandestine mission. He selected five other former prisoners he knew well and trusted. They set off in the darkness, a few feet from the southern wall. Cedano had worked in Gandolim's public works department and knew the location of the important electrical transformers that provided most of the electric power to the area surrounding Imperial Headquarters.

The detachment arrived at the power box with the transformers containing handheld explosives. They set the explosives with timers under Cedano's direction, then retreated into the darkness of night to return to the fighting. A few minutes later, the explosions shook the ground. The lights in the complex and surrounding area went out.

Isaiah's team turned on their night vision goggles and proceeded to enter the buildings within the complex. The complex had a video surveillance system that was no longer operational. The freed prisoners and most of the fighters from

Lyndon did not have the equipment needed to fight in the darkness indoors. Clearing the buildings of Noumeroi was a job for Shrah and Choluteca special forces.

Isaiah had supreme command. Michael led the team Janina was on, while Isaiah led the team Maya was on. All four fought to stay alive while killing Noumeroi. They moved quietly through the eastern maze of the complex after penetrating the property through the opening in the blown-out wall.

Janina was advancing when a Noumeroi zeroed in on her and raised his rifle. Janina's sixth sense kicked in, and she quickly turned and looked into the enemy's eyes before taking her life. It was Janina's first kill.

Noah, Tejad, and the rest of their team made their way along the northwestern portion of the wall before heading south on the eastern wall to enter behind the knights. Andy, Hope, Seth, and their teams entered the complex through the southeastern opening in the wall. Noah never left Kabel's side. Her life depended on his medical attention.

The fighting believers were making their way to the complex's main building by clearing out the smaller building and killing the Noumeroi inside. Many more believers were killed during the final advance. The streets surrounding the structure were riddled with well over 100,000 dead bodies. Thousands of the empire's fighters had defected from the fight and slipped away into the night. They had no interest in dying for their emperor after witnessing first-hand the ferocity of the Shrah fighters. Many of them were well on their way to becoming fervent believers.

The empire's command and control center was located in the main lobby of the building. Antipas and a small group of defenders were waiting there. The emperor and his pilot stood in the imperial chamber on the top floor of the building.

Andy and Isaiah co-planned all movements like a well-oiled machine. Isaiah thanked the Great Creator for the effectiveness and efficiency of his counterpart. The admiral's experience was invaluable to the mission and had saved thousands of Shrah lives. It had also cost the empire tens of thousands of theirs. The Noumeroi were decimated after so many deaths and horrific injuries.

Those who stayed behind to fight did so to their deaths. The surviving Noumeroi retreated into the lobby of the main imperial building. The leaders and combatants from Shrah converged near the center of the complex.

Michael, Maya, and Seth saw each other and shared a three-way embrace. Their fellow combatants allowed them privacy to be together for a brief moment. Emotions ran high as they celebrated that they were all still alive. They also shared the pain of losing so many team members. The deaths of Buluc, Danli, Obasi, Areni, and Morazan weighed particularly heavy on their hearts.

While the ajaws embraced, Andy hugged Isaiah. The general felt great gratitude for the expertise, courage, and sacrifice of the admiral. In Isaiah's eyes, Andy could see the pain of the lives lost in combat. No words were spoken.

At the same time, Hope and Janina embraced. Hope could sense how much Janina had matured. Janina hugged her with the confidence of a combatant woman, not a scared child. There was certain sharpness in Janina's eyes that hadn't been there before, accompanied by admiration and gratitude. Hope was the reason Janina was alive in the first place. They communicated with each other silently.

When the first round of embraces ended, the second round began. Michael went to Andy and hugged him with gratitude. Andy had risked his life and safety for the people of Shrah. The ajaw knew the great warrior had been brought to his people by the Great Creator. He also knew they owed their survival and victory to the Earthling.

Maya and Hope also embraced. Maya could feel Hope's pain at the loss of her beloved Yoro. Hope, in turn, could feel the agony in Maya's heart at the loss of so many of her people in the brutal battles on Tai-Anh. At the look in Maya's eyes, Hope knew that she finally had a place to call home. They communicated at a higher level, as Hope had evolved spiritually. She was now elevated and had been receiving lessons from Hamilton back on Shrah. The two strong females shared a silent moment of mutual spiritual understanding.

At the same time, Seth and Janina found their way to each other and embraced in a way they had not done so before. They had both grown into adults on the battlefield in the span of just a few moments. They looked into each other's eyes. Physical and spiritual attraction flowed between them.

Love flowed throughout the Shrah special forces and was shared, felt, and returned by the warriors already in the Eleventh Dimension. But the fighting wasn't over yet.

# CHAPTER 50: MATTERS RESOLVED

Noah confirmed that Kabel was still alive and stabilized. Her injuries were extensive. She had lost a leg and vision in one eye. Ovidius had arranged for medical assistance to be provided, and she was in transport for critical trauma care at the Lyndon Medical Center.

Obasi's body was in the same transport vehicle. Her injuries were not correctable. Her grandmother, who had predeceased her, had been awaiting her arrival in Crystal City.

The Shrah forces used shoulder-launched explosives. Once they entered the building, they found many dead Noumeroi who had been ready for a firefight that had never happened. They began the process of identifying the bodies. They turned them over and used their hand scanners to check their facial structures for identification.

They discovered that two bodies were missing: those of Emperor Exelcior and General Antipas.

Also missing were Michael, Maya, Isaiah, Andy, Hope, and Seth. While the Shrah special forces were sifting through the dead Noumeroi in the dark lobby, the ajaws were double-timing separately up through stairwells of the main building to the top floor. The middle floors of the building were completely unoccupied. They had received an intelligence report from captured Noumeroi that Exelcior, Antipas, and a small faction of Noumeroi were holed up on the top floor of the building. There was a rotary craft at the top of the building intended to transport personnel away. Michael double-timed along the northeast stairwell, Isaiah following close behind.

Seth climbed the southeast well with Maya some distance behind him. Andy was on the southwest well with Hope following. They had their obsidian knives at the ready.

Seth arrived at the top floor and opened the door, exiting the stairwell and entering the main passageway slowly and silently.

Down the passageway, he noticed an emergency light coming out of a door that appeared to be cracked open. He approached silently. When he arrived at the door, he could see inside the room. He turned off night vision mode on his visor. His pupils adjusted as he studied the room. There appeared to be one inhabitant wearing Noumeroi markings on a flight suit. Seth reckoned it was most likely a pilot preparing to depart with Exelcior and Antipas. The pilot had collected his gear and opened an automatic dispenser on the wall that contained a laser pistol. It was time to move in on him before he armed himself.

The pilot's back was turned to the door. Seizing the opportunity, Seth slid into the room. As he was closing in, the pilot suddenly closed the drawer and turned. Seth flew through the air and launched a sidekick at the pilot's chest. Both men fell to the floor, then stood up. Seth was quicker. He drove his obsidian knife into the Noumeroi's eye, piercing through the socket and stabbing through to the bottom of his brain. In a swift motion, Seth pulled the blade from the Noumeroi's eye socket and sliced across his neck, severing the external carotid arteries, superior thyroid, and trachea. The fight was over quickly. The enemy bled out on the floor.

A second Noumeroi came out of a room from across the passageway, carrying a laser pulse rifle, and proceeded to where Seth had killed the pilot. The Noumeroi leveled his rifle to shoot, but as he aimed, Maya approached and slit his throat from behind. Maya looked at Seth without saying a word, and they both hurried to the rooftop.

Mother and son arrived at the southeast extreme of the roof. Maya knew she had to be careful, as the rooftop was very exposed with few structures where she could hide. She moved stealthily toward the rotary craft in the distance. As she approached, she saw two tall male figures exit the door on the northwest corner of the roof. Moments later, they stepped out into the moonlight on the distant side of the vast roof. There were two more armed Noumeroi escorting them. Maya knew what she needed to do.

Michael and Isaiah arrived at the rooftop's northeast corner with obsidian knives at the ready. The ajaw had the advantage of emerging in a heavily shadowed northern portion of the roof. He advanced toward the west along the north side, managing to stay out of sight. He closed in on the two tall, strong men. Michael was outnumbered, but he found a prime spot in the shadows from which he could pounce at the right time. He could finally see the identities of the two men in front. They were exactly who he wanted to see: Emperor Exelcior and General Antipas. They were in a hurry to leave in the rotary craft, but that wasn't going to be easy. The Noumeroi intelligence forces had reported to them that the Shrah special forces and templar knights had breached the lobby doors. But they hadn't anticipated the bravery of the ajaws, who had separated from their main forces to intercept them alone. They had waited too long to leave.

The small detachment maintained radio silence to maintain their stealth. They would have to trust each other's judgment and warrior instincts. Their lives depended on them.

The blade sliced across her throat with precise swiftness. She dropped to the ground and exsanguinated rapidly. As soon as he sliced her throat, Andy had to deal with the other Noumeroi, who attacked with ferocity. The Noumeroi had a metal blade in his hand and an obsidian blade through his heart. Hope was standing behind him as he dropped to the floor. He'd never pulled the trigger.

Exelcior and Antipas were on their way to join the fight when they were tackled. Michael and Isaiah took both of them down with a force unlike anything they had ever used before, knocking them to the ground. The leaders of the empire were no longer concerned with defending anyone but themselves.

Michael took the mount position on Exelcior and punched him in the face twice. With his left fist, he broke two front teeth, and with the right punch, he fractured his eye socket. Michael rolled his right leg over the emperor's head, holding his left arm and placing him in an armbar. Michael put his strong leg on Exelcior's face, interlocked his feet, and thrust his hips upward. The pop sound was loud as the emperor's shoulder was pulled out of the socket, straining muscles and tendons, creating agony that caused Exelcior to swallow the loose teeth in his mouth. The blood from his eye injury blurred his vision.

As Michael stood back up, he saw Antipas and Isaiah in their own struggle to the death. Antipas had managed to thrust his metal blade into Isaiah's right kidney. As he drove the knife further into Isaiah's body, his throat was split open by an obsidian knife. With precision and ferocity, Isaiah's second slash was across the abdomen. The slash disemboweled Antipas. As Antipas tried to use his arm to hold in his intestines, a hand reached into his body and moved organs out of the way to grab a hold of his heart. His heart was torn out of his body as it gave its final beats. Isaiah held it up over his head.

Antipas left Tai-Anh and entered the Eleventh Dimension. He traveled through green fields on his way to Crystal City. When he arrived, he saw a blurry figure standing in front of him.

"I've been waiting for you," stated Yoro Copan with a smile on his face.

Maya elbowed another arriving Noumeroi in the side of his head with a force that made him drop his hands. In a fluid motion, she hammer-fisted her obsidian knife behind her opponent's right ear, driving the blade into his cerebellum, incapacitating him immediately.

Quintus Salvius succumbed to his wounds and died on the moonlit rooftop of Imperial Headquarters a few moments later.

The Ajaw of Shrah and the Emperor of Tai-Anh stood in front of one another. No one on the rooftop would intervene. It was Michael's fight to finish, so he gave his opponent the honor of standing up to fight. Exelcior noticed their proximity to the edge of the borderless roof and that Michael had his back to the edge. As injured as Exelcior was, he decided there was only one thing for him to do. Desperation took hold of him.

Exelcior decided to end both of their lives by tackling Michael off the edge of the building. He shot into Michael headfirst. Michael opened his legs, bringing his bodyweight forward to prevent them both from falling off the edge of the roof. He placed his right forearm under Exelcior's neck and grabbed his own left arm, wrapping it over the back of Exelcior's neck. Michael straightened himself up, placing Exelcior in a guillotine chokehold. Exelcior began losing consciousness and reached for the knife sheathed on his right side. Michael had no choice but to apply full force and break his neck. He turned and hurled Exelcior's body off the edge of the roof.

The Emperor of Tai-Anh's body lay dead and mangled on the ground of Imperial Headquarters in the falling rain. His spirit flew over windswept green pastures and arrived at a structure he did not recognize. It wasn't a city of crystal but of stone: the Pantheon of Warrior Gods. He felt a tap on his shoulder and turned to look into the eyes of Buluc Hix, who was certainly waiting for him.

# CHAPTER 51: ABOUT TIME

The space transport's engines fired. We were driven back into our seats as the craft cut through the rain. We climbed over the metal buildings of Gandolim and out into open space over Tai-Anh's vast Panthalassan Ocean. The raindrops eventually subsided, and the blue hue of the planet was contrasted by the increasing blackness of space ahead. The transport was being flown by a young but talented pilot from Lyndon. We were leaving in the shadows of the Kinich Ahau star system, the one with which I shared my Shrah name.

In the ship's medical bay was Kabel, who had already had her new leg printed and surgically attached to replace the one she'd lost in the final battle with the empire. She still had much recovery and physical therapy ahead of her. What treatment was left would happen on her home planet under the care of Noah.

Sitting next to me was Isaiah, who had survived his injury. In an ironic twist, it had been discovered that Isaiah had been born without a right kidney. Antipas's knife had entered only empty space. This had most likely saved Isaiah's life. One thing was for sure: Isaiah Gabriel was one bad motherfucker.

Behind us were the Maya and Michael, both brokenhearted over the thousands of lives lost on Tai-Anh. They would have to rebuild Temple Alom from scratch. But at least they wouldn't have to do it alone. Maya was asleep on Michael's chest. There was no better place for her to be.

In the seats across from us were folks from Lyndon and Tai-Anh who were traveling with us back to Shrah to undergo training in Atsalat, Ch'o'Jonik, and the Sacred Codices. Similarly, several folks from Shrah would be catching the return flight to Tai-Anh.

Hope would continue her military training with the Shrah special forces. She had replaced Obasi, promoted to the rank of captain. She was going home.

Directly in front of us were Seth and Janina. They seemed to have become quite cozy with one another in the months after the empire's fall. Seth was returning home a war hero. He had been promoted to the rank of lieutenant. He had also been knighted by the ajaws, replacing Buluc as grand knight of Temple Alom.

Hamilton had taken great care of the sick

on Shrah and had decided to return to Tai-Anh to manage the planet's health system and to continue to lead believers in discovering the Shrah Philosophy. Hamilton loved Shrah, but his home was on Tai-Anh.

Back on Tai-Anh, Ovidius had assumed the role of interim prime minister before being freely elected as such by the unified confederation that eliminated the boundary between Lyndon and Tai-Anh. There was only one nation on Tai-Anh, and Gandolim was its capital city. Elected congressmen were the war heroes Cedano Jole and Tejad Jazon. The future was bright with peace and collaboration between the two neighboring planets of the Kinich Ahau star system. At least there would be peace in that particular spot of the Andromeda galaxy.

As for me, I was retiring for a second time and would be assisting Isaiah in overseeing the training of Shrah's young warriors. We could never let our guard down. History had taught us that harsh lesson.

When the pilot activated the ship's artificial gravity, I stood to see how Kabel was doing in the medical bay. I waited for Noah to finish his consultation with her before I knocked on the bay hatch.

"Come in."

I stepped inside and sat next to Kabel. Her leg was wrapped in regenerative bandages, but she looked as beautiful as always.

We talked for a long while, but time always seemed to race when I spoke to Kabel. I was so very thankful to the Great Creator for her life. We laughed and cried, remembering all we had gone through together and all the wonderful lives ended by the war with the empire. Thousands had been killed on both sides. War was a thief of dignity anywhere in the universe.

Finally, I stood to leave. "I'd better let you rest."

"Andy, no. Please don't leave," said Kabel, looking as surprised by her request as I was.

I noted that it was the first time she had addressed me as Andy, not Kinich Ahau or admiral. "Okay, I can stay at your side for a while," I responded.

"No, Andy, not for a while," Kabel told me. "For the rest of my life."

I kissed her lips and accepted her request without saying a word. No words were necessary between us.

Made in the USA
Middletown, DE
13 February 2022